Cozy reading!

Kary Buchanan

POISON PATTY

By
Kary Buchanan

Poison Patty
by *Kary Buchanan*

Copyright © 2016 Kary Buchanan

All rights reserved.

For Mom, always a great travel companion who found the humor in pretty much everything. To my sister, who is just about the greatest.

Chapter One

Just my luck, thought Bee, frowning into her wine glass. She and her sister Bel had put together what was supposed to be an easy tour--one they could lead with their eyes shut--a repeat of one of the most successful tours that they had led three times before. The tour company, To Be Tours, specialized in leading small groups on "themed" tours, and USUALLY attracted intelligent, enthusiastic travelers with a taste for literature, culture, and fine food and drink. The guests were typically adventurous folks who enjoyed like-minded travelers and thoughtful conversation over delicious meals. This tour, Castles, Chianti and Classics, was one of their favorites, combining Bel's and Bee's "real" professions--Bel was a retired History professor, and Bee was a cookbook editor--producing an eight day visit to Italy complete with book discussions, historical sites, a cooking class, and wine. And then....Patty showed up, all 250 plus pounds of malice and money, porcine features and a talent for saying just the wrong thing. Between them, Bel and Bee had taken to calling her PP when reviewing the day's' disasters.

Piggy Patty had managed to insult, demean, and deride her way through two days of touring Rome--and they had six more days of her charming company to endure. Politely, Bee reminded herself, through gritted teeth. Even if it kills us, she thought grimly. They had already endured her dubious charms, her ceaseless appetite, and her incessant complaining while exploring the beauties of the Colosseum and the Pantheon. So far, the only thing that seemed to impress her was the gelato.

She sighed, and swirled the red wine in her glass. Ah, well. Tomorrow was another day, right?

"No one told me I'd have to WALK through the Vatican museum," Patty hissed as the sisters gathered the tour group after passing through security. Bel could only stare at her. Patty stomped away, muttering darkly about the review she would post about the tour company on Yelp. In all their years guiding specialty tours around the world, they had never been so appalled and personally maligned by a tour guest.

After drawing a deep, calming breath, Bee turned to Patty, and explained that in over 500 years, visitors to Vatican City had always walked through. There were no people movers here--just masterpieces, such as the Sistine Chapel.

"Well then," Patty snarled, "I must have a coffee right now!" Quickly, Mary Johnson, the cheerful, corn-fed Iowan, informed Patty anxiously that there were no restaurants in the museum.

"I have a mint if you want it," she offered earnestly.

"Oh, keep the damn thing and choke on it," Patty said with her usual grace and tact. Embarrassed to have her thoughtful offer rebuked so coarsely, Mary blushed and faded to the rear of the tour group.

Trying to focus on the positive, Bee smiled at Mary--the "sweet one" in the group; encouraged, her crestfallen face brightened. Bee counted heads before they set off on what should be the experience of a lifetime, IF Patty would cooperate. Bee raised an eyebrow to Isabella, known as Bel to the rest of the world. She nodded slightly, and positioned herself discreetly behind Patty to keep her moving with the rest of the group.

Patty's nephew James and his partner Bill edged as far away from Patty as they could. Mary and her husband Charlie obediently stepped forward, eager and intent, following every word Bee said. Margo, recently widowed, and her sister-in-law Lucy, both from rural Connecticut, smiled as Bee lifted a scarf above her head. This bright purple flag was hoisted on an antenna to help the group keep sight of Bee, as her five foot three frame could be hard to spot in a sea of tourists.

Margo emanated serenity and elegance as she waited, but Bel noticed a barely raised eyebrow shared with Lucy. Although discrete, Bee could tell the ladies shared a dislike for scenes, rudeness, and disruptions.

"Great," Bee thought, "Wonder what they think of Piggy Patty?" On a small tour like this, group dynamics could make or break the trip. A congenial group is like magic--a week of laughter, learning, and an appreciation of the country and culture visited, spiced by good food and wine, and creates mutual affection after eight days together. A disjointed group was another story--throw in a poisonous personality and the days drag on, people retreat from each other and the guides tap dance madly to try to save the tour. Bee shuddered. Her dancing shoes would be well worn by the end of this trip...

Caroline, a lively, independent woman from Texas, looked up from her guidebook. She asked if the group tour included a trip to the Hall of Maps. On her pre-tour information form, she had described herself as "a 40-something reference librarian with a particular interest in antique maps." Her green eyes sparkled when Bee assured her that there would be plenty of time to enjoy the area before moving on to the Sistine Chapel. Bel shuddered slightly--poor Caroline was Patty's assigned roommate; she hoped the Texan was as tough as she looked. The first two nights, jet lag had shortened the evenings and discouraged conversation. The rest of the trip didn't bode quite as well, she feared.

"James!" Patty's flat New England accent blared, jarring Bee back to the moment. "James! Help your dear auntie up the stairs." Her eyes glittered. "Willy, you don't mind if I steal James, do you?" she said coyly, although unable to hide the malice in her tone.

Bill assumed his best Parent/Teacher conference smile. "It's not stealing when it's freely given, Patty." She turned abruptly from him, and grabbed James' arm to heave her bulk up the stairs.

Bel and Bee gathered the group on the piazza overlooking the Vatican gardens. Bel, the purple scarf waving gently over her head, gave the "Castles, Chianti, and Classics" tour group an overview of the planned museum itinerary. All eyes were riveted on her, drinking in her thoughtful commentary--all but Patty's, of course. Her speculative gaze roamed over each of the group in turn. Bee just knew she was assessing their clothes, their accessories, and frankly, their potential worth. She did an involuntary check of her wardrobe, glancing down at her shoes (her favorite Clarks, comfortable and attractive), her Talbot's crisp chinos, the Ralph Lauren linen blouse, and her purse, a large and functional Longchamps. Patty would never know that Bel and Bee were thrift shop addicts, and nothing, other than the Clarks, had been purchased retail! Bee felt a smug grin starting, and quickly adjusted her face to reflect total engagement in Bel's introduction.

Patty's eyes narrowed when she lit on Caroline. Her gaze swept from Caroline's short, red hair, with just a few gray highlights, to her sensible Merrell walking shoes. Her speculative glance turned to a sneer.

Bel, finishing her introduction, reminded the group, "There are no flash photos allowed in the museum. These ancient treasures would be severely damaged by innumerable flashes every day." The group nodded as one, acknowledging her. "Rather like the Texas sun, eh, Caroline?" Patty commented. The redhead blushed--Bee hoped more from anger than embarrassment. Patty smiled a self-satisfied smirk and continued, "I use sunscreen every day to keep my skin unwrinkled!"

Probably the excess fat smooths your face out too, Bel thought, exasperated by the deliberately rude comment. She looked at Bee and the two of them had to look away--too often they shared the same thought and were known to burst out laughing without a word being spoken. That wasn't good for business, and Bee quickly moved to the front and took the purple scarf on its telescoping antenna (Hermès, she thought smugly, and Bee had only paid $2.50 for it!) and started to move forward, avoiding her sister's laughing eyes.

Margo turned as though to distance herself from Patty as the group slowly proceeded. She had joined the tour at the last minute, encouraged by her late husband's sister to enjoy a change of scenery. Lucy, Margo's sister-in-law, was as no-nonsense as expected for a well-known trial attorney. Her obvious fondness for Margo softened her stern edges.

Bee knew that as Lucy relaxed further into the tour she would be an interesting travel companion. Her knowledge of law was extensive, and her love of literature, already clear from her conversations so far, would make her an entertaining guest, Bel suspected. Bel made a mental note to sit next to Lucy at dinner soon.

The group moved without too much difficulty through the crowded halls, stopping frequently. Bel, a retired history professor, was responsible for this part of the tour. She loved history, loved lecturing--a natural combination for their specialized tour business. Bee admired how effortlessly her sister handled the eager, and often esoteric questions from their group. Her own forte was the meals--she had a wonderful list of restaurants to visit, vineyards for tastings, Tuscan farms for cooking classes, and of course, the very best places to stop for gelato and give the feet a rest. Tourists were like small children, she mused--they needed to be fed often, given rests, and allowed enough time to make their own choices with gentle guidance. She giggled at the thought, and was promptly sent the hairy eyeball by her professor sister. Once a teacher, Bee thought, always a teacher. Hmmm. There had been plenty of times when Bee had rescued Bel from an awkward situation--the elevator incident came to mind. Bee quickly put that thought aside, knowing she would truly have a fit of the giggles if she allowed herself to picture her sister trapped in the elevator with the elderly man and his incontinent dog... Besides, she thought loyally, Bel never--almost never, that is--reminded her of the time she left the thrift shop dressing room with her dress stuck in her pantyhose...at least it had been on Senior Discount day, and the elderly ladies had been too consumed with rushing to get the best bargains to really notice. She hoped.

Bee was glad to see her sister smile and shake her head ever so slightly. She knew! How did she know?! Once again, a life time of sharing adventures, joys, and griefs had made it impossible to keep a secret from her sister. Time to keep the little group moving and engaged. The crowd of tourists was beginning to build--she was thankful they chose "off season" for their tour, as the summer crush had yet to swell the crowds and lines to hours in the sweltering heat.

Bel had moved ahead, and the group followed in her wake like obedient ducklings. James and Bill had lingered in the Egyptian hall, fascinated by the mummies. Caroline had wanted to study each beautifully illustrated map, while Charlie and Mary stuck to Bel like glue, unaccustomed to the crowds of people and multitude of languages. Margo and Lucy had, as Bee expected, enjoyed the magnificent paintings. Patty had seemed less interested in the vast collection of treasures than she did in the location of the next chair or bench. She had just plopped herself into a chair beside a beautiful Greek statue--a chair reserved for the omnipresent guards. Bee sighed. It wasn't like obedient ducklings, she thought, it was cats. It was like herding cats. She squared her shoulders and headed for Patty.

"Patty, looks like you need a break. Let's find you a place to rest before we get to the Sistine Chapel," Bee said pleasantly.

"I'm fine here," Patty said looking mutinous. Bee could see the guard heading their direction, looking none too pleased with the situation. "Let's press on, Patty--we're almost there. Did you know it took Michelangelo four years to paint the ceiling? All while reaching over his head!" Patty gave a twisted smirk. "Everyone knows that he was lying on his back. Didn't you do your homework?" Bel sighed inwardly. Patty was just one of those people who have no real interest in learning new information. Her agenda was stubborn adherence to what she believed was true. Her own voice sounded phony chipper, even to Bel. The guard was already gesturing for Patty to leave. Soon he would be beside the women, and have plenty to say. Even Bel's basic Italian would leave no doubt as to what he would be saying. Bee and Bel couldn't afford to have their tour group noted in the list of "undesirable guides."

Patty, it was clear, was enjoying the discomfort--she knew full well she shouldn't be sitting there. As the guard arrived and the torrent of irate Italian washed over her, she smirked and heaved herself to her feet, moving surprisingly quickly and joining the group, her broad back to the guard, leaving Bel to apologize. She had a feeling that it wasn't going to be the last time, either. Mollified, the guard said some choice words, and Bel feigned ignorance. He rolled his eyes, and turned away with some classic Italian

hand gestures. Ouch. The group paused before the long hallw
Sistine Chapel. Bel continued her lecture, clearly relishing the oppc
to share her knowledge with educated, interested people.

"Michelangelo was commissioned by Pope Julius II to paint the Sisu
Chapel. He began his work in 1508, and finished in 1512. The ceiling,
especially The Creation, is believed to be his crowning achievement." Bel
continued her introduction to the Chapel, noting the various scenes the
group should look for. "There is no talking allowed in the Chapel, and
the guards take their jobs very seriously," Bel cautioned. Patty raised her
eyebrows, and Bel hurried on.

"Be sure to look at the reclining figure of Adam, as God reaches out to
him to give him life."

"You boys should like that one!" Patty stage whispered to James and
Bill. "I hear he's naked!" She giggled nastily. James' face tightened, and Bill
gently touched his arm. James relaxed, leaning away from Patty and toward
Bill's solid shoulder.

"Ready?" Bel asked, and the group began the long walk down the
corridor to the Sistine Chapel. Eagerly, the group surged towards the
chapel, each participant looking for what was the most interesting part of
the masterpiece for him or her. Bel and Bee took up positions on either
side of the group, silently pointing out different scenes they had discussed
before entering. They were lucky enough to all have a place along the wall
to lean back and rest while they soaked in the frescoes. All heads craned
upward, searching Michelangelo's glorious interpretation of creation and
judgement. Despite being visited by 5 million people a year, the assembled
crowd each felt alone with the majesty portrayed. A reverent silence in
the room was suddenly broken. "There's the ass of God!" Patty hissed. Bel
gritted her teeth. "Hush!" She whispered to Patty, who barely stifled her
guffaws. "Assogot?" whispered an Asian tourist nearby, anxious to have not
missed an important work. He scrutinized his open notebook, resting on
his forearms for easy reference. The noise roused the invisible guard seated
in front of a microphone. "Silence! There is no talking in the chapel!"
He reminded. Bel, embarassed, could see that one of the guards was

heading their way, alerted to trouble by the noise. She lifted up her purple scarf to call the group together. Silently, with puzzled looks, they gathered around Bel and all of them took the "Tours Only" exit, down the stairs and out of the Sistine Chapel. Behind them, the Asian tourist was madly scrolling through his iPad to find the "Assogot."

Once out on the steps, Charlie asked why their scheduled 15 minutes in the chapel had been shortened to ten. "Unfortunately, it was time to leave," Bel said, "because one of the group was unable to follow the rule of silence." Although she had not mentioned Patty's name, Bel noted that most of the company were shooting Patty vicious looks. Uh oh... time to tap dance.

Chapter Two

To Bee and Bel's great relief, Patty behaved remarkably well--for her--in the Basilica of St. Peter. She rolled her eyes at the pilgrims in their capes, on their knees reciting the rosary in front of the statues of the saints. Eye rolling at least was silent, and the pilgrims were devoutly focused on their prayers and never noticed. The rest of the group had stalked away from Patty. The sisters were glad to note that even she appeared impressed by Michelangelo's *Pieta*--the heart-rending statue of Mary holding her crucified son. It always brought tears to Bee's eyes; she felt the unspeakable sorrow of a mother cradling her lost child, his lifeless body nestled in her lap. The group stood silent before the Michelangelo. Bee swallowed the lump in her throat, and listened as Bel quietly shared with the group her knowledge of the work. It always amazed her that Michelangelo was just 24 years old when he finished the piece in 1499. It was the only piece he ever signed, she noted--his name engraved on the sash across the Virgin's breast--a moment of artistic bravura he forever regretted. Kind of nice to know he was human, too, Bee thought. It now stood apart from the world, behind bulletproof glass, the distance required after a mentally ill geologist smashed Mary's delicately carved marble nose with a hammer in 1972.

Bee sighed, remembering the first time she saw the *Pieta* at the New York World's Fair in 1964. She had stood in line with her mother and aunt for hours, waiting in the stifling heat. Bel had been left home with their father, recovering from her tonsillectomy with lots of ice cream to soothe her throat. At the time, Bee had wished they could change places, fretting and whining about the heat. Her mother and aunt prudently ignored her, fanning themselves and her with folded paper fans. She had sulked--yes, she admitted it--until they entered the darkened room and saw that glorious statue. Even at the tender age of 8, she knew she was in the presence of something other-worldly and divine. She made a point of visiting the timeless masterpiece on every trip to Rome.

Exiting the glorious basilica, the group squinted in the sun and headed to the right. Just in time, they were able to see the changing of the Swiss Guard, a ceremony that never failed to move Bel and Bee and fascinated their previous tour guests. This group was no different; the tour group members clicked away with cell phones and cameras, capturing the fascinating costumes and stylized march of the guards. Bee mused that every year, the guards seemed younger. She wondered if the current crop had started shaving yet. Patty waited impatiently for the ceremony to end; off she went to the guard stationed by the gate, and demanded that the group take her picture with the young guard. Bee winced; although other tourists stood next to the guards for photos, she had never seen one yet who coquettishly wiggled her immense rear up to the guard's pelvis. Patty did just that. Impassive, the Swiss guard held his ground, although Bee could see his surreptitious, if minute, step back from her. Time to tap dance, as Bel would say. The sisters hastily moved the group along the vast piazza to the Vatican Post Office. Due to renovations, it was located in a trailer. Patty grumbled as she climbed the steps. "Why are we stopping here?" she groused.

"It's a chance to send postcards to friends and family," Bel replied, "The stamps are unique, because the Vatican is an independent state." The group happily dispersed, choosing cards that showed the endless treasures, the Sistine Chapel, or St. Peter's tomb. Bel and Bee left them to make their purchases, knowing they would enjoy trying out their American accented "*per favore*" and "*grazie*" on the window clerks. Everyone was busy writing away at the long tables provided. Everyone, that is, but Patty. Bel looked at Bee, who raised an eyebrow. Simultaneously, they put out their right hands and chanted under their breath "Rock, paper, scissors." Bel groaned when she saw Bee had thrown paper. Damn. She shrugged and headed over to Patty.

"Patty, do you need help purchasing a card or stamps?" Bel asked.

For a moment--fleeting, but there--Bel saw the emotions wash over Patty's face. Was it shame, loneliness, or grief, Bel wondered? With all her self-described fortune, she appeared to be alone in the world. The moment passed quickly, though, and Patty sniffed as though smelling something bad. "I wouldn't spend my money on ANYTHING that supports the Catholic church!" she snapped, and turned away.

Bel rejoined Bee. "Yeesh," she said, "I bet there's a hell of a back story there." Bee giggled. "There's a hell of a back end!" Bee whispered back. Bel tried to looked appalled. "Really, Bee!" but Bee could tell she was struggling to remain indignant and professional.

Everyone was no doubt thirsty under the immense blue Roman sky, and would welcome the chance to sit for a while and absorb the treasures they had seen. Bel led the group down a cobbled side street and found a large table in her favorite Vatican City neighborhood street restaurant. Before the waiter had a chance to clear the table, Patty threw herself down in the chair at the head of the table. "Oh no," said the waiter, moving his hands in a generous gesture that is universally understood as negative, "not that one, *bella*!" Patty glared at the man. "My money's as good as anyone's!" Patty snarled, "I'll sit where I choose!" In her agitation, she squirmed in the chair, which promptly gave out; the leg went first, and Patty followed, wallowing in the Roman street for all to see. The group went silent, aghast yet fascinated, to see what would happen next. The waiter rushed to her side and attempted to help her up, but Patty shoved his arm away. "You'll hear from my lawyer!" she shrieked. The waiter looked imploringly at Bel, and shrugged. "*Scusami, scusami*," the waiter said repeatedly.

"What's he saying?" Patty said suspiciously.

"He's saying he's sorry," Bel said. She conferred with the waiter, who explained to Bel that he had asked her not to take that chair as the previous party had broken it, and he feared it would not hold her weight. "He can take his scuzzi and shove it," Patty sneered, unmollified by the glass of sparkling water offered. "Thank God for strong seams!" someone whispered, and the sound of muffled giggles was barely muted by the scraping of chairs being moved.

Time to move on. Bel and Bee guided the group to one of Rome's many public fountains, so they could fill their water bottles. Although Americans were usually hesitant to drink water from an outdoor source, Bel and Bee knew that all fountains in Rome contained fresh, uncirculated water, and were completely safe for drinking. Delighted, the group took turns filling water bottles and posing for pictures. A short time later, they settled the group at another street restaurant. This one catered mainly to tourists, as shown by the posted 'tourist menu,' so it was not one of the sisters' favorites. However, it would have to do, as everyone needed a break.

Most of the tour participants ordered pizza; in Rome, pizza was served individually, and most tourists loved it. Not Patty; she wanted a larger serving and complained loudly. "Really, Patty," said Caroline, "You'll find that it's quite satisfying and just enough for a lunch."

"Oh? And what would you know about satisfaction? If I were an old maid, I would keep my opinions about satisfaction to myself!" sneered Patty. Bee and Bel traded a worried glance; Caroline was Patty's roommate on this tour, since both were single travelers. Any disruption in the room assignments would mean a lot of work for them, so they hoped that Caroline could hang in there and let Patty's remarks go. Caroline's fair skin pinked, but she refused to dignify Patty's remarks with a come-back. She turned on her heel and joined the Johnsons, who were looking dismayed. Lunch concluded quietly.

Bel stood up with her purple scarf raised. "Let's walk down to our bus," she said cheerfully. "We are heading for the first castle of our tour--Castel Sant' Angelo. It was commissioned in 135 AD as a tomb for Hadrian and his family, on the banks of the Tiber River. Alaric plundered the mausoleum in 410, scattering the urns and ashes of all the emperors entombed there. Legend says that the Archangel Michael appeared on the top of the mausoleum in 590, signifying the end of the plague that was devastating the city. The statue on the very peak of the building was commissioned in

gratitude, and thereafter the place was known as the Castel Sant Angelo--
Castle of the Holy Angel." Bel paused to catch a breath.

"There's Paolo!" Bee pointed. Relieved, the travelers dutifully boarded
the Mercedes mini-bus. By unspoken consent, Patty took the seat next to
the driver. No one wanted to watch her try to cram herself into the back
seat. James, Bill, and Caroline volunteered for the back row, and settled in
comfortably, exchanging amused glances. The Johnsons and Bee took the
next row, Charlie folding his tall frame gracefully into the small space. Bel,
Margo and Lucy sat behind the driver and Patty, and Bel continued her
introduction to the Castel.

The short ride to the Castel was a relief to tired feet. Patty announced
that she would wait in the bus while the others toured. Paolo, however,
expressed his great and deep regret that it would not be possible. His fluid
tone, limpid eyes, and courtly gestures while he escorted Patty out of the
bus managed to have her deposited neatly on the walkway in front of the
castle before she could protest. He winked at Caroline as she went past, and
the redhead blushed--but smiled back.

Slowed by Patty's whining progress up the hill, the group listened
intently as Bel went on with her explanation of the history of the castle.
"In Puccini's opera "*Tosca*," Bel said, "the heroine, Floria Tosca, having
unknowingly caused her lover's execution, throws herself off the ramparts
of this castle. So," said Bel with a mischievous look in her eye, "be careful
in the castle!"

Entering the castle, the group began the winding climb up the
spiral ramp. Bel and Bee positioned themselves at either end of the
group. Bee took up her place beside Patty, since Bel had had the pleasure
in the Vatican--so to speak. She encouraged the sweating woman with
small talk as they wound through the dark, damp hall. "It's amazing
this building has been here for over a thousand years, isn't it?" Patty
just stared at her. The others moved forward while Caroline lingered to
read the informational sign, but Bee knew she would catch up with the
group quickly. Lucy and Margo turned, and asked about the *Passetto di
Borgo*. Distracted, Bee explained about the covered passage between the

Vatican and the castle, which provided the Popes with a safe way to flee from marauders.

Charlie joined the conversation, asking, "Isn't Michael the avenging angel?" Delighted, Bee answered, "Yes! He's the patron saint of paratroopers, police, and the ill, and was said to have been the leader of the forces in the triumph over the powers of hell. The populace believed it was his intervention that ended the plague, too." The conversation flowed as the group continued.

From below came a cry of distress. Bee turned and with a jolt realized Patty was no longer with the group. Quickly counting heads, Bee and Bel realized that neither Patty nor Caroline were there. With an exchange of looks, Bel nodded, indicating that she would stay with the group. Bee took off down the ramp. Around the corner a group of people had clustered-- guards, tourists, and...of course. Bel's heart sunk. There was Patty, splayed out on the floor, with Caroline standing over her, looking defiant. Patty spotted Bel.

"She pushed me!" she shrieked, jabbing a fat finger toward Caroline.

Caroline rolled her eyes. "I didn't push you. I tried to grab you as you were falling."

Patty moaned dramatically, and the guard spoke rapidly into his radio. Bel was genuinely concerned to see the large purple bruise rising on her forehead.

A chair rapidly appeared, and Patty was helped by two guards into the chair. Bel was sure she saw a malicious glimmer in her eyes, but quickly dismissed the thought. Patty's eyes must be watering from the pain, she thought charitably. Caroline came over to Bel.

"She was leaning against the wall when I came around the corner. As I walked by, she took a step toward me and tripped on the cobblestones. I think she was actually trying to push me!" Caroline flushed, both angry and amused, "That's what I get for trying to help her!"

Bel checked on Patty, the guards now discussing whether to phone for an ambulance. Alarmed, she turned to Patty. "Do you really think you need an ambulance?" she asked. Speculatively, Patty eyed her,

14

"Is it covered by the tour?" Surprise, Bel thought--she would milk this. "No, this accident has nothing to do with the tour--" Patty cut her off, "Then no. I'm fine."

Wearily, Bel helped Patty up from the chair and with a head nudge, suggested that Caroline join the group ahead of them. "Patty, are you really okay?" asked Bel. "A stint in a Roman emergency ward is not something to look forward to, but if..." Patty cut her off again, "No, I don't want to go to any hospital in Italy! They probably don't even speak English! But you can be sure that this attempt on my life is going into my Yelp review of this pathetic tour." With a flounce, Patty increased her speed and joined the rest of the group. "What are you looking at?" Patty snarled at an Asian tourist watching the excitement. Bee recognized him as the poor man startled by Patty in the Sistine Chapel. Small world, she thought, and gave him a weak, apologetic wave. She imagined him, home again, describing the bizarre events of his day in Rome to all his friends.

Bel gathered the group together again. Shaken, she said, "We need to ask you all to stay together. We haven't yet lost a tour member, and we don't want to start now!"

The Johnsons seemed to enjoy touring the castle as much as they had appreciated the Vatican Museum. They looked the part of first-time tourists with their brilliant white sneakers, fanny packs, and matching gimme caps which proudly proclaimed Sheldon, Iowa, as the home of a collection of exotic dirt. These caps had caused secret merriment among the sisters, but it was hard not to like the Johnsons. They were earnest, courteous, and awed by everything they saw. Bel wondered how they had found the resources to afford this specialized tour of Italy. She supposed small-town pharmacists made a decent living, but still.....

James, and his partner, Bill, appeared to be trying to enjoy themselves. They distanced themselves as much as possible from Patty, and were reserved, but courteous, with the other guests. The sisters had the feeling they were cautious, unsure of their reception as an openly gay couple. So far, though, the only one to even seem interested was James' Aunt Patty, and she had invited them as her guests.

Lucy and Margo were the "easy" tour members, Bel thought. They were knowledgeable, and had done their homework, reading up on all the sights before their arrival in Italy. They had come two days before the trip to adjust to the time change and spend time in the art museums before the tour began. Bel had, on occasion, seen fleeting looks of grief on Margo's face--it had only been six months since her husband had died suddenly of a massive heart attack. Ironic, the plump Bel thought, since both Margo and Lucy seemed so health conscious, rising early every day to take a brisk walk through the streets before the touring began.

Bel and Bee, anxious to be sure Patty was indeed unharmed other than bumps and bruises, decided to call Paolo to pick them up early and return them to the hotel. In 15 minutes he was there, bearing a cold compress and a bottle of sparkling water for Patty. She fairly simpered at him as she allowed him to lead her to the bus. Relieved, Bel and Bee turned to the other guests.

"Paolo will take anyone back to the hotel who would like to have a little break before dinner tonight. If you'd prefer, he can also drop you near the Pantheon or the Trevi Fountain." There were murmured consultations while the group made their plans.

"Paolo, you're such a dear boy--so attentive. Unlike some people..." Patty fairly purred. Bel wanted to gag, but forced herself to smile. Bill looked at James, who grinned and shrugged, determined to not rise to the bait.

Margo and Lucy decided to take the bus to the Trevi Fountain and then to walk to the Spanish Steps--a "lovely stroll" for them before dinner. Charlie and Mary decided to head back to the hotel and walk about the neighborhood, looking for a *Farmacia* to visit, while James and Bill chose to leave the group there, and wander back to the hotel, enjoying the sights along the way. Bel thought they might just need the privacy after spending the day with Patty.

Caroline hesitated before entering the bus. "I'd really like to see the catacombs," she said, "but it's so far out of town."

"One of my favorite places! Allow me to drive you there, *Signora*," Paolo said with a grin. "It will be wonderful to see the beautiful pines, and breathe the fresh air."

Caroline smiled, and climbed into the van. Patty frowned, and moaned gently when Paolo took the driver's seat. Paolo seemed oblivious to Patty, and chatted animatedly with Caroline instead. When they reached the hotel, just one block from the historic city center, the owner was there to greet them. A slim, young, woman, she hastened to take Patty upstairs. Bel and Bee guided Patty to the elevator, but Patty's girth made sharing the elevator impossible; tiny, it had been carved into the side of the formal marble staircase when the home was converted to a bed and breakfast.

Patty rode up sullenly. She felt she deserved more attention than she had gotten from the group. After all, she had been gravely wounded! And no one was nearly sympathetic enough, she sniffed. Well, she would use her time wisely while they all went out and left her behind.

Chapter Three

Bel and Bee collapsed on their twin beds, exhausted by the strange events of the day. They agreed that Piggy Patty--or PP--was the worst tour guest they had ever had.

"She's driving me crazy!" Bel moaned, "I could have killed her when she nearly got us thrown out of the Sistine Chapel." Bee cringed, thinking of the look on the guard's face as he came toward them through the crowd.

"Do you think her husband died or ran away?" Bee said. "Either would be better than living with that!" Bel retorted. "What do you think Jack would think of her?" Bel asked her sister. Jack, a recreational sailor with a salty tongue, put up with no nonsense and didn't suffer fools. Bee giggled, knowing her husband would have had plenty to say and most of it not repeatable. Bel knew that her husband, Nate, a quiet, resourceful literature professor, would be appalled by Patty, but few would know it. Nate was the essence of gentleman scholar.

Instinctively, both women reached for their phones to check for messages from home.

"Damn it, Bel, when did you have time to play Words With Friends?" Bee fumed. Although she never let on to her sister, she suspected that Bel cheated at the game. Or so Bee maintained--deep down inside she knew Bel was the better player, but hated to admit it to anyone--especially herself. In fact, when she lost the word games, as she frequently did, she was wont to suggest that excellence in word games was merely a neurological difference, having nothing to do with intelligence. Had Bee won, of course, she would have gloated over her sister and smirked about her better brain power. Bee shook her head ruefully.

Checking her mail, she was reassured to find a message letting her know all was well. Bel knew that Nate could take care of himself, but could the absent-minded philosophy professor look after the house this time? On their last trip, Bel came home to a cheerful husband who had finished his book, bottled his wine, but forgotten to water her prize orchids. Three of his bottles had popped their corks, leaving red wine all over the ceiling. When Bel had walked in she had thought she had entered a crime scene. Luckily, the only things actually dead were her orchids.

Bee had heard from Jack, too. A retired psychologist, he was relishing his free time. He had been good at his job, and had a long list of grateful patients who had worked through terrible life circumstances. His instinct and attention to detail made him a valuable resource. She worried about leaving him alone, though, knowing he would take the opportunity to sail as much as possible, often solo. He was a good sailor, she knew, but it made her uncomfortable when he went out alone. She was secretly thrilled when his text informed her that the weather on the bay was awful and he had been forced to stay on land. She texted back her condolences, not a bit ashamed by the big fib.

By unanimous agreement, the husbands stayed home when "the goils," as they affectionately called them, were leading a tour. They were always happy to go on the advance, scouting trips--the "Eat, pay, shove" trips, they called them--but stayed home when there were paying guests to attend to. The first trip the sisters had organized had not filled up. Desperate, they convinced their husbands to join the tour as "strangers" to make the tour look more popular. It was a disaster, funny in hindsight, but at the time, a real hand-wringer. Jack and Nate had happily shared a room, and had been tickled to realize that the elderly ladies on the garden tour had decided they were a couple. They eagerly embraced the roles, and the sisters had their hands full keeping them in line. The elderly ladies on the tour had been shocked when one of them discovered Jack leaving Bee's room early one morning, wearing nothing but his robe. They had been quite protective of

Nate, refusing to speak to Jack the rest of the day. Nate had been completely bewildered, having had an enjoyable marital evening with his wife as well, until Jack took him aside and informed him that the ladies "knew" he had cheated on him. To restore peace on the tour, the men staged a very public, very dramatic scene, worthy of a soap opera. The explanation was loud and ridiculous, the apology was florid, and reconciliation achieved, all within earshot of the very interested ladies. The sisters could barely look at them for the rest of the trip. It was the very last time the "boys" were invited on a tour.

Having touched base with home, the sisters turned to reviewing the evening plans. Dinner was to be a traveling meal--cocktails and *aperitivo* at the hotel, then dinner at one of their favorite cafes on the Piazza Navonne. A great spot for people watching, close to the hotel, and perfect for the after-dinner stroll to Bee's favorite gelato shop.

Bel groaned. "Who gets PP duty tonight?" Bee stuck out her fist, and together they chanted "Rock, Paper, Scissors" and both women burst out laughing when they realized they both threw paper. They chanted again, and this time, they both threw rocks, and laughed even harder. The third time, they were silent when they both used scissors.

"Dang." Bee observed soberly. "Even the universe doesn't want to sit with Patty." They looked at each other. "Time to use the 'Deciding Factor,'" intoned Bel.

"NO!" Bee moaned. "You know what day it is! No fair!" Bel just shook her head, and smiled serenely. When the girls were little and couldn't agree on whose turn it was, their mother had decreed 'The Deciding Factor' to end the petty childhood squabbles. On even days, Bel had first choice, having been born on an even day. On odd days, Bee chose first, having been born on an odd day. It was an even day, and they both knew it. Bee sighed. "Ok. 'Deciding Factor' it is. But you get to walk with her to the restaurant!"

Two hours later, the group convened in the B and B serving area. The sisters had arranged with the concierge to offer the guests a choice of Chianti or prosecco, and to provide an antipasto platter, focaccia, and olives. The sisters did a head count, and were reassured to find all present, even Patty, a large and unnecessary bandaid on her bruise. James, restored by his walk through the city, offered her a glass of prosecco.

"I want a Diet Coke," she muttered petulantly. "I don't think there is any, Patty," he said, trying not to grin. She frowned, "What kind of a country is this?" The others laughed, assuming she was kidding. Her face tightened, and she silently accepted the proffered glass.

Caroline was sharing her adventure with Paolo with Margo and Lucy. They listened raptly as she described the eerie catacombs where early Christians had been buried. Unable to bury their dead within the city walls, they relied on wealthy benefactors to donate land where they could carve out niches in the tufa below the earth. She went on to explain how the burial niches had been carved out of the volcanic material, pliable and easily worked, but hard as stone once exposed to air. Thousands of early Christians had been interred there, and small oil lamps and a few beautiful frescos were all that remained after Visigoth raiders had swept through the tombs, looting the graves for the gold jewelry buried with the bodies. Caroline's knowledge and her enthusiasm made her listeners jealous that they hadn't explored the passageways too. Her green eyes glowed as she described the lovely pines----umbrella-like trees--under the beautiful, startling blue skies, in stark contrast with the chilly, dark underground necropolis below.

Patty interrupted her description of the idyllic afternoon. "I'm glad you had fun," she said acerbically. "After you pushed me down, I had a horrible headache all day." Caroline's green eyes snapped, "Seriously, Patty. You need to get a grip." She walked away, and Margo and Lucy followed. The three of them helped themselves to another glass of prosecco and laughter flowed from their little group.

The second glass of wine seemed to relax the group and stimulate conversation. James and Bill were joined by Charlie and Mary, and the four chatted like long lost friends. Bill, a soccer coach at his high school, was delighted to hear that Charlie and Mary had a son in college on a soccer scholarship. "Oh man. Now you've got him started!" James rolled his eyes. Bill laughed, and put his arm around James' shoulder, "We can't all be gourmet chefs. Some of us just run around the field and work up an appetite. I appreciate your cooking!" The affection between them was obvious, and Mary eagerly took James aside to discuss the spices he had bought that day in the street market.

The concierge brought out the *aperitivo*, and the group hungrily tasted the typical Italian delights. Bee took the opportunity to educate the group, discussing the differences in olives, the rich foccacia, and the platter of assorted meats, cheeses, and pickled vegetables. There were many questions about the differences between salami, pepperoni, prosciutto, and lardo. The adventurous eaters tasted almost everything. Bee was delighted to see Mary and Charlie close their eyes and taste the lardo--and enjoyed the surprised look of pleasure on their faces. "You know," Charlie exclaimed, "for a piece of fat, that sure tastes pretty good!"

"That's disgusting," said Patty, and ate her third plate of cheese. Glances were exchanged all around the room.

Bee laughed, "That's what I thought before I tried it, too. But it's a regional specialty, and they're fiercely proud of it. It's actually quite delicious. You just have to forget what it is and be willing to just go with it." The rest of the group gathered around, and one by one, helped themselves to a slice. Bee was happy to have James contribute to the discussion--he had enthusiastically begun pickling foods just the summer before, and was able to explain the process as the group sampled the antipasti. Mary added to the conversation when it turned to the difference between bread and focaccia. She was a bread baker, and loved the earthy flavors of rosemary and olive in the dense, moist bread. Margo joined the discussion, eagerly asking Mary about making gluten-free bread.

Lucy stood to the back of the group, watching Margo. She smiled when Bel joined her. "This is the happiest I've seen her in six months," she told Bel. Indeed, Margo's face was flushed and animated as she described their visit that afternoon to a bakery that offered gluten-free desserts. "It's been rough. Margo lost her father tragically at a young age, and now, to lose

Frank so young, too..." Lucy's voice drifted off, and the loss of her brother reflected on her face. Despite her Talbots catalogue good looks and Ralph Lauren legs, there was a sad little sister somewhere inside the fashionable, competent attorney. Impulsively, Bel hugged her. Startled, Lucy smiled, and shook her head ruefully, "A great comfort I am. I wanted her to think of something different, and all I can think of is how happy she and Frank were, and how much I miss him." The catch in her voice brought tears to Bel's eyes. Lucy cleared her throat, and said lightly, "Let's grab some cheese before Patty eats everything!"

Dinner was a success--the easy stroll in the cool night air piqued appetites, and the group happily settled around a table in a cafe overlooking the Fountain of the Four Rivers in the Piazza Navonna. Bee waited for Patty to choose a seat, then swooped in and sat next to her, eliminating the awkward shuffle of people trying desperately to avoid sitting near her, while avoiding looking like they were avoiding her! Bee felt very noble when she saw the obvious relief on everyone's faces as they sat. Taking one for the team, she thought to herself. Bel owes me BIG. Turning, she saw Bel looking at her from the other end of the table, amused. She knows! thought Bee. How does she do that?! Bel smiled at Bee, and picked up the menu to explain the different dishes to the group.

The group was engaged in making their choices. Margo, a gluten-free eater, was delighted to learn the restaurant had gluten-free pasta and she could choose freely. Patty announced loudly that she was allergic to peanuts, and demanded to know what was "safe" for her to eat. The waiter, dressed in a white shirt, bow tie, and long black apron, turned questioningly to Bel. Bel, using her charm as well as her Italian, clarified the situation, explaining Patty had an allergy and was concerned that peanut oil might be used. Mildly insulted, the waiter turned to Patty. "You're in Italy! We use only olive oil!" he said in heavily accented English. "But I will check for *Signora*." He bowed stiffly, and left the table. Under his breath, he spoke rapidly to the waiter at the next table, who burst out laughing. Bel was rather certain she heard the words nuts--but wasn't at all sure he was referring to the legume in question.

The food was delicious, brought in stages. The *primi piatti*--soup or salad for most of the group, artichokes for Bee and James--was accompanied by a large bottle of house wine. Patty was thrilled when the waiter brought her a Diet Coke, and she drank it in almost one gulp. She smacked her lips. "Now, that's good!" she gloated. The waiter, with a clipped nod of his head, turned to bring her another.

The *secondi* was just as good--fish for Lucy and Margo, pork for Charlie and Mary, and octopus for James and Bill. Stubbornly, Patty insisted on a pizza. She had no interest in "foreign food." Caroline eyed her with obvious distaste. Uh oh, thought Bel as she ate her veal piccata.

The group was distracted momentarily as a flower seller approached the table, carrying an armload of roses. "For the beautiful lady?" he repeated over and over, approaching each man at the table in turn. Bill, seated next to both Mary and Lucy, gallantly purchased roses for each of them. Charlie, not to be outdone, bought a rose for his dinner companions, Margo and Caroline. James laughed, and motioned the ecstatic flower seller over, and bought roses for Bel, Bee, and Patty, earning him a round of applause. The waiter, seeing the roses covering the table, produced a wine chiller filled with water, and the ladies added their flowers, each in turn.

"Ouch!" exclaimed Caroline, as a thorn snagged her thumb. A drop of blood landed on the white linen table cloth. "Ah hah!" cried Patty smugly. "I knew you had blood on your hands!" She laughed heartily at her own joke.

Mary, the perpetual scout leader, promptly drew a band aid from her fanny pack and offered it to Caroline. She accepted it gratefully, but with a grim set to her jaw that worried Bee.

The group lingered over dinner, enjoying a second bottle of wine. The night was cool, and the breeze carried the sound of the splashing fountain over the cries of the street vendors. The helicopter toys they were selling flew high into the air, colorful arcs in the night. Others hawked scarves, knock-off designer purses, or "original" art. Bill, Charlie, Caroline, and Lucy had all read Dan Brown's *Angels and Demons* from the reading list, and were discussing the scene where the Cardinal meets an untimely end in the fountain. Caroline, with her knowledge of ancient maps, was eagerly pointing out the key locations in the book on her map of Rome. James, Mary, and Bee were happily engaged in trying to figure out what spices had been used in the delicious sauce they had enthusiastically passed around. Margo, a faraway look in her eyes, was smiling at a distant memory, while rolling her wine glass between her fingers.

Maybe, thought Bel. Just maybe we can pull this off...please, please, please, she prayed to the universe. Maybe we got all the kinks out today. Or maybe not. At her age, she knew enough to be hopeful and sceptical at the same time.

After dinner, Mary and Charlie declared themselves too full for gelato, and decided to walk back to the hotel early. "Too full for gelato?!" Patty snorted. "Too full of Mallmart ice cream, you mean!" She laughed, a harsh sound in the soft night air. Charlie looked startled, and turned away, his arm around Mary. The couple hurried off, with the briefest of goodbyes.

"What was that about?" James demanded of his aunt. "Oh, nothing. You know all those hicks shop at Mallmart," she narrowed her eyes at him. "You wouldn't be caught dead in a Mallmart, would you, pretty boy?" James flushed.

Bel paid the waiter, adding an uncustomarily large tip in gratitude for the service. She sighed. Theirs had not been the easiest of groups to serve tonight. The ladies gathered their roses, and the group wandered into the piazza. Arm in arm, James and Bill gazed into the fountain.

"Young love," said Margo quietly, and tears filled her eyes. Lucy and Caroline linked arms with her, and stood quietly together. The streetlights made halos around their hair, catching the women in silhouette. They were striking in their differences--Lucy with jet black hair, pulled back close to the head, Caroline, with her short red hair, and Margo, with her blonde curls, looking the most angelic of all.

Chapter Four

B ack in their room, the sisters chatted about the day. "So far, so good," said Bel. They agreed it had gone better than expected, what with Patty's nastiness and accidents. "That woman is so mean," said Bee, "it's no wonder nobody wants to be with her! Even though she paid for her nephew and his partner to go on this trip, it's clear they aren't comfortable being around her."

"I wonder why they agreed to go, then?" Bel mused, "I mean, it's a great opportunity, but seriously, would you want to be indebted to her?" Bee shook her head.

"I could have killed her today when she threatened to sue that poor waiter, after he told her not to sit in that chair. Really, that fall was her fault." Bel and Bee agreed that she was among the nastiest of tourists they had had the displeasure to know.

"Of course, the best ever was Mom," said Bel. "Remember the time we toured Scotland together? You, me, mom, and our two daughters--a girl's trip. I think that's what motivated us to start the specialty tours. Mom was such a trooper, as old as the hills but game for anything." "Sure!" Bee agreed, "Remember the time she approached that young man who was wearing a kilt in Edinburgh? I'll bet that was the first time an octogenarian asked him sweetly, "Please, sir, I always wondered what a Scotsman wore under his kilt." "Madam," he replied seriously, "I canna tell ye but I can show ye. We have a sitting queen!" With that, he turned his back, bent over, and flipped up his kilt, baring a gloriously naked derriere." They roared with laughter at the memory. "The best part," gasped Bee, "was that mom ever after insisted that that was the highlight of the trip!" Bel, wiping away tears of laughter, disagreed. "No," she giggled, "The best part was listening to her describe his backside to her friends-- "oh, it was lovely and firm!"" she mimicked. They dissolved into laughter again.

"She was a gem," said Bel. "But Patty is just a big, fat, pain in the ass. I'm not slim by any means, but she hogs the lion's share at any gathering, and the others resent her surly attitude and nasty digs. What are we going to do?" Bee thought for a moment. "The main thing is for Caroline to continue to room with her," Bee said. "Otherwise it will be a nightmare for us and we'll lose money on the tour, having to request another room. Who knows if the remaining places will even have an extra room? One of us will have to room with PP if they don't!" The sisters sobered, considering.

"Maybe she will just drop dead and save everyone a lot of grief-- including her nephew!" Bel remarked, annoyed by the idea. "Bel! Don't even think it!!" Bee grimaced.

Thoughts turned back to planning the next day's activities, and the women checked their schedules, divided duties, and reviewed the sites they were to visit, being sure to include references to their beloved literature--the "classics" part of their tour. Shakespeare, Dante, Machiavelli, Irving Stone, G.K. Chesterton, and Dan Brown formed the basis of their reading list, hoping to appeal to a broad spectrum of guests. So far, it appeared that the tour group members had done their homework; each of them had seemed to have read at least two of the suggested books. Of course, it appeared that each had read what appealed to them most. Talking it over, Bee and Bel thought they could have easily predicted what each guest had read. The only surprise to them was Charlie and Mary--they had delved deep into Machiavelli--an odd choice, they thought, for the Iowans. The scheming Florentine prince seemed more Patty's style, Bel mused.

"More like Lucretia Borgia!" snorted Bee. "She's poisonous!"

There was just enough time to relax before sleeping. Having checked their email, the sisters turned to one of their passions: Words with Friends. Fingers flew madly as the sisters competed. They were great competitors, but neither kept track of wins or losses. "Seriously?" Bee groused.

"Do you even KNOW what "quired" means??" Bel tried to look sup
"Don't you?" she challenged. "I asked YOU!" Bee roared. Bel shrugged.
"It took the word. I don't have to define it!" Bee glared at her sister, and Bel
studiously stared at her phone, pretending to be absorbed in what she saw
there. "Ha!" Bee crowded, and Bel saw that her sister had added an S to
quired, doubling her points at the same time. Damn! Equanimity restored,
the sisters played happily until bed time.

Alone in her room, Patty was busy. Caroline had disappeared, making
a feeble excuse about wanting to see the night sky, but Patty had seen
Paolo waiting by the back door of the B and B. Industriously, she used
her iPad to access the public records information so helpful to real estate
agents like Patty. At home, she was involved in securing tenants for some
of her clients, and the landlords wanted to know that their prospective
tenants were free of serious criminal activity. Of course, Patty subscribed
to a service for the information, and found it amusing to investigate her
neighbors and acquaintances as well. This had landed her in hot water
when she publicly accused her next-door neighbor of stealing from the
school system where she worked as a teacher in a previous position. Patty
had gone to a Board of Education meeting in her hometown, and loudly
denounced the teacher at the meeting. "Once a thief, always a thief!" Patty
had thundered. However, the teacher had a common name, was not the
one arrested, and was immediately cleared. The resentment that simmered
next door to Patty, however, did not. It broke out from time to time in little
ways: dog waste in her flowerbeds, very early lawn mowing on weekends,
and other fairly benign reminders of the neighbor's annoyance. Patty took
her revenge; on a day when her neighbor was away at school, she snuck
into her yard, and poked a very stinky piece of cheese into the house's vent
system. She fully expected the evil smell to keep her neighbor searching
madly for the source, for years to come.

Tonight, however, she had tour participants on her mind. Her small
eyes glittered, and her tongue poked out of the corner of her mouth as she
concentrated. She scrolled through her iPad. Interesting, she thought, and
smiled. It wasn't a nice smile.

Chapter Five

Bee and Bel were up early, ready to greet the travelers as they arrived in the breakfast room. A typical Italian breakfast was laid out for them. Rich, dark coffee perfumed the air. Bel, a tea drinker, was thrilled to see steaming hot water and her favorite black tea available. She always traveled with tea bags, just in case...but she was in luck. The concierge had remembered her preferences--that was one reason they kept coming back to the quiet little B and B, tucked away on a back street, away from traffic but centrally located. The high ceilings, natural light and comfy beds made up for the tiny showers. Bel shuddered at the image of Patty crammed into the corner shower, and quickly tried to think about the delicious cheeses, breads, and fruits before her. She filled her plate with protein, knowing it would be a busy day. Her hand wavered over the pastries, her conscience warring with her tastebuds. As usual, her tastebuds won. She resolutely ate her yoghurt first, though, to try to justify the treat. She wasn't even fooling herself.

Bee fought the battle of the bulge. She envied Bel, her older sister. Taller, blonde, blue eyed and a sharp wit, she carried the occasional extra pounds more easily. Bee sighed. As a teenager, she had, in frustration, confronted her mother. "Bel is blonde, tall, and blue eyed. I'm short, chubby, have braces, and have mousy brown hair and dirt brown eyes." Her mother's eyes had swept over her, amused and affectionate but not buying into the self pity, "You were the last child. I was tired!" They had both burst out laughing and helped themselves to ice cream. Bee shook her head fondly at the memory, and enjoyed every bite of the warm, flaky pastry.

Patty was one of the first of the tour group guests to arrive. Thankfully, the sisters noticed that she was no longer wearing the bandage over her bruise. She had a smug, self-satisfied look on her face, Bel noticed. She helped herself to breakfast, and looked around for a convenient table. She spotted Bee and Bel, and started toward them. The concierge, approaching from the kitchen, stopped at the table to confirm details with the sisters. Bee and Bel rapidly engaged in perhaps an overly detailed discussion, and Patty changed course and headed to an empty table.

By ones and twos the others in their group filed in and helped themselves to breakfast. There was a pleasant hum in the room as everyone chatted congenially. A good night's rest does wonders, Bee mused. The last to arrive was Caroline, looking flushed and angry. She headed straight to the sisters' table, and leaned in close.

Quietly, icily, she spoke, enunciating carefully.

"I'm sorry to tell you that you will have to find another room for me. I will kill that woman if I have to spend another night sharing her room." She stared at Bee, and then at Bel. The sisters waited silently for her to continue, dreading but not surprised by the ultimatum.

"Do you know what she did? I went out last night. When I came back, the room was dark. No problem, that's fair. But when I went to turn on the bathroom light, nothing happened."

She scowled. "Good thing I have a flashlight app on my phone. She had taken all of the light bulbs out of their sockets!"

Bee started to speak, but Caroline held up her hand. "There's more. She set her alarm for 5:30 this morning. Loud. I tried to sleep through her shower, which was a whole lot easier than sleeping through her getting dressed, slamming drawers, replacing the light bulbs, and opening the drapes." Again, Bee started to speak. Caroline, giving her a look, held up her hand again. "I'm not done. When she finally left the room I went to take my shower. She had used ALL the towels. And then thrown them in the bidet." This time Bee was speechless.

Caroline smiled grimly. "I know it will cost the tour extra money to arrange another room. But I will. not. share. with. her." The punctuation was slow, deliberate, and final.

Bee and Bel exchanged glances, and smoothly, calmly, Bel assured her, "Of course not. We will make whatever arrangements necessary. You will have a room to yourself for the rest of the tour." Despite her outward calm, Bel's heart sank. There went any hope of a profit on this tour. The tap dance shoes might not survive this group.

The red-headed Texan thanked them gratefully, and headed off to get her breakfast. She did NOT sit with Patty, choosing instead to sit with Charlie and Mary, who welcomed her to their little table.

Bel raised an eyebrow to Bee, and Bee answered in kind. "While you introduce today's activities, I'll phone the B and B in Siena," Bel said, and Bee nodded her agreement. "If they don't have a room available...." They looked at each other, horrified. "Oh, no!" Bee said. "You don't mean..."

"Don't say it!" groaned Bel, "Just keep your fingers crossed!" Fingers! thought Bee. She was ready to cross fingers, legs, toes,and eyes to keep from having to share a room with PP!

Bee gave the group time to finish up their meals, then suggested everyone grab a second espresso or latte and join her in the sitting room where they had enjoyed their *aperitivo* the night before.

Assembled, the group looked at her expectantly. Bee took a breath before she began. Unlike Bel, she didn't speak to groups for a living. Being an editor was a much quieter job, and Bee had to get psyched for the task. Once warmed to her subject, though, she was a witty and intelligent speaker.

"I hope everyone had a good night," she began, and out of the corner of her eye noticed Caroline blushing. That was odd, she thought. She was indignant not half an hour ago, and now she's embarrassed? And why was Patty smirking? Bee continued. "Today we say *arrivederci* to Roma. We hope you enjoyed your visit to the Eternal City, and if you tossed a coin in the Trevi Fountain, you'll surely be back." The group smiled its agreement, heads nodding. "Paolo will be here in an hour to load your luggage into the bus; please have it in the lobby promptly so we are not delayed in our departure. We will drive through the countryside up to Siena, where we will have our first cooking class." James and Mary high fived each other, delighted at the prospect of getting first-hand knowledge of Tuscan cooking.

"Our instructor speaks very little English, but is a well known cook at one of the oldest inns in Tuscany. They are giving us their kitchen, their garden, and their larder to create a sumptuous meal, and we will stop in at a vineyard on our way, and taste some marvelous wines. We'll learn about Chianti, Chianti Classico, and Super Tuscans." Bee was glad to see the group looking eager and engaged. Hopefully the thought of the delicious wines would keep them happy on the three hour long ride north.

"I can't tell you exactly what's on the menu--our instructor bases her choices on what is fresh and ready in the garden, the weather, and other factors my Italian just couldn't keep up with." The group laughed sympathetically. "I will tell you, though, that I've never left her table hungry, and it's always been delicious. Have any of you ever made pasta by hand?" Mary and Lucy raised their hands. Bee was surprised by Lucy. "Really?!" She blurted out. Lucy laughed. "I love pasta!" she said. "You sure don't look it," said Bill, mildly, and Lucy smiled and batted his arm. "Thanks. It's amazing what you can eat if you run five miles a day!" Her voice had a rather pointed quality to it. Bee noticed that Patty was eating her third pastry, and winced.

Just then Bel rejoined the group, and gave Bee the slightest nod and a thumbs up. Relieved, Bee grinned back at her.

"What's so funny?" Patty asked suspiciously. Bel came to Bee's rescue and said, "The weather forecast has been revised. We'll be under the Tuscan sun in no time--instead of the Tuscan rain clouds!" Bee let out the breath she'd been holding. The group cheered, and with that, Bee dismissed them to pack up and finish their morning routines, reminding them to be in the lobby at 10:00 a.m. sharp.

As they all headed out of the room, Patty said loudly, "I wonder what a reference librarian does at night in Rome? Just what would she research? The mating habits of the locals?" and laughed nastily. Caroline, her face flushed and set, walked out of the room.

34

Chapter Six

Bel and Bee were in the lobby early, having settled with the concierge and assured her of their return and a favorable review on Travelocity. They were careful to reiterate their thanks for her attention to detail--the tea, gluten-free food for Margo, and the use of the lovely sitting room, normally for the owner's family only.

At ten o'clock, all the luggage was in the lobby. Funny, thought Bel. You can tell exactly which luggage goes with which person. The Johnsons had plain black nylon wheeled suitcases, practical and straightforward. Margo had an old suitcase--good quality, but obviously well used. James and Bill had matching suitcases from L.L. Bean, with leather trim. Caroline's was new, sturdy, and green. Lucy had a designer bag, with designer tags, discreet but obviously expensive. Bel and Bee had matching bags, too--bought with the profits from their last tour. They were wonderful--wheels that rolled 360 degrees, a lovely chocolate brown, and easy to lift into overhead bins. And Patty's bag...Bel giggled. Like Patty, it was overfull, bulging at the sides, and garish.

By 10:35, Paolo had all the bags loaded, and the group began to file onto the comfortable little bus. Perfect for a small group, it seated 12 and had room in the back to hold the luggage. It was a tight fit for the luggage, but Paolo had obviously played way too many games of Tetris as a child, and made everything fit perfectly.

The group enjoyed the road trip into Tuscany, and Bel and Bee had discovered through experience that most tourists were ready for a break from the city after a visit in Rome. Conversation flowed freely in the little bus. James and Bill were delighted when it turned out that their daughter Avery was attending Caroline's alma mater. They traded stories about the campus, town, and the opportunities available to the university's graduates. Mary and Charlie, seated with Margo, discovered a shared passion for Shakespeare. The couple had met as cast members of a production of Romeo and Juliet. Charlie proudly recited the lines from Tybalt's death scene--the glory of his acting career forty years earlier! Margo applauded vigorously, and Mary beamed. She had, she announced with dancing eyes, excelled in the role of Nurse. Patty was happily ensconced next to Paolo, who graciously parried her attempts to engage him while he navigated the twisting roads. Lucy read her guide book, looking up often to drink in the scenery. Bee and Bel sat together, enjoying the opportunity to just sit, relax and take a breath. They sat in companionable silence, until Bee looked at her sister and and asked "So how much is the extra room for the rest of the trip going to set us back?" Bel sighed. "How much is it worth to keep a happy customer?" She added, under her breath, "How much is it worth not to room with Patty?" Bee held up her hand, unconsciously copying Caroline's dramatic conversation that morning. "So...we need to call the other B and B's ASAP and reserve that extra room!"

The undulating Tuscan Hills were newly green-- another great reason to plan the trip for springtime-- and spiny artichoke plants were visible in nearly every garden that they passed. Soon, the hills took on a pointed quality, and the road became steeper by the minute. As the bus arrived in Siena, Bel told the group about the *contrade* of Siena-- the competing neighborhoods, which had vied for status and power for generations. In the past, she told them, the *contrade* actually waged war on each other; now, though, the neighborhoods competed primarily with the famous Palio. The Palio was a wild, 90 second horse race that took place each year, granting the winner boasting rights that the neighborhoods took very seriously. Each year, the *contrade* vied for jockeys, horses, and position, and there was no requirement that the jockey be aboard the horse when it crossed the finish line. In fact, there were very few requirements at all, and there were open rumors of collusion and bribery to ensure a victory.

The serene Campo, a lovely place to people-watch, enjoy a glass of wine, and toast the Tuscan sun as it set behind the famous tower, became a seething mass of spectators, horses, and gamblers, and was best avoided, thought Bee and Bel.

Bel continued her introduction to Siena, describing the unique system of neighborhoods, each with its own symbols, history, and traditions. "My favorite is the Noble Caterpillar," said Bel. "Quirky!" agreed Caroline, with a smile.

The bus pulled up to the hotel where the group was staying. Piling out of the bus, James remarked on the cobbled streets. "Good thing I wore my walking shoes," he said. The narrow, twisting streets of the ancient city reflected its medieval roots. An extremely hilly town, the walking would be a challenge for some of the group. "We'll meet in the main square in an hour," said Bee. "Unpack, get your bearings, and head for the tower you can see just over there." The group lined up obediently at the rear of the bus, accepting their suitcases in turn as Paolo unloaded the neatly packed storage area. Bee, behind Caroline, thought she heard Paolo murmur "*Bella...*" as Caroline reached for her bag. Interesting, Bee thought; a budding romance between the 30-something Paolo and the 40 plus Caroline? She looked at the green-eyed librarian speculatively. Maybe...she was an attractive woman, fit, and single. Bee made a mental note to tell Bel later--a juicy tidbit to share in the privacy of their room.

An hour later, right on time, the group assembled in the square, obediently gathering by the purple scarf. "We have a little surprise for you," said Bee. "Remember our discussion of the *contrade* of Siena? We bought scarves representing each of the neighborhoods for you as souvenirs." The items were a bit tacky--certainly not Hermes--but they were a fun reminder of this gracious town and its ancient heritage, and the group eagerly reached for the scarves, looping them around their necks *ala Italiano*.

Bee was amused to see which contrada each group member chose. James took the Dragon, traditional home of the bankers of the city; and Charlie, the panther-- a fitting nod to his profession as a pharmacist. Lucy took the Tortoise, symbol of the sculptors--"Slow and steady," Bee thought, that's an accountant! Margo was enchanted by the Unicorn, the home of the goldsmiths--perfect for the blonde, ethereal woman. Patty grabbed the scarf for the She Wolf--enough said! Bill laughed as he took the Ram--home of the tailors. "I may not dress like a tailor, but..." he winked at James, who blushed. Mary was delighted to take the Goose, because, she explained, she kept a stone goose on her front porch, which she dressed according to the seasons. Caroline was delighted to have the quirky Noble Caterpillar, traditional home of workers in the silk trade, and one of four "noble" *contrade*, earned by their bravery in 1369. "Just a bit before my time!" she drawled, exaggerating the Texas accent.

Bee and Bel led the group to the elaborate Duomo--an amazing building constructed of alternating stripes of green and white marble. One of the most fascinating facades in Italy, the central portal was capped by a bronze sun. Begun in 1284, it was the most striking building in Siena. As lovely as the outside was, the interior delighted the group as well. The whole interior floor was made up of dramatic mosaic panels. The group was fortunate (good planning by Bee and Bel, of course) to be in Siena during one of the rare times when the floors were uncovered--the ancient art work spent much of the year under protective wood panels. The group wandered in twos and threes, soaking up the beauty of the magnificent Duomo. The ladies in particular were delighted by the cathedral gift shop, and busied themselves finding treasures to bring home to friends.

After the cathedral visit, there was time for shopping, sightseeing, or relaxation. Bee and Bel, happy that day had gone so smoothly, offered to lead the group back to the hotel through the main square, allowing the travelers to go their separate ways at any point.

Back in the Campo, they stopped at the Fonte Gaia-- a favorite fountain of Bel's. She was always charmed by the pigeons who stood on top of the lion's heads-- and drank water from the lions' mouths! It was an odd and unique sight, and many in the group whipped out their cameras. The beautiful white fountain, ornately carved, was a dramatic addition to the simple, warm brown city center (burnt sienna, mused Bel), paved with cobblestones. While the group took photos, Bel gave them background information on the fountain.

"Fonte Gaia, or Fountain of Joy, was built in 1419, bringing water into the city center. Hundreds of miles of tunnels were constructed to bring the water here, and drain the surrounding fields. Take a look at the bas-reliefs of the Madonna, surrounded by virtues--both Classical and religious. The fountain was designed by Jacopo della Quercia. There was a bit of scandal during Victorian times, because the statues included two female nudes. Having stood since 1419, they were replaced in 1866 to placate those offended by the naked female form."

Bel artfully began to move the group to the side, allowing a Japanese tour guide to move her group up to the fountain. Bel, warm under the spring sun, envied the guide her bright flowered umbrella--her signal to her tour group. It provided the woman with shade, even though others might consider it obnoxious as they were forced to duck and weave when she plowed through a crowd, her umbrella held above her.

Suddenly. they heard Charlie bellowing. "Oh my God!" he shouted. "Help!" Bel and Bee turned as one to see Mary frantically clawing at her throat, and Charlie ineffectually trying to help her. The sisters could see that the long, flowing goose *contrada* scarf had caught on the iron railing surrounding the fountain. The scarf was choking Mary and her brown eyes were terrified. Every struggle seemed to tighten the scarf around her neck. Bel and Bee pushed their way frantically through the crowd. Before they could reach Mary, though, one of the Japanese tour members deftly slipped the scarf up and over the pointed spindle. Bee got to Mary's side as the hero of the moment turned away.

With a shock, she recognized him--were they going to meet "Assogot" everywhere they went? Grateful, she thanked him profusely, while Bel and Charlie helped Mary to a chair in a nearby cafe. The Asian man looked at her, a flash of recognition in his eyes. Before he could speak, however, his tour guide lifted her umbrella and was off. Dutifully, he followed after a quick bow to Bee. How very strange, she thought. How had he reached Mary so quickly? In fact, just how had Mary's scarf gotten tangled in the railing? Bee turned to follow the Japanese group, but they had vanished, swallowed by the crowds of tourists.

Bel and Charlie were relieved to discover that other than some bruising and a shock to the system, Mary had suffered no long term ill effects.

"What the hell happened?!" Charlie demanded. "I don't know," Mary whimpered. "I wanted one last picture of the pigeon on the lion. Patty was next to me." Here Mary dropped her voice. "She was...crowding me..." It was obvious the polite little Iowan was uncomfortable saying anything negative, "When I turned to go, I was caught." Charlie fumed. Standing up abruptly, he slammed his fist on the cafe table, making the cups and glasses jump. His flashing brown eyes suggested a dangerous rage. "Don't be upset, Father," gasped Mary, "you know what happened the last time." Bee looked up quickly, alert to the situation's potential for disaster. Mary was able to soothe Charlie; grumbling, he sat back down. "As long as you're okay," he said, "but if anyone messes with you..."

Bel quickly ordered a cup of tea--her solution to any crisis. Bee wished there were martinis available at this hour, but kept the thought to herself. Bee made a drink motion and looked at Bel questioningly. Bel shook her head, and the tea arrived. Bee rolled her eyes. Seriously? This called for more than tea, but Bel shot her a warning glance. Sighing, Bee ordered coffee for the whole group. She wasn't about to drink that rotten tea.

Patty was on the edge of the group, trying to look sympathetic, but failing. She came up and patted Mary's little hand with her own sausage fingers. "Poor dear. Sometimes our actions come back to strangle us, don't they? Perhaps when you get home you can get a replacement scarf at Mallmart." Why the obsession with Mallmart, Bel wondered. It was the second time Patty had snidely suggested the Iowans visit the big box store.

Patty continued, "Too bad Paolo wasn't here to offer some mouth to mouth, eh?" Patty leered as she lumbered past and settled herself at a table, refusing the tea and demanding a Diet Coke. No one took notice of her, other than Caroline, who looked exasperated.

40

Lucy and Margo volunteered to sit with Charlie and Mary while the group explored the City building with its marvelous frescoes, testimony to the beneficence of the various city guilds and its democratic government.

Charlie gratefully accepted the company, his hands still shaking slightly as he looked at his petite wife, her neck ringed in a red welt. "I've seen the frescoes before," said Lucy. "I was in Siena years ago on a school trip," she laughed. "Let me tell you about it while we enjoy our tea and catch our breath."

"It involves the Unicorn contrada fountain, a stolen pizza, and a LOT of vodka." Margo raised her eyebrows. "Lucy!" Margo looked shocked but amused. "I would love to hear the story!" Her blue eyes sparkled for the first time on the tour. Margo's drooping posture had worried Lucy, but now her sister-in-law sat straight up and leaned toward her. "Tell us, please!" she begged. Lucy began. "We were 19 years old, full of ourselves, and broke. We had just enough money for either a pizza or a bottle of vodka. Being 19, we chose vodka, of course. We sat here on the Campo, watching the sun go down, passing the bottle between the three of us..." Lucy lowered her voice, and continued her story.

For the next half hour, she regaled them with her story. Diners at the other tables heard a burst of laughter, and the gurgle of Margo choking on her coffee. "....and that" Lucy concluded darkly, "is why I have never had vodka again!" "Oh my," said Mary, forgetting her incident entirely. "Really?! A police dog?!" Lucy nodded gravely, and said, "Ruined me for pets for life." Margo nearly fell off her chair laughing.

Bel and Bee came trotting up to the congenial group with the others straggling behind them. James and Bill had climbed the tower, enjoying the magnificent views of the surrounding countryside. Bill was enthusiastic, but James looked winded and sweaty. Patty had ungraciously waited for the climbers at the foot of the stairs. Caroline was engrossed in the frescoes, and chose to spend the time studying the fascinating panels. Bee was available for suggestions for dinner in the quaint city if anyone wanted a recommendation, and Bel encouraged everyone to plan an early dinner.

The Tuscan cooking class was scheduled for the next day, and they needed to get an early start.

The two sisters ate dinner in their favorite restaurant, *Gallo Nero*, far from the Campo and its tourist menus. The restaurant featured traditional foods of the region, both ancient and modern, and locals filled the tiny restaurant's tables. After ordering a bottle of house red wine and their first course, Bee and Bel reviewed the highlights--and low points--of the day.

"I can't believe it was "Assogot" who freed Mary!" Bel exclaimed after Bee had related the eerie coincidence. "Gives me the creeps," agreed Bee, happily forking in more pasta. Troubled, Bel mused, "You don't think..."

"Noooo..." Bee said. "But which is worse? An unknown Japanese tourist, or Patty? Remember what Mary said about her crowding her?" The two ate in silence. Beside them, a large and raucous party of an extended Italian family gesticulated, laughed, and talked through their meal. There appeared to be great merriment at the expense of one young couple, obviously about to become first time parents any minute. Bel took in the blooming belly of the blushing wife, and giggled.

"Don't!" Bee moaned. "Remember?" Bel started. "Didn't I say don't??" Bee eyed her sister. "You're going to anyway, aren't you?"

"Remember when you were pregnant with Teddy? You and Nate took Katie out for dinner at a fancy restaurant as a "last" evening out before the baby." Bel could barely speak, suppressing the laughter. Bee shuddered at the memory, even 30 plus years later.

Bel continued, fueled by another sip of Chianti (not bad for a house wine, she thought, fleetingly). "Your water broke, right there at the table."

Bee interrupted her. "What would you have done?" She demanded. Bel shook her head, admiringly. "I think it was brilliant! You sneaky thing. You knocked over Katie's glass of water, pretending that she spilled it all down your lap." Bee remembered very clearly. "Good thing she wasn't old enough to be indignant at being blamed wrongly!" They had exited the restaurant quickly, after loudly proclaiming that Katie had spilled all over her mother, and that she needed dry clothes...and left a big tip. Half an hour later, Teddy was born. They had barely made it to the hospital.

"Back to Mary's "incident"!" Bee proclaimed, ready to think of something else. "Could it have been a simple accident?" "Of course it was," said Bel, with just a hint of doubt in her voice. "Why on earth would anyone want to hurt Mary?"

Chapter Seven

After a leisurely stroll in the cool spring air through the cobblestone streets of Siena, the sisters were happy to reach the hotel. As they were entering the building, James and Bill approached from the opposite direction. They had enjoyed the evening relaxing in a tiny cafe, watching the crowds flow by. James was excited about the cooking class and peppered Bee with questions. Bill took the opportunity to take Bel aside.

"James would kill me if he knew I said anything, " he started. Bel smiled, understanding the delicate nature of relationships. "But he is really struggling with Patty and her non-stop, snide comments. He's just about had it." Haven't we all? thought Bel. "The problem is, after we agreed to accompany her on the tour, Patty had informed us that James is her heir. She seems to think that gives her license to deride him and make homophobic comments." Bill looked both angry and pained. "What can I do to help?" Bel asked sympathetically.

Bill took a breath. Bel could see him struggle to relax his body. "Anything you can do to keep her away from us would be great. He feels obligated to sit with her, walk with her...I don't mind being odd man out," he grinned ruefully, "but she just upsets him so." Bel nodded, having seen the tense set to James' jaw a number of times.

"She certainly has a way with words", Bel ventured, trying to remain discreet. Bill shook his head. "She's managed to alienate everyone in the family--she hasn't spoken to her daugher in 19 years." Shocked, Bel couldn't think of a thing to say--a rare occurrence, indeed. She couldn't imagine not speaking to her own daughter, even if she did make her a little crazy through the teen years! But to miss out on 19 years of her life--Bel was saddened, disgusted, and frankly, curious. "What on earth could make a mother turn her back on her own child?" Bill shrugged, a little embarrassed. Bel could see he was uncomfortable with having shared so much. Briskly, she moved the conversation along.

"We'll certainly do our best to position ourselves strategically, and to give you as much breathing space as we can." she promised. Just then, Bill's cell phone buzzed--he looked at, and his face lit up. "Excuse me, it's my daughter." He turned to James so they could share the call. It was obvious that they were devoted to Avery and she to them. Bel wondered briefly about Avery's parentage--from the photo James and Bill had proudly shared, Avery looked most like James, Bel thought.

Bee and Bel left the two men catching up with their daughter. In the lobby, the sisters were happy to see Margo and Lucy relaxing. Dinner had been an adventure for them--they had walked up and down the hills of Siena in the dusk. Margo's fair skin was flushed with a healthy glow, and Lucy's bright eyes were laughing. They were recounting their adventure to Charlie and Mary. They had walked to the Basilica of San Domenico, and seen the head of St. Catherine, preserved there for over 600 years. They had then wandered back toward the Campo, and had been delighted to find a gluten-free restaurant for Margo. She had been amazed at how many options were available to her in a country often defined by pasta. They had shopped along the way, and brought out their treasures to show off. They surprised Mary with a new scarf to replace the one that had been unceremoniously left behind earlier. Mary's face glowed, and she tucked the scarf into her ever- present fanny pack.

"You'll forgive me if I don't wear it tonight?" she asked anxiously, unready to put it around her neck. "Of course!" Margo exclaimed. "It's yours for later," she assured her. Charlie patted his short wife--the strain of the day still showing on his face. "Goodness, Mother. Don't do that again!" he ordered, obviously doting on her. "My heart can't take the strain!" Mary laughed gently, and reached up and smoothed back his graying hair. The older couple excused themselves, and headed up the stairs. Margo and Lucy got to their feet as well, and gathered up their bags, full of souvenirs destined for family and friends back home in Connecticut.

Bee and Bel left the comfortable lobby, thankful that the day had ended well, despite poor Mary's unfortunate entanglement. Back in their room, the sisters relaxed together over a bottle of wine-- a fair vintage, considering it had been bought in a local wine shop, sold by the paper cup, soda bottle, or liter-size soda bottle. Each vintage was displayed in a large, glass carboy, with a plastic tube feeding out of the bottle for serving the wine. Not the most elegant presentation, but economical and practical for locals and tourists in the know.

"Mmm, not too bad," murmured Bee. "the price was right, at least!"

"And better than the thousand-dollar bottle you ended up with at the university auction" chuckled Bel. Bee winced, recalling the look on Jack's face when the auctioneer had said "SOLD!" and pointed at her. She had had a little too much wine, and gotten carried away at the auction, not seeing Jack's frantic "quit" hand motions across the room.

"And much better than the swill your husband makes in the garage!" Bee laughed. After that remark, Bel felt much less embarrassed about the exploding wine. Encouraged by his early success at wine-making, her husband had conducted what turned out to be an unfortunate experiment, and passed on several large bottles to Bee and Jack to try. Despite the bottles being stored properly in the basement, Bee had discovered what appeared to be a murder scene in her family room... Ceiling, floor, cushions, walls...... all covered with red wine. It had taken hours to clean up the mess. There was, she mused, still a small spot of red on the ceiling. It was a beautiful shade of red, she had to admit.

"Beautiful!" She murmured. Bel looked at her, eyebrow askance, waiting. Hastily, Bee followed the train of thought through.

"Did you hear Paolo this morning?" she demanded of her sister. Silently, Bel shook her head, waiting.

"I THINK I heard him whisper "*Bella*" to Caroline this morning when she gave him her luggage, and the way she blushed, I don't think he was talking about her suitcase!" Bel's eyes danced.

"Looks like we're beginning a menagerie!" Bee whispered. "First Piggy Patty, and now Cougar Caroline!"

The sisters enjoyed a few minutes of gossiping speculation--hoping that Caroline was worldly enough to handle such a fling. How much sexual sophistication did one expect from a librarian from Texas?! One thing they both agreed upon was that Caroline certainly looked happy, and as long as Paolo did his job, it was frankly none of their business.

After sending a few quick emails to husbands and children, the sisters turned off the lights. From one side of the room came a decidedly porcine snort, and the room was filled with giggles. When everything had quieted once again, from the other bed came a pathetic attempt at a feline growl, which produced yet another fit of laughter.

"Oh, Lord, now I have to pee!" Disgusted, Bee flung back the covers, muttering about the joys of middle age as she stumbled in the dark to the bathroom. "Don't make me laugh any more!" she said sternly. The only response was a musical rendition of a tinkling waterfall from the other side of the room. "OOOOOf!" Bee made it just in time, no thanks to Bel's excellent imitation of a waterfall.

Chapter Eight

The next morning, Bee and Bel hurried to ready themselves for the day. First would be a quick visit to Monteriggioni, a local castle built in 1213, and then on to the vineyard. The castle stop provided a magnificent view of the country side, and helped work up an appetite for dinner.

The cooking class was usually one of the favorite activities of the trip-- in fact, not only had they never gotten a complaint from participants, it was always considered a highlight. The cooking lesson was elementary enough that all the tour members could follow the directions, but unique enough that even the more accomplished cooks would be challenged. The reward at the end-- eating a fabulous Tuscan meal-- was the icing on the cake, or, rather, the truffle sauce on the pasta. Bel's mouth watered just thinking about it. Last year, she had made a bit of a pig of herself at the table. Bee had given her The Look; when she glanced down at her front, Bel was horrified to see that she had, again, dripped greasy sauce on her white blouse. Ah, the perils of having an ample bosom, she sighed, remembering.

Bee seemed to be reading her mind, and shot her a reproving glance. How DID she do that??

"Let's use your napkin as a bib," she whispered, "instead of as a hat as you did at the last family wedding." That was unnecessary, thought Bel petulantly. Is she going to be the bitch of the day??

Stamping up to them came Piggy Patty, a snarl already on her lips. Nah, thought Bel. That role's already filled.

"Good morning, Patty." Bel chose to assume the positive. Her sunny tone was lost on the fractious woman.

"Good morning my foot." Patty glared.

"What seems to be the trouble?" Bee stepped into the conversation, hoping that the two of them would present enough of a coalition to moderate what appeared to be an oncoming barrage. A good idea, but unsuccessful.

"What's this about assigned roles at the cooking class? Maybe I don't want to be with Lucy and Margo in the kitchen." She looked like a sullen, overweight two year old denied a treat. Bee wished she could send her to her room for a time out.

Bel responded. "Patty, remember the interest sheet you filled out before the tour? We simply used that to create like groupings for different outings, including the cooking class. You indicated that you had food sensitivities, so did Margo. For that reason, we put you together to work most closely with the chef; we thought you would value the individual attention to your needs."

Dang, thought Bee, admiringly. She's good. They had separated the group last night, in an attempt to buy James and Bill some peace. Bel had been quick on her feet, remembering Patty's allergy to peanuts and Margo's need to be gluten-free.

Somewhat mollified, Patty relaxed a bit. "Oh. But..." Quickly, before she could continue, Bee exclaimed "Here's Paolo! Why don't we go ahead and get settled in the bus? That way you can choose your seat first."

Seizing the opportunity to hog the best seat once again, Patty trotted off, simpering at Paolo as she hoisted herself into the front seat.

Bee shook her head admiringly at her younger sister, who tried hard not to look smug. "You're going to hell for lying, you know that, right?"

Bel smiled serenely. "I wasn't lying. I just...adjusted the timeline of the conversation...."

The rest of the group filtered through the lobby to the waiting bus. Mary, bless her, was wearing the new scarf around her bruised neck.

A rush of affection surged through Bel; she knew the scarf was a wonderful symbol--of faith in Bee and Bel, of friendship for Margo and Lucy. And, she thought practically, a way to cover the faint but present bruises.

The ride to Monteriggioni was pleasant, and the group chatted congenially about the day ahead. Paolo swung the little bus up the hillside, while Bel provided the history of the area. Montereggiano was half-way between Siena and Florence, and historically, was a strategic resource, controlling both the road and information. At the base of the fortifications, Paolo parked the bus and handed out water bottles to the travelers. The group gathered at the gates, listening to Bel's description of Dante's impressions of the castle--he had written that "Monteriggioni is crowned with towers", ensuring the safety of the Republic of Siena until 1554. The castle fell only because of betrayal--a secret plot that between the Captain of the garrison and the Florentines insured that the fortress was handed over without a battle.

The group was encouraged to explore the castle walls, and to wander through the timeless little village. There were pleasant little shops and cafes for those who weren't tempted to climb the stairs--thankfully broad, modern stairs with handrails--to the city wall ramparts to enjoy the view of the undulating Tuscan hills, green with spring growth. James and Bill set off immediately for the walls, as did Caroline, Margo and Lucy. Their laughter as they climbed the many steps could be heard below. Charlie and Mary headed for the little shop in the square to buy a postcard to send their son, while Patty headed to the cafe for a diet soda. Bee and Bel, taking advantage of a rare moment when they were not tap dancing madly, headed for one of their favorite little shops, where they always found quirky local crafts to bring home. The challenge was to purchase an item without one's sister seeing it--so that it could reappear at Christmas as a wonderful memento of the tour. Neither sister was quite sure she wanted a reminder of this tour, though--instead, they focused on looking for gifts for their friends at home. After a lovely hour of browsing, the sisters reluctantly headed back to the designated meeting space-- a charming little outdoor cafe at the center of the village.

Arriving a few minutes ahead of schedule, Bee and Bel found Patty right where they had left her, but beside her was the cafe owner, speaking rapidly in Italian, gesturing angrily.

"Patty, what seems to be the problem?" By unspoken agreement, Bee engaged Patty, and Bel spoke quietly to the cafe owner in Italian. Patty looked up sullenly, her chin set defiantly. "I wasn't finished with my drink!" she hissed indignantly. "He took it away before I was finished. I won't pay for something I didn't get to drink!"

Bel, having gotten the other side of the story, sighed and shrugged. "It's just a simple misunderstanding, Patty. It seems you had three refills, and when he asked if you wanted another, you said no."

"But that didn't mean I wanted him to take my glass!" Her eyes narrowed. "I'm not paying!"

The rest of the group had entered the courtyard, and stopped, hearing the angry voices. No one wanted to be associated with the petty squabble. Bel turned back to the cafe owner, and spoke rapidly in Italian. Throwing his hands in the air, he spun around and stalked back into his cafe, loudly exclaiming in Italian. Even those who didn't speak the language had a pretty good idea of what he was saying.

"Let's go ahead and meet Paolo, since everyone is here," Bee suggested. Patty triumphantly rose from her seat, and stalked off. With a nod to Bel, Bee followed her, pointing out architectural details enthusiastically to Patty, who barely acknowledged her. Bel quickly headed into the cafe, where she had promised to meet the owner and cover the charges. He had calmed down with her assurances, and met her with a rueful smile. "How long is your tour?" he asked Bel, reverting to his excellent English. She grimaced. "It's been four days--four very LONG days--and we have four to go." She sighed. "*Mi dispiace, Signore.* She has been--" Bel paused, not wanting to be unpleasant-- "Well, she has been a challenge. Allow me to pay her bill."

The cafe owner shook his head. "No, *Signora.* I think you have already paid a very high price with that one. Thank you, but it's my gift to you. I think it will be a very long tour for you, and she will cost you much more than the price of a soda in the long run. *Buongiorno, Signora."* With that, he bowed and offered her his hand. Grateful for the sympathy and understanding, she shook his hand. *"Grazie, mille grazie!"* Bel exclaimed, and hurried after the group.

During the short ride to the vineyard, Bee pointed out the changes in the landscape from Rome. The Roman pines were gone, replaced by the lovely cypress trees, some of them decades, if not centuries, old. The trees were said to have been brought to Italy by the Etruscans, thousands of years ago. A coniferous tree, the cypress keeps its leaves in the winter, lending it supernatural qualities in ancient times. Because of its strong scent, the cypress was planted around homes, churches, and cemeteries to "freshen" the air-- or mask unpleasant odors.

Bel also pointed out the olive groves dotting the hillsides. Their silvery gray leaves fluttered in the morning sun. "You won't get any fresher olive oil than what we will taste here in Tuscany," she promised. "You'll soon understand why Italians use olive oil instead of butter on their bread!"

"And their pasta, and polenta, and their vegetables!" teased Bee. From the front of the bus, Paolo chimed in. "It's good for you! Good for your heart, good for your skin, good for everything! That's what makes Italians the best lovers..." he grinned in the mirror. Everyone laughed, and Bel stole a glance at Caroline. Sure enough, she had a becoming blush. Bee smiled to herself, and saw Bel nod at her, an amused smile on her face.

Their next stop was a small, family vineyard. While their wines were not yet the best, they were knowledgeable, welcoming, and eager for the exposure to the American market. Bee and Bel had decided to include them in the tour because of the vintners' fluent English and enthusiastic presentation. After an hour at his table, everyone had at least a basic understanding of Chianti, Tuscans, and Super-Tuscans. James and Bill ordered a case of wine delivered to their home, much to the delight of the vintner. Bee and Bel were flattered to be given a bottle of Chianti to take with them; the vineyard may have been young, but the owner understood marketing and good will. Bee and Bel made a note to return next time as well.

The bus hummed with contented chatter. Fresh air, exercise, and three or four glasses of red wine relaxed everyone. Bel was peppered with questions about the cooking class, their appetites whetted. Bel answered as best she could, promising only that it would be a delicious meal.

They soon arrived at their destination, eager to begin. It was a lovely afternoon, and the vineyard was hosting other tour groups as well, but theirs was the only group lucky enough to share the kitchen and prepare a traditional sumptuous Tuscan meal. As the group tumbled out of the bus, Bel stepped to the side of the parking lot to organize a group photo. She noticed a tour bus leaving, passing close to her in the narrow space. Looking up, she saw the bus was filled with Japanese tourists. One of them pointed a camera at her, and Bel could have sworn it was "Assogot"! Bee's voice called her back to her task, and she hastily turned to snap a group picture.

"Say *'Formaggio!'*" called Charlie, and the group grinned.

They assembled on the patio, where tables had been laid under a grape arbor, ready for a wine tasting. The group would tour the wine-making facility first, and then visit the kitchen garden to gather herbs and vegetables for lunch. They would then do a "fat" tasting. Bel and Bee were glad they had explained lardo earlier, eliminating some of the squeamish responses and thus not embarrassing their hosts--or themselves. At that point, they would work in teams to create their midday meal. Patty, Margo and Lucy would work with the head chef, and James, Bill, and Caroline with one assistant. Bel, Charlie, and Mary would work with another. Bee was to float from group to group, helping as needed. As a cookbook editor, she was comfortable with all types of cooking styles and cuisines. Her kitchen skills were legendary in the family. Because she was such a good cook, no one in the family ever let her forget the time she roasted the Thanksgiving turkey with the neck and organs inside. A rare mishap, prompted by too much company, a dog throwing up in the living room, and a very delicious mimosa or two--not necessarily in that order.

Truthfully, Bee could have taught the class herself, but the experience just wouldn't have been the same for the participants. Here, in the vineyard, surrounded by the Tuscan hills, was an experience that even she relished. The musical Italian accent of their instructor, the warm spring breeze, and the beautiful ancient bricks in the large, sunny kitchen created a wonderful memory for all.

Touring the vineyard, Bel missed Nate. They had visited here together, early in the season on their scouting trip. He had spent hours with the elderly Italian wine master, the two of them like kids in a candy shop. They had talked wine, philosophy, and more wine. They had sampled all the wine put in front of them, and desperately needed a nap after enthusiastically comparing Chiantis, Chianti Classicos, and Super Tuscans. Bel was concerned about her husband driving the little Italian rental car through the winding hills, but he was so pumped from all the information he had gathered, his adrenaline negated the effects of the wine. All the way back to the hotel, he had excitedly sketched out his ideas for his next winemaking adventure at home. Bel had closed her eyes and murmured "that sounds great" every time he paused for breath, until she fell asleep, warm in the sun. She wasn't even sure Nate had noticed. Bel made a mental note to have some of the estate reserve sent home--he would be delighted, having long since finished the case they had purchased last time.

Ever eager, Charlie and Mary were front and center, intent on the information the oenologist was sharing. James and Bill were close behind them. Margo and Lucy were absorbing the introduction to wine making, and Bee was surprised to see Paolo beside Caroline, the two of them shoulder to shoulder. Usually, Paolo preferred to wait in the bus, listening to his music and chatting on the phone with friends. Patty was on the edge of the group, having fallen behind as the group moved up the slope. Bel was with her, Bee noted guiltily.

By virtue of the Deciding Factor, it should have been Bee delegated to babysit Patty. But because cooking and wine were Bee's forte, Bel had, not quite graciously, agreed that she would assume the duty. Joining them, Bee gave her sister a discreet, sympathetic squeeze of the shoulder.

"Beautiful, isn't it?" Bee murmured, looking out across the countryside.

Bel smiled, and looked out over the rows of grapes, the small fruits forming. "Magical, I think. How do you think the first person figured out how to make wine?" she mused.

"Rotten grapes." Patty's voice was a jarring note on an otherwise serene landscape. "How much further are they going to walk?" she whined.

"Well, I think you might be right! Fermentation is just about the most important part of making wine. My husband struggles with that occasionally." The sisters giggled, but composed themselves quickly when Patty glared at them.

"I think they're just about through. Shall we turn back and beat them to the patio?" Bee suggested. Patty turned on her heel, and losing her balance, grabbed at a vine to steady herself. The delicate branch snapped off in her hand. "Oops." She tossed it on the ground, and walked away. Horrified, the sisters looked at each other. Silently, Bel picked up the beautiful vine, and cradled the branch as they followed Patty's ponderous steps down the hill.

Once inside the kitchen, the group assembled, eager to get started. Bee introduced the head of the kitchen--an older woman, Lucia had the look of one who didn't worry about makeup or fashion--and as a result, appeared younger than her years. Lucia had grown up on the estate; her father had been a tenant farmer there, as had his father before him.

Lucia had helped in the fields during the harvests, and in the kitchen after school and summers. Her mother had wanted her to get an education and leave the farm, so she had gone off to university to study teaching, and hated every minute of life in the city. She had found her way to a quiet restaurant serving "country" food, and worked in the kitchen because she was so homesick. After coming home on vacation, there had been a loud and passionate scene when Lucia announced she would not return to the university. Her mother had cried, she had cried, and her father had been called in to mediate. Flummoxed, he had floundered about for a solution that would protect him from the wrath of either of the women he loved. Finally, he hit upon what he had felt was a brilliant solution--to send Lucia to cook in the manor house of the estate. He was sure she would love the work, and be able to leave the farm by her own choosing, rather than being callously sent away. Lucia went happily off to work each day, apprenticed to the head cook and away from the fields (and the field hands that made her mother so nervous). Now, years later, she was still in the estate kitchen, recognized as one of the best Tuscan cooks in the region. She had even been featured in a travelogue shown in the US, and toured as a guest chef in the US, sponsored by a Tuscan olive oil company.

Lucia gave a brief speech, showing off her few words of English. "Hello! Hello! We are happy to cook you!" she said, smiling broadly. "Today we cook many delicious things." She then reverted to Italian, pausing to give Bee and her assistants time to translate. The menu would include a pear, gorgonzola and walnut appetizer with prosecco. The *primi piatti* would be picci, the typical Tuscan pasta which they would make themselves, with a choice of two sauces. The *secundi* would be a veal course, made with lemons and capers, with a side of sesame-coated roasted potato slices. For dessert, they would enjoy tiramisu. Each course would be complemented by a wine produced there at the vineyard.

The whole group was invited out to the kitchen garden, and there divided into the teams the sisters had outlined earlier. One group was assigned to gather the herbs needed for lunch, and they happily began snipping away. Another was picking the vegetables to be used in the sauces for the pasta. The third group dug the potatoes to be roasted for the *secundi*. They met again in the kitchen a short time later, flushed and laughing after their time in the garden.

Lucia had her assistants hand out aprons, and had everyone wash their hands in the huge farm sink. The group was enchanted by the foot pedal that operated the water flow; using their feet prevented them from getting their dirty hands on the faucet handles, and made filling heavy pots much easier. Charlie was delighted, and declared it was exactly what their farm needed at home.

Bee had informed Lucia of the dietary considerations of the group earlier that week, and was relieved to hear Lucia ask, "Who's no peanut?" Patty raised her hand. "And who *sans glutino*?" Hearing the phrase she'd learned earlier, Margo raised her hand. Lucia beckoned them closer. "You tell me." She looked at Bee, who listened as Lucia spoke rapidly in Italian.

"Lucia wants to know about your food sensitivities. She is known for her homeopathic healings of dietary problems, and likes to understand what and why certain foods bother certain people." Bee hoped that Patty wouldn't create a scene; she was uncertain whether the prickly woman would be thrilled to be the center of attention, or threatened by being questioned.

"You tell me?" It was more of a command than a question, but softened by the earnest look on the Italian's face. Margo complied. She told Lucia of her years of troubled digestion and its unpleasant side effects. Unconsciously, Margo grimaced, remembering the years of belly aches and embarrassing incidents. Lucia looked at Bee, and asked questions. Bee turned to Margo, and passed along the questions. "She would like to know how far back you remember symptoms. Did it change at puberty? And does anyone else in the family have the same symptoms?" Margo answered quickly--her entire life had been lived assuming tummy aches after every meal were normal. Everyone had assumed the delicate girl was reacting to losing her father. It wasn't until much later that a doctor picked up on her mild comments of routine stomach aches that her food sensitivities were explored. It wasn't long before he recommended eliminating wheat, and since then, life had been much more pleasurable. Lucia nodded sympathetically, and patted her hand. "Sans glutino is good". Margo smiled, gently amused to hear her doctors' recommendation so soundly endorsed.

"Now you." She pointed at Patty. "When?" Patty was thrilled to be the center of attention. Bee was relieved, and looked at Bel. Bel rolled her eyes as discreetly as possible, but Patty was eagerly relating her story.

"I wasn't allergic to peanuts as a kid. I ate peanut butter every day. I even hid a jar under my bed so I could eat it after I went to bed!" Patty looked triumphant at her long ago sneakiness. "When I went to college, I didn't have it very often. I discovered Nutella instead." Lucia gestured, and Bee thought she detected a bit of impatience, but Patty plowed on. "When my daughter was about five" (here heads snapped around, surprised at the mention of a daughter), I had an appendicitis attack." It was her turn to grimace at the painful memory. "I went in to the hospital for surgery." Her eyes took on a peculiar look--Bee wasn't sure what it was, but it wasn't pretty, and it made her shiver.

Patty continued. "Right after the surgery, I went into anaphylactic shock. Nearly died. The stupid anesthesiologist had bungled his job. I complained to the hospital, and threatened to sue them, sue him, and everybody else. " Now the look on her face was pure greed. "They begged me--begged me!--to keep from suing. They fired the guy, didn't charge me for the surgery, and sent a nurse home to take care of me. No charge!" She gloated. Bee glanced at Lucia, and the group, and saw distaste mirrored on all the faces. James had turned away. Lucia motioned her to continue. Patty laughed shortly.

"I never told them that my daughter had brought me a box of chocolates in the hospital. I knew you weren't supposed to eat before surgery, but I was hungry. I didn't think one chocolate would be a big deal." She raised her chin, defiant. "I only ate one. But it had peanuts in it, and that's what caused the allergic reaction, not the anesthesia". The group gasped, and Margo got to her feet and got a drink of water, obviously repelled. "When we went on vacation the next month, using the money we saved since we didn't have to pay for the operation, I had some peanut butter, and my throat closed up and I couldn't breathe. The doctor in the emergency room tested me for allergies. That's when we found out I was allergic to peanuts. You can bet we didn't tell anyone when we went home!" She laughed harshly, her voice sounding overly loud in the silent kitchen. After a stunned silence, Bel translated the information to Lucia; she left out the more distasteful details of Patty's scamming the hospital. Looking around, she could see that the others were as sickened as she was. That poor anaesthesiologist! She thought. A ruined career-- all because of Patty.

"Where did you live?" asked Margo, her voice tight as it broke the uncomfortable silence. Patty narrowed her eyes as she turned towards Margo. "That's my business!" she responded. "And none of yours!" Margo's eyes were flashing in a dangerous way. Lucy turned to her normally mild mannered sister-in-law, a concerned expression crossing her face. Margo smiled at her, but it was a thin smile, Bee observed, the kind that people use when they want to reassure someone that you are fine, thank you, and both parties knew it was a lie. Uh oh, thought Bee, time to tap dance again. She assumed a falsely cheery smile and clapped her hands gently. "Well, let's commence our cooking lesson! I know I'm hungry!"

Lucy, Margo, and Patty went to Lucia's side, and found that they were going to work on the picci pasta, and create one of the sauces as well. In addition, they would make a gluten-free version. The chef had developed a master list of needed ingredients, which was then translated for the group's use. They began assembling olive oil, water, flour, and eggs to begin making the pasta. Lucia made a bowlful first, demonstrating the techniques to the three women. Patty, bored and left to her own devices, surreptitiously stuck her finger in some chocolate sauce and licked her finger. Lucy and Margo happily imitated the cook's actions and soon had a second bowl of gluten-free dough ready to be shaped into pasta.

Bill, James, and Caroline were working on the appetizer, a second sauce, and the roasted potatoes. There was a cheerful buzz of conversation in the room, with nearly everyone engaged and interested. Mary, Charlie, and Bel were enjoying making the tiramisu and the veal dish. Mary took a number of photos of the three groups, promising to mail them out to the others after the pictures were developed. "Oh, why not just email them to us?" asked Margo. "We don't have a computer," said Mary with a reddened face. "there was one at Charlie's store, but…"

"Now, Mother," chided Charlie gently. "Let's not go into all that. These nice folks aren't interested in the details of our lives." Catching a glimpse of Patty's malicious smirk, Bee wasn't so sure.

In a couple of hours, all of the meal preparations were done, and it was time to set the long wooden table that spanned most of the length of the adjacent dining room. The appetizers were universally loved, and the prosecco went down oh, so smoothly. So did the second bottle. Bel loved prosecco, and hoped no one saw her refill her glass for the third time. The toasted walnuts which topped the pear and gorgonzola appetizers were the perfect accent. Gently warmed, they were rich, earthy, and delicious, despite being so easy to prepare. The group was especially delighted because they had picked the produce themselves in the kitchen garden.

Each participant got to sample the pastas with each of the sauces-- a rich mushroom and truffle sauce with cream on one dish, and a lovely sausage and fennel sauce on the other. They were delighted to discover the gluten-free pasta was delicious, and Margo was pleased to be able to enjoy the pasta too. A delicate shaving of parmesan on the fennel dish was just the right finishing note. The group took a break from eating, and most chose to drink a glass of sparkling water to clear their palates-- all the better to enjoy the main dish. "Roast potatoes with sesame seeds-- who would have thought?" remarked James. "But the perfect accompaniment to the savory veal dish", answered Caroline. "And so simple to do!" Mary beamed, resolved to make them as soon as she got back to Iowa.

Accompanied by satisfied murmurs, another bottle of the vineyards' Tuscan wine was opened, and dessert was served with a flourish. The tiramisu came to the table on a beautiful ceramic platter, created by a local artist. Patty brusquely asked if there were peanuts in the tiramisu. Bel checked the Italian for "peanut" on her phone translator to be sure. With a raised eyebrow and exaggerated patience, Lucia reassured her that the traditional coffee flavored dessert had no peanuts. Bill closed his eyes while tasting the concoction, the better to enjoy it; everyone savored the decadent dish. "Oh, man." He sighed with pleasure. A perfect end to a delicious meal! A near reverent silence in the room was marred only by Patty's sucking the spoon. Patty helped herself to seconds, then thirds, when she thought no one was looking. Margo noticed, and grimaced. So did Bel. Tapping time, she thought wearily. Again.

Hastily, Bel stood and raised her glass. "A toast to Lucia and her fine assistants! Our thanks for a wonderful meal!" "Lucia!" the group echoed, and conversation resumed. *"Bravo! Bella!"* Charlie enjoyed trying out the few words of Italian he knew. The group lingered at the table, enjoying the comfortable feeling of being happily full, having drunk wonderful wine, and spent a lovely day in (mostly) companionable company. Gratefully,

Bee and Bel exchanged a "virtual high five" across the room, raising their glasses and eyebrows to each other across the long wooden table. Bel hoped Bee hadn't noticed how many glasses she had raised that evening; Bee, on the other hand, was too busy enjoying her glasses of wine to care how many Bel had.

It was time to head back to the hotel. Lucia walked with them out to the bus, where the group were slowly loading their satiated selves into the comfortable seats.

"*Ciao*, Bella and Bee-ah!" The sisters grinned at Lucia's transformation of their names.

She kissed them on both cheeks, and held the sisters at arms' length while she looked into their faces. In Italian she said, "Come back soon. I love your groups--they are always so interesting! But that one--" she nodded seriously towards the front seat where Patty was once again ensconced-- "don't bring that one again. You didn't translate everything, I know. She's poison, that one. Be careful." And with that, Lucia turned and walked back into the kitchen. Bee and Bel exchanged glances, and made their way slowly to the bus.

There was a companionable silence in the bus as they wound through the Tuscan landscape. The little hill towns were lit against the coming night, warm yellow lights winking in the distance. Stars began to come out, and in the warm bus, Mary leaned into Charlie, nestled into his arm. "Got the recipes, Mother?" he whispered. Mary smiled up at him in the dark, and patted her fanny pack. James rested his head on Bill's shoulder, and Bill flipped through the photos on his Iphone of the day's' adventure, pausing now and then to send the best shots to their daughter. Margo and Lucy and Caroline murmured quietly together. From the front seat, came an odd noise--a snort, and then a sigh. Patty was snoring.

The group arrived back at the hotel, and stumbled out of the warm, comfortable bus into the light, rubbing their eyes and stretching. Bill and James invited anyone interested to join them for a nightcap, emphasizing loudly that they were planning on walking to a bar a few blocks away. Charlie and Mary declined, claiming fatigue, and headed up to their room.

Bee and Bel accepted, happy to stretch out the evening just a bit. Lucy, looking interested, turned with a questioning glance at Margo. Margo shook her head, saying "Please excuse me for this evening. I have some, um, research to do. Go ahead, Lucy, I'll be fine." With that, she left the group, Lucy looking after her, obviously torn.

"Come on, Lucy--she needs some quiet time, I think." Bel linked arms with Lucy. "And you need some time off from taking such good care of her." Relaxing, Lucy smiled appreciatively at Bel.

"I'm in! Caroline?" Lucy called to the green eyed Texan.

Caroline yawned ostentatiously and checked her watch. "Well, it's been a long day," she noted, "and I have correspondence to catch up on." "Ready to get off your feet, eh, Caroline?" Patty said with a twisted grin. Flushed, Caroline left the lobby rapidly.

James and Bill stood up. "Well, we're off, too," said James, "Coming?" and they left in such haste that Bel and Bee were certain they were trying to avoid giving Patty the chance to join them. Patty frowned, and headed into the lobby alone. As the small group crossed the parking lot, Paolo called "*Ciao!*" to them and raised his hand in greeting.

That's odd, thought Bee. Why hasn't he left yet? He's usually in such a hurry to get to some girl...and then Bee smiled, remembering that Caroline now had her own room.

Chapter Nine

The little group walked comfortably down the narrow, winding streets. They found a small cafe, with tables set on the sidewalk, where they could watch the world go by and enjoy a drink in the cool night air.

James and Bill had heard from their daughter Avery. They had sent her photos of the cooking class already. She had changed her facebook photo to one of the two of them, dressed in their aprons, grinning as they showed off the appetizer they had created. They were flattered, and Bel could see the love wash over their faces as they eagerly told the group all about her.

"After the doctor, James and I were the first people to hold her when she was born." Bill looked emotional, remembering that long ago day. "She's been the light of our lives ever since." He grinned. "Of course, that light was a little crazed during the teen years..." James laughed, remembering the regular discussions about fashions and what was or was not acceptable to them. "And that whole sex education bit....whew. That wasn't comfortable one bit. No sir!" The group laughed, understanding the discomfort.

"Did you have a woman have "The Talk" with her?" asked Lucy, curious. The men exchanged glances. James spoke first. "Both our moms are gone, and neither one of us has sisters. My cousin offered, but we knew she wasn't really keen on it. She was being very loyal, but....we decided that as her parents, it was our job." Bill nodded. "You can't sign up for just the good stuff. I tell the kids in my class that every year. Funny, it's easy to do the sex ed unit with my classes. But when your own little girl is sitting there...." He shook his head. James squeezed his hand. "You did great. You made it all the way through the conversation. I was so ready to bolt for the door when you got to the details about puberty. Avery was a trouper. Imagine having that conversation with your dads!"

The group laughed, and shared their varied experiences--on either end of the conversation. Bel recalled asking her mother "Just what is that penis thing, anyway?" when she was about four. Her mother had coughed for quite a while--choking, probably--before she handled the question. Bee hadn't been home--her usual source of interesting if misguided information about the grown-up world. Hearing this dubious reflection, Bee protested--her information had always been solid, she argued. "Oh yeah?" Bel countered. "And what about the time you told me that mommies got pregnant by getting stung by bees, and then you told me since your name was Bee, if you punched me I would get pregnant."

Bee laughed at the indignant look on Bel's face. "That was a good day," she said, "You didn't bug me for at least two hours!" The group exploded into laughter, and even Bel joined in ruefully. "I didn't mean to be a pest!" she protested. Bee raised her glass to her sister, and they toasted a long ago childhood.

Lucy turned back to the men. "Was the cousin you mentioned the daughter Patty referred to?" James looked away for a moment. "Yes. They haven't spoken in years." "I'm so sorry," Lucy said hastily. "I didn't mean to intrude. Forgive me." James waved his hand. "It's ok. It's an old story, and best left in the past. Sad, but families..." his voice drifted on. Bill spoke up. "We've made the best of it, and we've managed to remain on reasonably good terms" --here he rolled his eyes-- "with everyone involved. I think it's much healthier this way for all."

Feeling that the lovely evening had taken a melancholy turn, Bee signaled the waiter for another round of drinks. These, she announced, were on her, in honor of an intrepid group of travelers. The group drank a toast to *Bella Italia*, and then to Bee, and the conversation returned to happier ground.

Soon, the party broke up. James and Bill strolled off through the neighborhood, hand in hand. Lucy, Bel, and Bee walked the narrow lane back to the hotel, musing. "I'm so sorry I mentioned Patty." Lucy apologized. "I'm afraid I upset James and spoiled the evening."

"It's not your fault that Patty can't get along with anyone!" Bel exclaimed. "That horrible story of hers today...it really seemed to upset Margo." Lucy nodded. "I talked with her on the bus back. Her father was an anesthesiologist. I think it just hit her badly."

"He died young, didn't he?" Bel asked gently.

"Yes. He was gone before my brother and Margo met." Lucy sighed, the mention of her brother bringing tears to her eyes. "Margo has had an awful couple of years. Losing Frank was...well, I wasn't sure she would survive it. And then..." Lucy took a deep breath. "Turns out Frank had taken out loans to support his business. The economy has been difficult in New England for the last couple of years. He had a lot of faith in his business, and himself, and didn't worry about carrying a huge debt. He was sure he could repay it." Bee felt a knot forming in her stomach, knowing where this was going. "But he was wrong. He had cashed in his life insurance as well, and when he died, he left Margo with nothing. Nothing but debt, that is."

They had reached the steps of the hotel. "Please don't say anything to Margo--she's so very proud. She would barely accept this trip as gift, and if she knew I had said anything..." Bee hastened to assure Lucy that her privacy was sacred to them. Impulsively, Lucy gave them each a peck on the cheek. "You were right, you know. I did need a night off from watching over Margo." Smiling, she mused, "I suspect she needed a night off from Mother Hen me even more!" Lucy thanked them, adding, "It was great to laugh and relax, and not feel guilty for having fun. I appreciate it." Lucy said goodnight, and left the sisters in the lobby.

Suddenly drained, the sisters took the elevator to their room rather than the two flights of stairs. They leaned against the walls, feeling the clank and hum of the machine hauling them upwards. They exited at their floor, walking quietly so as not to disturb those who had turned in early. As they rounded a corner, Bel thought she heard Caroline laugh, and a deep masculine voice echo her laughter. Raising an eyebrow to Bee, she began to giggle. Bee shoved her unceremoniously into their room.

By Deciding Factor, it was Bee's turn in the bathroom first. "Make it quick!" Bel implored. Bee stuck out her tongue--a very immature act for a woman in her fifties--and sauntered slowly into the tiny bathroom. Bel settled down on her bed, and checked her emails. Nate had sent her a brief description of what their daughter was up to, and informed her that he himself was coping nicely. He had already watered the orchids twice, he assured her. They wouldn't dry out this time! Bel sighed, thinking of her new batch of orchids, drowning under his over-zealous care.

The message from her daugher was longer, chattier, and included a list of things she would like Bee to bring home to her. Shopping? thought Bel. Not much on this trip! She hadn't even had time to look for her required souvenir. Bel collected spoons--not the tacky tourist ones, although Bee insisted on giving her one now and then--but lovely wooden ones. She found them in thrift shops, in farmers' markets, and in craftsmens' shops. She loved their organic forms, their practical nature combined with function and beauty. Her shopping just got more complicated. Well, she would make a list. She and Bee had built in a few extra days to relax, evaluate, and wind down after the trip before heading home. They would have a LOT to talk about after this one, she thought.

Bee strolled over to the bed, and bounced up and down on it. Bel narrowed her eyes and said slowly and distinctly, "You make me pee this bed and you're the one who will sleep in it." Bee casually got up, and flung herself down on her bed, reaching for her phone. "Wouldn't be the first time you wet the bed!" she whispered under her breath. A pillow flew across the room, smacking her upside the head. She snickered as Bel stalked past to the bathroom.

Bee's messages were much the same--a quick note from Jack, grumping about the continuing bad weather. Restless, he had gone to the boat anyway, and spent the night there, listening to the wind humming through the lines. The rain had sounded so lovely, beating against the tight, snug cabin, and he had slept like a baby. She smiled, imagining his snores coming from the vee berth in the cabin. He had not, he confessed, continued to enjoy the rain the next morning. He had packed up and headed home. Bee was relieved, and again sent him a sympathetic note. She told him a bit about their group and the misadventures they had faced. Bee was surprised to get an immediate response--Jack was not a night owl. Checking her watch, she remembered the six hour difference. He would be in his beaten up leather chair with a cup of coffee, checking the weather forecast. She smiled at the mental image.

"Good God. Sounds like a recipe for disaster. Be careful, old thing. I want you home in one piece. I need you to sand the bottom of the boat." Bee snorted. She wasn't sanding his old bucket of a boat. She could read what he hadn't written, though--he missed her, and was ready for her to come home. Sometimes it's nice to go away, she thought; the people staying home get a much clearer idea of what they don't have, than what they DO have when you're there!

She was a little uncomfortable, though--it was the second time in one day that she had been warned to be careful.

Bel came over to the bed to retrieve her pillow. "You're frowning. What's up?"

Bee shook her head ruefully. "Nothing. Jack just echoed what Lucia had said earlier today, and it gave me a weird feeling."

Bel nodded, instantly on the same page. "Be careful?"

It was Bee's turn to nod. "Weird, eh?"

"Well..." Bel thought for a moment. "think about it. So far on this trip, we've nearly been thrown out of the Vatican museum. We've had to spring for an additional room. Patty fell and whacked her head in the Castel. Mary was nearly choked at the fountain. Patty confessed to fraud. And apparently we're being stalked by a random Asian tourist. Not your typical tour!"

Bee smiled. "When you put it that way!" she said. "No wonder I'm exhausted."

"You're exhausted because you had four glasses of prosecco." Bel said primly.

How does she DO that?! Bee wondered, as Bel turned out her light.

Unsettled, Bee returned to her emails, eager to connect with her "normal" life--anything that didn't involve Patty! Her last message was from her boss. Bee sighed, and decided not to answer. She had used up all her politeness for the day. She plugged in her phone, turned out the light, and willed herself to sleep, trying to block out the not so gentle snores from the bed next to her.

Chapter Ten

Bright and early the next morning, Bel hopped out of her bed and into the quaint, tiny shower stall. "Ah, payback," she grinned. Running the water as hard and loud as possible, she wiggled into it sideways (the only possible way to enter) and began singing at the top of her lungs. "O sole mio," she shrieked, but didn't get any farther before the devil, in the guise of her sister, came charging into the bathroom.

Bel saw a plump little paw enter the shower stall and knew that it was there to turn off-- or worse, turn to cold-- the water. "Oh no you don't!" she shouted. Holding onto the tiny soap with one hand, Bel used the other to cover the faucet. "Wakee wakee!" she yelled with glee. Bee was definitely not a morning person.

Bel diverted a little of the shower spray to hit her sister; "Okay. Now I know to keep an eye on my little dog, you wicked witch!" said Bee. Bel chuckled.

"Four glasses of prosecco might actually help you, you know!" Bee said. A glass of cold water was unceremoniously dumped over the shower curtain, and Bel heard Bee gloat, "Revenge is a dish best served COLD!"

The bathroom was decidedly damp when the two finally finished their morning toilette. Guilty, they mopped up the floor before leaving the room. That was the problem with rooming with your sister, Bee thought-- you could get yourself into trouble so easily... she grinned, knowing she enjoyed the mischief they inevitably found.

Despite the morning water fight, the women were up and out early, making sure they were in the breakfast room and ready to greet their group before any of the others arrived. They walked quietly down the hall, aware that many of the other guests would be sleeping in. They were startled to come around a corner, and see Patty crouching in the hall. Instinctively, they stepped back, and exchanged apprehensive glances. What in the world was Patty doing now? They peeked around the corner, trying to stay out of sight. Bee giggled to herself--it appeared they were spying on a spy. Indeed, in just a moment, the door of Caroline's room opened, and Paolo slipped out into the hallway. The door closed quietly behind him. The sisters could see Patty's round shadow draw back as Paolo headed toward the stairs.

"Oh dear." Bel looked thoughtful. "I have a bad feeling about this. How much you want to bet that Patty will make a scene?"

"I don't know..." Bee mused. "Her specialty seems to be more dropping poisonous bombs into seemingly innocent conversation--blindsiding people."

"Nasty piece of work in any case." Bel looked like she had smelled something unpleasant. "Should we warn Caroline? I hate to look like we were spying on her, too, but knowing Patty will try to embarrass her, she might appreciate being forewarned. " Bee looked thoughtful.

"Maybe if only one of us speaks to her. That way it might not look like we thought it was a big deal." "I vote for you!" Bel quickly interjected.

"You're not getting out of it that easy. Shoot for it!" This time, Bel lost. "Best two out of three?" she said hopefully.

"I'll save you a seat!" Bee hurried away. Sighing, Bel turned to the door; she raised her hand to knock, then put it down again. Just how was she going to put this? Well, she thought. I'll just say it.

She knocked on the door quietly, hoping that Caroline was still asleep. Within a few seconds, however, the Texan opened the door, looking wide awake and lovely in a pale green robe that did wonders for her eyes. She looked surprised to see Bel.

"Good morning, Caroline. I'm sorry to bother you so early," Bel started off well. "May I come in for just a moment?"

"Good morning to you, Bel. It's a little early for visiting, isn't it?" Her green eyes looked a bit guarded, but she opened the door wide and gestured her in.

"I wanted to speak with you privately. I was up early and heading down for a cup of tea a few minutes ago..." Bel hesitated.

"Yes?" said Caroline, her voice cool and steady.

"Well, hell. I'm just going to lay it out there, Caroline. This is bloody awkward. I don't give a damn what you do--you're an adult, and an attractive, competent one at that." Bel saw just the tiniest bit of easing in Caroline's tense posture. "I'm only here because when I came down the hall, I saw Patty crouching at the corner. Just then Paolo came out of your room. I'm not here because Paolo came out of your room, I'm here because Patty saw him coming out of your room. Knowing her, she will make some sort of nasty remark publicly to try to embarrass you. I don't want you be taken by surprise and subjected to her unpleasantness." Bel ran out of breath.

Caroline turned from Bel, and walked to the window. Bel was afraid the woman was too angry to speak, and was relieved when she turned back with a wistful smile.

"Thank you, Bel. Thank you for caring enough about my feelings to do something that was obviously uncomfortable. Thank you for not judging me."

Bel grinned. "Judge you? We're just jealous! Paolo is adorable!" Caroline's eyebrows went up, a small smile lifting the corners of her mouth. Bel added hastily, "Bee was in the hall too. We just didn't want to overwhelm you with the two of us."

Caroline nodded. "And now what?" she asked slowly.

"What?" Bel asked, feeling dense. "About what?"

"About Paolo..." Caroline lingered over his name.

"Whatever you want, Caroline. It's none of our business, and it hasn't affected his work." Bel stopped, and corrected herself. "Actually...it has, for the better! He's never been on time the way he's been on this trip!" She smiled at Caroline and shrugged. "We're not in the business of digging in our guests' personal lives. Our job is to share Italy with you to the best of our ability, and to make sure you have a good trip."

"You guys are terrific." The gratitude in Caroline's voice was audible.

Bel stepped to the door, but paused with her hand on the knob. "You'll be ok when Patty says something awful? I really do think she will." She shook her head, regretfully.

"I'll be fine." Caroline said firmly. "She can say what she likes. Knowing that you two know, and aren't angry with me--I'll enjoy my Roman Holiday, and take home some amazing memories to enjoy. She can just drop dead."

"See you at breakfast, then." Bel closed the door behind her, and took a big breath. Was it going to be one of those days?

She found Bee seated in the sunny window, enjoying a latte. Gratefully, Bel saw that Bee had brewed her a cup of tea. She slid herself into the seat and took a long, slow slip of the wonderful tea. Ahh, tea...she thought, and closed her eyes, taking in the delicious, subtle aroma. She thought of the first time she went to the UK and discovered the art of making tea. "Bel!" Bee disturbed her reverie. "Bel! How did it go?" Bel, startled, opened her eyes to see her sisters' concerned face.

"Awkward at first, as you can imagine. But I just blurted out the facts, told her we didn't give a damn what she did and just didn't want Patty to take her by surprise. She was grateful for the heads up."

Bee sat back in her chair, relieved. "Whew. Thanks for handling that one. Could have been a mess." She rolled her eyes.

"You know, I have a feeling that there's way more to Caroline than we know. There's something steely there, and I think she'll be just fine, no matter what PP says." Bel was thoughtful. "You know, most of the librarians I knew as a child terrified me. Do they all know how to give that cold stare? Do they teach that in librarian school?"

Bee laughed. "Maybe it's a Texas thing, for taming wild horses!"

The sisters turned their attention to the breakfast buffet laid out. Cold meats, cheeses, and rolls. Hard boiled eggs, yoghurt, pastries. Tomatoes, olives, and pickles. Muesli, nutella, and fruit. They tucked in happily, and enjoyed the quiet meal before the others arrived. They talked over the plans for the day--today they would pack up and move on to Florence. Bee and Bel always enjoyed Siena, one of their favorite small towns. But it had been an odd visit, and they agreed that it was most definitely time to move on. Florence offered a completely different experience--a bit more urban, with a tremendous emphasis on art and literature, and of course, the wonderful political intrigue of the Medici family.

Bee and Bell were excited to return to the Uffizi and the Accademia and the amazing treasures housed there. The Vatican Museum was filled with amazing treasures, too, they agreed, but somehow everything seemed more accessible, more "doable" in the Uffizi. The sisters both felt a little overwhelmed in the Vatican Museum--there was simply too much; one couldn't take it all in. Sensory overload and tired feet caused the brain to shut down and just glance at treasures one would have oohed and aahed over in a small gallery.

The trip to Florence was a short one--less than two hours in the bus. They had arranged a short visit to another castle and, following that, a vineyard for another wine tasting and a picnic lunch. After checking in to their B and B, the group would have time on their own to sightsee, relax, shop--Bee and Bel were hoping to get in some shopping at last--and meet again for wine and aperitivo before dinner.

Arriving at the vineyard, the tour group gathered for an interesting discussion of the merits of the local wine. Paolo attended the talk as well, and Patty's sly grin suggested a nasty scene to follow. Indeed, as they sat down to a beautiful picnic lunch laid out for them in the vineyard, Patty cleared her throat and leaned toward Mary and Charlie-- the only ones kind enough to sit near her. "Mary, dear," Patty sniggered, "what would you think of a Cougar in our midst? One who is DOING IT with ---" she gave it a dramatic pause-- "the HELP?' Mary, startled, recoiled from Patty, and Charlie whispered, "Keep your voice down, ma'am!"

"Well, Father," Patty said sarcastically, "does Mother know that our esteemed librarian is not what she says she is? Does everyone here know what a SEX SURROGATE does?' She laughed nastily; nobody joined her. Faces were turned to the table in embarrassment.

Caroline stood up. "Well, now that Prying Patty has let the cat out of the bag," she said, "I will set the record straight. I am in no way a sex surrogate, but I am a licensed sex therapist. I don't usually let strangers know my profession right away-- it tends to put ideas in people's minds. That's why I say I'm a librarian. And frankly, this is my vacation-- free advice is not something I want to get into. As for Patty's other revelation-- done with panache and class, I might add-- we are both adults and it is nobody's business what we do!"

Despite her strong and confident words, she was flushed. She turned even pinker when Lucy stood up as well, and began to applaud her.

"Bravo!" said Lucy. "Patty, I for one am sick and tired of your nosiness and meanness. This is my vacation, and I don't want it spoiled by your petty insults and innuendos. Leave us all alone!" Most of the others in the group applauded her sentiments; Patty just looked defiant.

"Oh, yes?" she sneered. "Maybe you'd like to hear about how sweet Mary and Charlie were able to afford this trip!" Mary gasped, and her face crumpled. She turned to Charlie, tears in her eyes. He leapt to his feet, eyes blazing. He slammed his hand on the table, making them all jump. "Stop!" He roared.

"Charlie!" Mary's voice was pleading. "Sit down! Please! Remember what happened last time!' She grabbed his arm, tugging back into his seat, her anxious eyes wet with tears.

"Now, Mother, don't cry," said Charlie, patting Mary's back, shooting an angry glance toward Patty. He sat down, his face white with anger.

Bel and Bee exchanged THE LOOK. It was way beyond tap-dancing time, but they felt Caroline had acquitted herself with dignity and honesty. Charlie's angry outburst had stunned them. He could easily have grabbed Patty and shaken her, they felt sure. But could Mary stand up to Patty's wickedness? She seemed more fragile than the others and the sisters were concerned for her emotional welfare. And who knew what other revelations Patty had in store? Time to put a stop to the ugly behavior.

76

"That's enough of that kind of talk! " Bel said, clapping her hands. "Let's finish this excellent lunch and get on the bus to Florence, and its treasures and intrigues!"

Hmmm, treasures and intrigues, thought Bee. That would be a great title for another tour....meantime, they had a sex therapist in their midst! Perhaps she could just casually mention the...."Bee!" said Bel. "Earth to Bee!" "Oh, sorry, just remembering something...um...." "Never mind," said Bel. Her sister was known for these little lapses in reality, and it was best to bump her out of them as soon as possible.

"Everybody on the bus!" Bel said crisply. There was quite a rush for the tour bus; the sisters knew that it was because the others did not want to get stuck with Patty. Paolo refused to make eye contact with her, and refused to engage in his usual banter with her. Bee noticed him glancing in the rear view mirror and smiling at Caroline. Good for him, she thought. She frowned. It was a conundrum; having Patty sit up front eliminated the stress of wondering who would end up her seat mate, but it also meant that Paolo bore the brunt of her company every drive. It seemed a little unfair to him, but at least he didn't have to spend the whole day with her... Bee knew she was rationalizing, but it worked for her, she thought cheerfully!

Exchanging glances, the two sisters nodded grimly at each other in the bus. They would have to take Patty aside and inform her that she would either have to stop antagonizing the other tour guests, or... Or what? Bel puzzled over the rest of that sentence. Never in all their tours had they had such an obnoxious client. Bee was obviously thinking along the same lines, Bel guessed, observing the frown on her sister's face. The bus was subdued-- none of the cheerful chatter that had filled the small space just the evening before. Bel sighed, a barely audible exhalation, but Bee heard it, reached out and squeezed her hand.

There was no point in false cheery chatter. They needed to get to the city and allow everyone to check into their own rooms. A little distance from each other would go a long way to making everyone more comfortable again. As they got closer to Florence, Bel took the opportunity to make a few remarks about the city, its history, architecture, and of course, the amazing art found in the Uffizi and the Accademia. She passed out a list of suggested spots to visit during the afternoon "free time", including the Galileo Museum and the Ponte Vecchio.

"Florence is, by the way," she continued, "known for its wonderful leather goods. If you'd like a lovely handbag or briefcase, this is a terrific place to shop!"

From the back of the bus, Bee could hear James stage whisper "It's almost my birthday, Bill. I could use a new briefcase!"

She relaxed her shoulders just a bit, the stress having made her muscles tighten. The diversion of thinking about afternoon activities was easing some of the tension in the vehicle. People began to talk quietly, making plans for the afternoon. Murmured questions, answers, and quiet laughs signaled arrangements made. Patty stared straight ahead, rigid in her isolation.

They soon arrived in the city, and Paolo adeptly navigated the cobbled streets, bringing them right to the door of their hotel.

After the lovely little medieval town of Siena, the bustling city of Florence was awe-inspiring. The flora was now distinctly different from the plants and trees of Rome, and people seemed just a bit better dressed and sharper; most seemed bent on their own business, and tourists were mainly to be found in the major squares of the city. The group found the flat topography less charming than the area further south, but it promised much easier walking.

In the hotel lobby, Bee and Bel handed out room keys, and the group quickly dispersed after picking up their luggage from Paolo. He very pointedly asked Caroline, Lucy, Margo, and Mary if they needed help with their luggage. They declined, with thanks. He picked up Caroline's green suitcase, and followed her up the stairs. He directed a stream of Italian behind him, and Bee and Bel were glad they were the only ones who understood Italian. They were pretty sure the rest of the group got the general idea, though.

Patty lumbered toward the elevator, towing her suitcase behind her. The sisters swiftly followed, and cornered her before she could enter the tiny lift.

78

"Patty." Bel could have a very commanding voice when needed, Bee thought, admiringly. Must be all those years lecturing to sleepy students.

"What?" she snarled. "I want to go lie down." Her little eyes darted to the elevator, as if calculating whether she could scuttle there fast enough to escape the coming conversation.

"Patty." Bel repeated herself, calmly but firmly. "Listen to me. I am giving you an ultimatum." Patty sneered.

"We are hereby officially putting you on notice that your presence on this tour is probationary."

Patty began to bluster, but Bel calmly went on, talking over her. "If there is ONE MORE incident--" Bel held her finger up as if she were speaking to a child-- "you will no longer be considered part of our tour. You will not be allowed on the bus, and your room reservations will be cancelled. You will be issued a refund for the remaining three days, minus our termination fee."

The large woman stared at them, and quivered with rage. "How DARE you speak to me like that?" she bellowed.

It was Bee's turn. "Patty, we have documented every incident with you. You signed a contract, which included termination information. You have knowingly and deliberately disrupted the tour. That is grounds for a termination of the contract. We have made every effort to fulfill our part. Either you do the same, or our association ends."

The two women held their breath, wondering what would happen next. However, like bullies everywhere, Patty didn't know what to do when their victims stood up to them. "I'll call my lawyer!" she sputtered.

"That's fine" Bel said calmly. "You have a choice, Patty. We are offering you the opportunity to remain with us, and we welcome you---IF, and only IF you can be civil to everyone--and I mean EVERYONE--in the group." She took a breath and continued. "We will expect you to apologize to everyone over dinner."

Patty glared at her.

"Do we have an understanding, then?" Bel stared straight into Patty's eyes.

Mutely, Patty nodded, her chin stuck out and her brow furrowed.

Bee and Bel turned as one, leaving Patty standing in front of the elevator. They took their bags, and calmly, deliberately, went up the stairs. It was only when they had closed the door behind them that they looked at each other.

"Oh, my God." Stereo voices. They looked at each other. Bee blurted, "I'm about to pee my pants I'm so stressed!" She ran for the bathroom. "Hurry up!!" Bel pleaded. "Me too!"

Minutes later, with empty bladders but still shaken nerves, the two sisters sat down to craft their "Emergency Tap Dancing Plan" as they called it. This tour was falling apart at the seams--no, wrong analogy--this tour group was slowly being poisoned, with each tour member being targeted, one at a time. James and Bill had been repeatedly humiliated. Caroline had been spied upon and slandered. Charlie and Mary had been threatened with....well, what? Bee and Bel were sure that Piggy Patty--no, Poison Patty--had been about to reveal an exaggerated version of some information that she had somehow obtained. But what? Charlie and Mary had obviously been uncomfortable, so there was something there they hadn't wanted shared. Charlie's violent outburst suggested something significant. Their natural curiosity was, unfortunately, in high gear, and led to wild speculation.

"Do you suppose they run a brothel?" Bee giggled. "Mary doesn't strike me as the Madam type!"

"Drug runners?" Bel offered. "No one would suspect a nice elderly couple from Iowa! And they probably already have a mule!"

"You goofball. That's not what that means!" Bee rolled her eyes at her sister, who happily stuck her tongue out at her.

"Noooo...." mused Bee, suddenly serious. "Patty kept mentioning Mallmart, remember?"

Bel nodded, thinking. "It must have something to do with that." She shook her head. "I don't even want to know."

"What would we have done if Patty hadn't agreed to our terms?" Bee wanted to know.

"I haven't got the foggiest idea!" Bel looked drained. "I guess call the last two hotels and cancel her reservation, and tell them we wouldn't be responsible if she tried to book a room and charge it to us." She looked unhappy, just thinking about the possibilities. Bee knew her sister needed a boost.

"Come on." Bee grabbed her purse. "We've got three hours. Let's go spoon hunting and get away from all this!"

Chapter Eleven

Alone in her room, Patty brooded. Her plan to turn everyone against Caroline had backfired. Her attempt to show Charlie and Mary's true nature was short circuited by Lucy, and she resented it. Everyone thinks I'm the bad guy, Patty thought to herself. What about people who sell out their friends and profit from it? There was a nagging discomfort as she considered this line of thought--the truth was, she didn't have any friends. Well, what about people who had flings, or lied about their careers? Didn't that say something about their characters? Really, it was disgusting. She would never demean herself by engaging in such a base fashion, giving in to such animal urges.

Patty's face darkened. Just such behavior had ruined her relationship with her daughter. Discovered in an inappropriate, compromising affair, her defiant daughter had refused to apologize, refused to beg forgiveness. The little tramp--until she came crawling back, Patty had threatened, she could expect nothing from her mother. It had been 19 years, and she hadn't seen or heard from her once. Her loss! Patty had grimly changed her will, leaving everything to James. It galled her to know that everything she had worked for would go to him, but the satisfaction of knowing her daughter would get nothing--nothing!--was enough to produce a thin smile as she signed the document. Besides, she had reasoned at the time, she could always rewrite the will if she--Patty couldn't even bring herself to say her name--came to her senses and admitted what a willful fool she had been.

Patty struggled with warring emotions--self-pity and anger. Here, she had almost no power to get her way--and she had gotten her way for decades. It was easy to manipulate people, she thought. Most were stupid, gutless, and weak. Even hint at their indiscretions and they caved. Many a real estate deal had gone her way, simply because she had done her homework, paying attention and keeping her eyes and ears open. She marveled at how naive people could be; she had entered many a home when the sellers were out, gone through their desks and medicine cabinets, culling their most intimate secrets so easily. And they never understood how she knew so much, thinking her references to the hidden part of their lives indicated a far deeper awareness. Patty let them think that. It didn't take much to get them to sign whatever she brought them.

This trip was her reward to herself for a particularly brilliant real estate sale. She had represented both the buyer and the seller, and kept the entire commission for herself. The president of the local bank was being transferred out of the area, and his beautiful home was for sale by owner. Patty had toured the house--and the contents of his desk--and found an invoice for a noted divorce attorney in the next town. She had easily convinced him that her help in selling the house was far more beneficial to his career. With her profit, she decided to visit Italy, a dream destination for James.

It had amused her to invite James and Bill, dangling the trip as both a threat and a prize. They owed her, and they knew it. She wanted them to come and be her escorts, and they had little choice. Embezzlement was illegal, and if James' new employer had even a hint of it, he'd be fired immediately. If he had only told her why--what did he do with the money?-- she might have let it go. But her weak and sickly husband had, for once, put his foot down. He insisted she stay out of it and threatened to publicly leave her if he heard even a whisper that anyone knew of the inconsistencies at the factory. She had already been forced to endure the disgrace of a daughter who left town under a cloud, and had no desire to be abandoned by her husband, as much as she despised him. They had never spoken of it again.

84

She frowned. They hadn't spoken much about anything, she thought. After SHE left, he rarely spoke, and never laughed at home. Once, she had walked into a restaurant at lunchtime, and heard his voice. He was at a large table, filled with colleagues. His laughter startled her--she hadn't heard it in such a long time. Abruptly she had left the place before he had seen her. Her anger built all day long, erupting and flowing over him like lava that night. The worst part was that he had simply stared at her, and left the room silently, her anger unabated or satisfied. He had died a few months later, sitting at his desk in his office. A massive heart attack had finally released him from their loveless marriage. Patty had been relieved, and found the role of grieving widow bought her some temporary sympathy in a town tired of her. She had played the part to the hilt, swathed in black, dabbing at her eyes. His company had given her a very generous compensation package. Their daughter had not come to the funeral.

Patty sat in her room, the city of Florence laid out beneath her window. Lost in thought, the ancient city was invisible to her. All she could see were the imagined injustices done to her. For some reason, she had no memory of the nasty remarks, the calculated comments, or deliberate cruelties she had inflicted on others. And now Bee and Bel. How dare they threaten her? She would make sure they never forgot her.

Bee and Bel were oblivious to the malicious thoughts being directed their way. They practically raced down the narrow stairs of the B and B. They paused for a second to admire the lovely garden patio with its ancient rock wall, then sped onto the streets of Florence. There was a brief but costly stop in their favorite stationery store, where they bought beautiful, renaissance-inspired note cards, hand-printed wine and jelly labels, and embossed stamps for friends at home. "Amazing attention to detail!" murmured Bel. "Craftsmanship is alive and well in Italy. I guess after centuries of exquisite workmanship, customers come to expect expertise." After paying for their purchases, Bel crowed "Now, on to the real hunt!" The two were die-hard aficionados of second-hand shops, flea markets, and the like.

Turning the corner of a small square, which was anchored by the ancient duomo, Bel remarked on the age of the cathedral. "This Duomo was originally built in the 1500's," she said; always the tour guide, she just couldn't help herself. "We should step inside and confirm their hours." They stepped up to the church entry but saw a sign posted stating that mass was in progress, and the cathedral was closed to casual visitors. "Maybe on the way back," said Bee, disappointed. Turning another corner, they passed the expensive perfumery founded by monks in the sixteenth century. Many tourists visited the shop, but few could afford the enticing but pricey concoctions. Bee and Bel had shopped here previously, where each had a perfume custom blended for her. They referred to the perfume as their birthday gifts to themselves....... two of many, that was.

Their favorite antiques and junk shop was ahead, and Bee could feel herself salivating. This treasure trove was quite a find, and few Americans knew of it-- the sign was tiny and did not indicate what was within. Sometimes they felt as though they were opening Pandora's box when they cracked the door to the shop. Although they adored shopping together, each sister suspected that the other was in league with the devil on these expeditions. Their tastes were so similar that they loved the same things, so there was a general race to find the goodies first. And then there was the encouragement, the prodding-- "Go ahead and buy it, you deserve it----how many packs of cigarettes would this represent?" Bel had quit the nasty habit a year ago, and she and Bee still used the cost of smokes as a compensatory tool. It came in quite handy.

"Bee, you know you want it. When did you last have one you loved as much as this?" The search was on, and the two knew well that they would find ways to rationalize their purchases with little trouble.

"Ah, *Signoras*!" said the shopkeeper, a short, rotund man with startling blue eyes and lush black moustache. "I have kept some special things for you!" From a cabinet behind him, he reverently removed a sterling silver spoon-- just exactly the type that Bel collected, as he knew well. The bowl was etched with tiny flowers. The handle was something special-- entwined roses and ribbons. Yes, Bel had to have it. She stroked it gently with one finger. Bee, meanwhile, was searching the glass jewelry case for anything pretty with a bee motif-- her signature passion. Disappointed, she moved away. "Nothing today, I see, Alberto?" she said. He shook his head, but advised her to return the next day. He explained that he had a delivery of estate jewelry coming to the shop from a local castell. The sisters eagerly agreed to return. If only things had worked out that way.

Chapter Twelve

After a couple of hours of shopping, the sisters stopped at a cafe to get off their feet, gloat over their treasures, and enjoy a cappuccino and a cup of tea. They also justified getting a pastry and splitting it, on the grounds that it had been a very difficult day. They justified the second one on the grounds that the first one had been delicious. While they ate, they reviewed the plans for the evening and tomorrow morning's tour of the Uffizi, a quick lunch at the rooftop cafe, and then an afternoon visit to the Accademia. It was a very full day, but their groups always enjoyed this part of the tour.

Bel was the designated guide for the group in the museums. She loved Renaissance paintings, and Botticelli's 'Venus' was one of her favorites. She loved the intricate detail, the rich symbolism, and the spare simplicity of Venus herself--unadorned with anything but her glorious hair. Bee made a mental note to be near the front of the group at that painting--Bel could go on and on about it in her enthusiasm. They would have a lot of ground to cover before sensory overload dulled the group's interest and their aching feet made them cranky. It was Bee's job to keep things moving so the group would have the opportunity to see all the highlights with Bel's expert explanations. Afterwards, they would be given additional time in the museum to go back and visit their favorites. Most of them headed straight for the gift shop.

They finished their beverages, feeling much better after the sugar and caffeine boost.

Bel licked her spoon contentedly, then looked at it speculatively, thinking it would look nice with her collection. "NO!" Bee's voice startled her.

"What?!" she said, guiltily. How does she DO that?? she wondered to herself. Bee looked at her sister, amused.

"You do know why you always lose at poker, don't you?" Bee asked.

"No, I don't! And what does that have to do with anything?" Bel was indignant.

"My dear big sister. It's written all over your face." Bee laughed at Bel's startled look. "That spoon was headed for your purse. I know it, and don't bother to deny it."

Bel turned pink. She primly picked up her coffee cup, and pretended to drink from it. They both knew it was empty, but Bee graciously refrained from comment.

"Well." A discrete change of subject was in order. Bee attempted to sound business-like. "The restaurant is expecting us at eight, and we've requested wine and aperitivo at seven at the hotel. We can have our book discussion before dinner."

"Sounds good. It's an easy walk to the restaurant," Bel noted, "but with lots of turns. I'll be in front of the group, you take the rear. That way, if we get separated, we'll still get everyone there."

Alarmed, Bee hastened to point out that she should be in front to explain the meal they were about to enjoy. She didn't want to have to try to make small talk with Patty, especially after the conversation they had recently had.

"Fine." Bel agreed. Bee was instantly suspicious. "I'll walk with Patty, let's just say it." Bee waited, wondering where this surprisingly agreeable conversation was going. "Oh, and by the way….Deciding Factor means you get to sit next to her at dinner." Bel smiled smugly. Bee opened her mouth, then shook her head and shut her mouth, caught in the trap the canny Bel had laid for her.

Bel reached across the table, and grabbed her arm. "Look!" she hissed. "What??" Bee snapped her head around, searching in the direction Bel indicated by the thrust of her chin.

"Over THERE!" Look at that tour group!!" Exiting the Duomo was a small group of Asian tourists, following a guide with a purple umbrella held high.

"Couldn't be!" Bee exclaimed. "Could it?!"

They watched the group gather about the guide, listening as she gestured first toward the Duomo, then the bell tower. After a few minutes, she appeared to have concluded, and bowed to her group. They bowed in return and applauded, and the knot of people broke up into small groups, heading towards the little shops lining the piazza.

One man in particular caught their attention. He had his notebook aimed at the Bell Tower, then turned toward the Baptistry to take a photo from that angle. Bee and Bel gasped. It almost looked like the tourist was taking a photo of them.

"It's him!" they shouted together, prompting the other cafe guests to look at them curiously. They grabbed their bags and ran. Fleetingly, Bee was glad their waiter had presented them with the bill promptly, and they had put down Euros while they were talking. That's all their tour company needed--a visit from the police! She giggled at the mental image of the two of them sharing an Italian jail cell. What would Jack and Nate say about that!

They ran into the square, determined to speak to "Assogot". As they made their way across the square, a group of laughing school children swarmed past their overwhelmed teacher. Shrieking and shouting, the group of children ran into the square, having been released from the solemn environs of the Duomo. Bags in hand, the sisters had to pause to be certain they didn't collide with the unruly students. Frustrated, they watched their target move slowly away into the eddying crowd and disappear down a side street filled with pedestrians.

Bel stamped her foot.

"Damn!" Bee swore. "This just keeps getting weirder."

They turned and silently headed back to the hotel.

Passing a small corner grocery store, they nearly bumped into James, carrying a bag of groceries. He blushed when they saw him, which made them smile.

"Find anything interesting?" Bee asked eagerly. She loved visiting local grocery stores, enjoying the window into everyday life. It always intrigued her to see what was on the shelves--not for tourists, but for hungry people on their way home from work. That was how one really got a sense of the culture, she thought--seeing what they ate for breakfast, lunch and dinner on a routine basis. It was amazing to see the commonalities, and even more fun to try the foods that weren't available at home. She had discovered some very delicious local specialities, and also a few bizarre flavors she never wanted to taste again.

James paused before answering. "No...just looking for some interesting pastas to bring home. And some snacks for the bus." He looked uncomfortable.

"I'm really sorry about my aunt." He sounded miserable. "Frankly, I've been on pins and needles, wondering when something would happen. It's kind of a pattern with her." He shook his head, his immaculately styled hair sweeping across his forehead. "It's why we moved out of state. We just couldn't stand it anymore." He looked anxiously at them. "What happens next?" he asked. "Would you like Bill and me to leave the tour to make things easier?" The women shook their heads, frowning.

Bee patted his shoulder, her heart going out to the young man. "No apology needed, James. You're not your aunt's keeper. We don't hold it against you." Bel nodded, and Bee continued.

"We've spoken with Patty privately. We've made it clear what our expectations are, and she agreed." Here James looked startled. Bel interjected, "Well, perhaps agreed is too strong a word. But Bee is right-- we've made our position clear, and she understands it."

Relief flooded the young man's' face. "Thanks for not holding it against us. That means a lot to me. But..." his face darkened. "You don't know Patty. She won't let anything go that easily. She may lay low for a bit, but she'll find a way to manipulate this. She always does." His jaw tightened.

92

"Please be careful." With that, he hurried away, leaving the two women startled and uneasy. So much for the relaxing afternoon--one conversation and they were right back in it.

"Huh." Said Bee. "That's the third person who's told us to be careful. That's not a pattern I like." Bel pursed her lips. "Let's check in with Jack and Nate," she said thoughtfully. "Time to call in the research specialists."

Chapter Thirteen

Back in their room, the sisters picked up their phones. No games for them, though--they both felt the need to connect with their families, people who were loving, funny, and had no Patty to worry about. Bee and Jack connected immediately--he was home and lonely, and responded to her text right away. All was well at home, he reported. Her orchids were looking a little yellow, so he had watered them. Again. Bee sighed, knowing they wouldn't survive his loving attention. They caught up on the details that are the fabric of married life--their children, the garden, his elderly parents, the contents of the fridge (how long would Kentucky Fried Chicken stay edible in the fridge, he wanted to know. Was a week too long?) She strongly urged him to throw it out, adding a frowning face emoticon to be sure he knew it was a bad idea.

Feeling a need for a sane opinion, she told him some of the revelations of the day. "Who is this person?????" he typed back. Smiling to herself at his dramatic use of question marks, so unlike her normally quiet husband, she gave him Patty's name.

"Could you google her and let me know if you find anything?" She texted him. "She makes us uncomfortable and I'm not sure why." He wrote back immediately, "Perhaps because she is rude, obnoxious, slanderous and just plain vile!!!" Bee knew her gentlemanly husband was upset--he would never say anything like that out loud. But it was nice to be validated--sometimes on a small tour like this, little things could bother people that wouldn't seem so egregious in a large group. Tempests in a teapot, her mother used to call them. But not this time.

It was poison in a pill named Patty, and she took an odd comfort in Nate's protective reaction.

He promised to look into her background, if any could be found. Bee gave him her hometown information--they had a copy of everyone's passports in case of emergency. She flipped through the file of passports, waiting for Nate to get back to her. "That's weird!" She nudged Bel with her foot. "Hey. Listen to this!"

Bel looked up from her phone--she had written to Jack, but he wasn't online. She was disappointed and cross. "What!" She heard the peevishness in her voice. "I mean, what's so weird?"

"Margo and Patty were born in the same town!" Bee frowned. "Talk about your seven degrees of separation! Come all the way across the ocean on a tour group of ten people, and one of them is from your hometown!"

"And just your luck, it's Patty. Ugh." Bel made a face. "At least they don't live in the same town now. Margo must have moved away, while Patty stayed put."

Nate's messages resumed. He was eager to explain to Bee that the septic system was to be serviced in the morning. Bee cut him off, writing, "Darling, I just cannot deal with that shit right now. Literally." She added a happy face, so he would know she was being facetious. His "haha" assured her that he had gotten her play on words. Glancing at the clock, she sighed, and sent Nate lots of x's and o's, telling him that she needed to get ready for dinner. Her husband sent back an equal amount of love, and they signed off.

Over on her bed, Bel was brooding. She had a visual image of Patty as a huge, cruel spider, presiding over a sticky web. Poor James seemed caught in that web, and it looked like she was trying to snare Mary and Charlie, too. Caroline was "the one that got away;" she had denied Patty her nasty triumph of salacious gossip. What other traps were waiting? Bel shuddered at the visual image. She did NOT like spiders.

There was an insistent knock on the door, startling the two sisters. They looked questioningly at each other. "Did you...?" they asked each other simultaneously. Mutely, they both shook their heads, and Bee jumped up to open the door. Mary and Charlie were there, looking grim.

"Please come in!" Bee opened the door wider, and beckoned to them. Bel hastily shoved her bag of snacks under her pillow, wiping her cheesy fingers on the pillowcase surreptitiously. Bee shot her a look.

"What can we do for you this evening?" Bee asked, dreading the answer.

Charlie cleared his throat, while Mary twisted her hands in her lap. Charlie remained standing, and towered over the little woman who had seated herself in the boudoir chair beside the window. The couple looked at each other, and the silence in the room was awkward. Bel smoothed the coverlet on the bed where she sat, and spoke softly.

"It's about Patty." It was a statement, not a question. The Iowans nodded.

"Her behavior was inexcusable, and I trust you know we do not condone anything she has said and done." Here she paused, and looked at them, willing them to acknowledge that the sisters were not responsible for the actions of a tour group member.

"Well, thank you." Charlie hesitated. "It's just that..."

"We can't go on like this!" Mary choked out. "We came to get away from stress, not have more!" Her eyes were red, Bee noticed. It had been an awful day for them, and Bee felt guilty for having had such an enjoyable afternoon. They should have gone straight to Charlie and Mary and checked on them, she reproached herself. Guilty, she reached out and stroked Mary's small hand, and noticed it was trembling.

Charlie picked up where she left off. "That WOMAN has made Mary a nervous wreck, and frankly I'm pretty damn sick and tired of her myself." His fists clenched. "She had better stop making those nasty comments, or else..."

Mary hastily interjected "We're just thinking perhaps it would be better if we left the tour."

Startled, Bee and Bel both spoke at once. Bel stopped, and let Bee continue with a nod and a small smile.

"We certainly hope not. You have been such a wonderful part of our group. Everyone--" here she grinned a bit, "well, almost everyone--would be devastated if you left."

Bel took over, as she usually did, "Without invading anyone's privacy, I think it's fair to let you know that we have had a very serious discussion with Patty. We have made it quite clear that she has one opportunity to set things right tonight at dinner, and that any other disruptive behavior will result in her being barred from the remainder of the trip."

Bee added helpfully, "In plain English, she'd better shape up or she's out." Bel shot her a look.

"Patty knows she is to apologize to the group tonight if she wishes to continue with us, and she indicated her willingness to do so."

Charlie and Mary exchanged glances, and Bee and Bel could see them visibly relax.

"It's our goal to make everyone on this tour comfortable," Bel spoke slowly. "We'll do what it takes to make that happen. While we can't guarantee what will come out of her mouth, we CAN guarantee that we won't tolerate any more of her nasty comments."

"Well, Mother?" Charlie looked down at his wife. "It's totally up to you. I'd just as soon bash her and be done with it, but that's frowned upon by polite society." He smiled grimly, his hands opening and closing reflexively.

"Charles!" Mary looked at him anxiously. "That's not funny."

"I'm sorry, my dear. You know how I get crazy when anything upsets you."

She smiled at him, and patted his arm. She turned to the waiting sisters. "Thank you, ladies. We'll stay."

Bee and Bel exhaled, not even realizing they had been holding their breath.

"Come along then, Mother. The ladies need to get ready for dinner, and so do we. We'll see you downstairs shortly."

Charlie gave a gallant little bow, and shepherded Mary into the hall.

Bel collapsed onto her bed, and Bee did the same. "What the hell?" Bel muttered.

Bee, without raising her head, added, "Worst. Tour. Ever."

Chapter Fourteen

To cap off a rather bizarre day, Bel discovered that her favorite outfit was ripped. She sat by the window, trying to hastily repair the damage. She squinted while trying to thread the needle. "Where are my reading glasses?" She fumed. Bee snorted. Without turning around, Bel knew. They were on top of her head. With great dignity, she reached up and perched them on her nose.

"Mom used to say growing old isn't for sissies." Bel snorted. "What do you think mom would have said about this mess?" Bee looked thoughtful. They considered the question.

"Well..." Bee smiled, thinking of their bright and perceptive mother. "She wouldn't have liked Patty, that's for sure."

"No." agreed Bel. "But she'd have tried to figure out what made her behave this way. Then she'd focus on finding one nice thing about her."

"She'd have her work cut out for her." Bee doubted that even the most generous observer would have an easy time finding something positive about Poison Patty.

"She has a good appetite?" Bel suggested. The two of them laughed. "You got that right! She's a chow hound for sure."

Soberly, Bee considered. "You know, I bet mom would say that all that eating was a way to insulate herself--keep eating, and you create a barrier between you and the world."

Sighing, Bel considered her waistline. "I don't want a barrier. I just want fettuccine!"

"And that, dear sister, is why your dress ripped!" Bee ducked as a pillow came flying across the room.

Repairs completed, the two women finished their preparations for the evening. It was important, they agreed, that tonight they look both professional and polished, to establish that it was their tour, and they had the ability to make decisions about the tour and follow through with those decisions. Although Patty had nominally agreed to apologize, they weren't certain it would be gracious, immediate, or comfortable for all involved. They needed to be able to command the situation. It had indeed been a long day, and it wasn't over yet.

"Not till the fat lady apologizes!" Bee giggled. Bel shushed her, but by the glint in her eye, it was obvious she agreed.

They headed out the door. Opening it, they were startled to see Paolo, his hand raised to knock. He was as surprised as they were, turning his knock into a wave.

"Oh, Lord, now what?" Escaped from Bel's lips before she could stop herself.

Hastily, Bee said "Paolo! How nice to see you! What can we do for you?" as cheerfully as she could, hoping he was there to confirm pick up time in the morning.

"*Buona sera, Signora* Bee, *Signora* Bel." His large, dark eyes weren't smiling.

"How long have I driven for you?" he asked, and answered his own question. "Four years, twice a year sometimes. Have I ever asked a favor?" His English was heavily accented, but outstanding. He had been an English major at university, but the depressed economy had forced him to find other ways to use his language skills. One of the reasons Bee and Bel continued to engage him as a driver was because when he waited for a group in the van, he could often be found with a piece of classic American literature in his hands, notes scribbled in the margins. He would sometimes ask the proper pronunciation of the English words; his dream was to find a position teaching English Literature, and the sisters enjoyed bringing him classics from home.

"Please, *Signora*. *Basta*. Don't make me sit next to HER in the bus anymore." His eyes narrowed. "She is evil. She is cruel. She is sweaty."

Bel tried hard not to smile at the last comment. Bee sighed. "Paolo. Think of it from our side. If she sits next to you, she isn't sitting next to Caroline and making snide remarks."

At the mention of Caroline, his eyes softened. "*Bella* Caroline!" he breathed.

Bee and Bel looked at each other, eyebrows in full alert. They had assumed the relationship was a casual, convenient recreational outlet for the two of them. But Paolo didn't look like he was taking this casually. Could it be something more? Startled, the two were momentarily speechless.

Paolo shuffled his feet. Bel, sensing his resolve weakening, pressed the point. "Paolo, you know we respect you and your privacy. We know you would never do anything to jeopardize one of our tours." He looked just a bit guilty, knowing that beginning a physical relationship with one of the customers was not really ethical. Not wrong, exactly, between two adults, but...

Bel continued. "Please, Paolo. It's a very difficult situation. If we can have Patty sit in the front of the bus, everyone else is much, much happier, and she is happier, too. And that means we're all so much happier." Except Paolo, thought Bee, guiltily. Bel went on "And that means so much to the success of the tour. Please, Paolo?"

The man shrugged, a classic Italian gesture. "*Signora*, when you put it that way. You are saying that the success of the tour is on me, eh?! What can I do then?" He smiled at Bel, his eyes twinkling. Relieved, they linked arms with him, one on each side, and he escorted them down the broad staircase.

Downstairs, the group had gathered in the lovely reception room. Since the B and B was on the small side, they were the only guests staying there. They filled every available room, as both Patty and Caroline now had single rooms. The hosts, a lovely Italian woman and her British ex-pat husband, were already handing around glasses of wine.

They greeted Bel and Bee, looking anxious. "Is there something wrong with your accommodations?" Roger asked.

"What do you mean?" Bel was surprised by the question.

"Everyone seems so tense. We were worried that you were unhappy with the rooms."

Embarrassed, Bee shook her head. "We've had a bit of a problem with one of the group members making herself unpleasant."

"Ah. *Signora* Patty." Sophia's voice made it clear what she thought of the person in question.

Without agreeing or denying it, Bee continued. "The issue should be resolved shortly. We have an understanding."

Roger appeared reluctant to speak, but was obviously tempted. A look from Sophia gave him the impetus to proceed.

"Are you aware that *Signora* Patty has made...." he paused, searching for the right word. "Well, frankly, she has made threatening remarks to Sophia. Said she's going to ruin her on the internet if we don't upgrade her room for free, provide her with free wi-fi, coffee every morning in her room, blah blah blah." Roger looked both apologetic and angry, a rare combination. Bee loved the British.

"We don't have any other rooms available. Your group, as you know, is using all of our rooms now."

"Roger, we're so sorry. I wish you had told us earlier!" Bel blurted out.

"No worries, we're used to that sort of bluster. Just not from one of your customers." Despite the embarrassment, Bee and Bel noted and appreciated the compliment.

Sophia shrugged. "She's not going to bully me. I'm not afraid of her." Her beautiful brown eyes were amused. "My family's from Sicily. It would take a lot more than a rude American to scare me."

Again, Bel apologized. "This one is problematic for all of us," she said. "We are working hard to resolve this; in the meantime, by all means, don't give in to any threats! Our praise for this lovely B and B will balance any negative feedback from her." Sophia and Roger, however, shared a worried look. "It's just," Roger said, "well... we applied for a loan to upgrade all the bathrooms and one stipulation from the bank is getting consistently positive feedback from customers." "Ah," said Bel. "In that case, I can see your concern. We will work on Patty." The sisters turned when Lucy and Margo entered the room.

Lucy looked annoyed, and Margo was tearful. Lucy had fire in her eyes. She strode purposely to the tour leaders, brandishing a letter. "What do you think this is?" she demanded. Horrified, Bel and Bee shrugged. "Please tell us," Bee said, resignation in her voice and drooping stance.She glanced at her sister, and out of the corner of her mouth, Bel whispered, "It must be a Poison Patty letter."

"I have about had it," Lucy said. "Take a look at this!"

Bel gingerly took the letter and held it so that Bee could read it too. "When is a doc not a doc?" it read. "When he has to leave his job in disgrace after nearly killing a patient!" Both women gasped. "What's this about?" asked Bee.

"It probably alludes to Margo's late father" said Lucy. "He was an anesthesiologist in Hartford, and had a case of near death from anaphylactic shock. He had to resign to keep the hospital from being sued; the patient recovered, but he never did. He became more and more depressed, and when she was only 14, Margo found him dead of an overdose. It was suicide, complete with an apologetic note. He simply could not go on. And now we hear from Patty that she had a similar experience--and it was due to eating peanuts, not the doctor's mistake!"

"What a waste of a decent human being! I'm so angry, I could just kill her!" Margo burst out.

Lucy said softly, "Well, Margo, we aren't sure it was Patty. She doesn't live in Hartford, does she?" Lucy asked Bee and Bel. They looked at each other, and the answer was readily apparent on their faces.

"Oh, no!" moaned Margo, and she swayed against Lucy. "That does it!" Lucy snapped. "We are done with this tour. Anything to do with this despicable woman is too much. We're leaving!" Lucy turned on her heel, but Bel put out a gentle hand to stop her. "Please, just wait a day," Bel said. "I think you will be interested in what Patty has to say tonight."

"We don't have anywhere to stay tonight," Margo said. "Why not wait and see? We wouldn't be able to leave til morning anyway." Lucy's angry face softened when she looked at Margo. "Ah, you've been through so much, Margo," she said. "if you want to wait a bit, it's fine with me." The two turned away together, and found a seat with Caroline. Lucy sat with her arm protectively around Margo.

Chapter Fifteen

Heads turned as Mary and Charlie entered the room. "Greetings, all!" said Charlie. He and Mary looked just a bit worse for wear; their faces seemed a little more lined, and their usual spiffy outfits looked wrinkled as well. "I hope they hold up okay," thought Bee. "They're such wonderful people-- salt of the earth and all that." The thought of salt reminded her-- "ahhh, *saltimbocca* tonight!" She licked her lips appreciatively as she thought of the wonderful dinner awaiting.

James and Bill entered the room, Bill with his arm protectively around his partner. They sat with Mary and Charlie, and Bel heard them quietly apologizing to the Iowans for Patty's behavior. Just as the sisters had, Mary assured the men that they held nothing against them. "You aren't responsible for your aunt," she said.

James nodded gravely. "Still," he muttered, "I am so sorry for your trouble on this trip." Just then, Patty entered the room. She was wearing a lacy top that must have cost more than tonight's dinner for ten. Unfortunately, on her, it looked like an exploded poodle had entered the room. The polyester slacks and huge designer handbag, although hideous, were pricey as well, the sisters knew. Bee especially liked to keep her eye on fashion trends-- the better to score at the local consignment shops. Patty's too tight kitten mules looked absurd on her clodhopper feet. Bel sighed. How would this evening go?

The answer was forthcoming. "Good evening, all," said Patty, eyes sparkling with with either fun or malice. "I have been asked to apologize for being mean to you nice folks. So-- I have composed a little ditty which should cover it all. " "Oh God, " thought the sisters. "What now?" They looked at each other. There was a sudden breathless stillness in the room. "Do I have your undivided attention?" demanded Patty, a grim sneer on her face. "Good. Here goes."

Taking a wide-legged stance against the fireplace, she recited:

"Roses are red,

Violets are blue.

Sell out to Mallmart,

Won't you two?"

Turning to Mary and Charlie, she said, "I sincerely apologize to you both for underestimating your cleverness. How do the other town residents feel? Hmmmm?"

White-faced, Charlie leapt from his chair. Mary pulled frantically at his sleeve. "We can't have any more incidents!" She cried. Muttering, Charlie subsided. The group sat, shocked. Droning on, Patty continued.

"Roses are red,

Violets are blue.

Stole from your boss?

And I know it, too!

I deeply apologize, James. I had no idea you were bright enough to hide the stolen funds!"

She turned to face Bill and James. James looked as though he was going to faint. "Why, you nasty old hag!" Bill said. "You'll get what's coming to you!" James was white-faced and silent, but Bill continued, "All the money in the world is not worth putting up with her!" Without pausing for breath, Patty continued in her sing-song voice,

"Roses are red,

Violets are blue.

Antics in the bedroom

Are disgusting, you two!"

Here she turned to Caroline and Paolo, who was still in the room. Paolo gasped. The sex therapist looked humiliated for the first time.

"So sorry, Caroline. I didn't ..."

Oh Lord, thought Bee!

"Enough!" Bel commanded, and strode toward her. "Bel, watch out!" shouted Bee. Patty had reached behind her and grabbed a fireplace poker. The room came alive. James, Bill, Paolo and Charlie all rushed to Bel's aid. James wrestled the poker away from his aunt, knocking her down, while Charlie sat on her. Squawking and red-faced, Patty was flopping like a landed fish, trying to get out from under Charlie. "You will all pay for this!" Patty snarled. "If you think this was bad, just wait to see what Miss Patty has in store for your entertainment tomorrow!"

"There will not be a tomorrow," said Bel icily. "As of now, you are eliminated from this tour. We will return the unused portion of your tour money to you." Drawing herself up to her full height, she pointed at Patty and said, "You will be gone by tomorrow morning! We have had enough of this behavior. Now go and pack!" The room erupted in applause and Charlie let out a whistle of approval.

"You can't do this to me!" Patty yelled. "I paid in full for this stupid tour! I am going to sue you-- just like I did Margo's father!" There was a gasp from Margo, who looked faint. Lucy stood up and said, "If you're not gone tomorrow, there will be real trouble!" There was sincere menace in her voice. Patty marched to the concierge desk and demanded room service. She obviously intended to make the appetizer course her meal.

"I am so sorry," said Sophia, although she didn't sound sorry in the least. "There's no one available to bring you anything right now." Patty turned and flounced away. The other guests sighed with relief, hearing her make her slow and noisy way up the stairs.

Immediately, Sophia entered the room. "Ladies and gentlemen, you have had a dreadful evening so far. Please, go and enjoy your dinner. But let us promise you a sweet end to a bitter evening. Come back after dinner, and I will provide you with a very special dessert--a family recipe that I assure you will make up for the unpleasantness," she said, a sparkle in her eye.

Bee and Bel were thrilled to be given an exit strategy. They quickly rounded up the dazed group, and shepherded them to the restaurant a few streets away. The group was silent, walking in pairs through the dark streets. Bee and Bel hoped the change in scenery would provide a welcome diversion from the ugliness Patty had spread. As promised, the quiet little restaurant was close by, and the fresh air and movement had been essential to reviving the group. At the door, Bee quietly asked the host to remove one place setting, hoping to make the absence less dramatic. Although, she mused, it would be hard to top that scene.

Despite the traumatic events earlier, the group was surprised to discover they were hungry. Patty's poisonous poetry had united them, rather than separated them from each other. Bee and Bel quickly ordered carafes of wine for the table, and made sure that Margo had the gluten-free menu. Wine was poured, and a silence descended on the table. Bill was the first to break the silence. "Here's to Patty." All eyes were on him, shocked. "May she have a pleasant dinner all alone, and choke on it." There was a brief silence, and then a resounding "Here, Here!" from the group. Bee and Bel exchanged glances, raised their glasses silently, and took long sips of wine.

After that, conversation flowed. The topics ranged from the gallery trips planned for the morning, to options for the free afternoon. It seemed that everyone was determined to make the best of the trip, not in spite of Patty, but to spite her. Since they were all attacked by her nasty comments, no one felt singled out or on the spot. They did not, however, discuss the vicious little barbed "apology".

Dinner was marvelous; the veal was tender, the pasta was luscious, and the wines complimented the main dishes as well as the artichokes. The service was seamless, leading to a long discussion on the differences between the European profession of waiting tables, and the casual approach in the states. After a delightful couple of hours, the group pushed back their chairs, eager to enjoy the special treat Sophia promised them. They wandered back to the B and B, a far more relaxed group than had left it just hours ago.

Dessert was superb. Roger and Sophia had set up the lovely terrace with candles, cafe tables, and bottles of chilled prosecco. There were delighted murmurs of surprise as the gracious hosts welcomed them back. They proudly presented each guest with a moist, rich slice of tiramisu. It was decadently rich. It was even more delicious than the tiramisu they had made at the vineyard, which they would never have thought possible. Most of the guests had seconds, including Bee and Bel. "What do you do that's different?" Bee asked Sophia, always interested in tweaking traditional recipes. "We use a little finely ground hazelnuts between layers and on top," Sophia said. "We find it adds just a little more interest to the dish. The texture, the aroma..." The guests' spoons scraping on plates indicated agreement. "Delicious!" exclaimed James. "It's to die for!" agreed Bill.

Sophia smiled, as she gathered up the empty plates. "I'm so glad you enjoyed it! Roger loves it, too, so I always have to make extra. I have another in the fridge, if anyone needs a midnight snack." There were soft moans, as no one could contemplate another bite.

The grating sound of a door closing in the background turned heads; then the heavy sound of footsteps on the stairs made everyone sit upright.

"Patty's spying on us," whispered Caroline.

"Let her," spat out James. Bill reached over and took his hand, and James smiled grimly.

The next morning, Bel and Bee woke slowly, and Bee confessed that she had a headache already. Bel was sympathetic, but was feeling snappish herself. They hadn't had enough wine to produce this sickly feeling. Something just didn't feel right today. When Bel's cell phone rang, she snatched it up quickly when she noticed that the call was from Nate. "Honey, hold onto your hat!," he said. "You won't believe what I found----" a rapid pounding on the sisters' door interrupted his call and Bel asked to return his call later. Bee was advancing slowly towards the door, almost as though she dreaded what was on the other side. When she opened the door, the B and B's maid was standing there, wringing her hands. "*Signore, per favore,*" she said, her face white and her knees shaking. "It's the mean one, I mean the *Signora* Patty. She not looking good!" The maid went on to stammer that she had brought Patty her morning coffee as Patty insisted--Americano style, of course-- and after knocking on her door with no response, she had used her key and peeked into the room.

Her command of English was disintegrating quickly, as her distress became more and more apparent. The sisters hurried to Patty's room; hesitating on the doorstep, Bee turned to Bel and and said, "Now what?" Bel, less cautious, elbowed her out of the way and strode purposely inside.

"Bee!" hissed Bel. "Come in here, quick!" She had flipped on the bedside light and pointed to a very still, very pale Patty. Her eyes looked glazed over, and her tongue protruded from her mouth obscenely. Bel checked for a pulse in Patty's neck, and Bee waved her hands in front of Patty's face. Even to an inexperienced observer, it was obvious she was dead. They simultaneously took an uncertain step back; on the floor next to the bed was a white dish with what looked like a chocolate dessert of some kind. Indeed, there was a nasty smear of something brown around Patty's finally still lips. The women glanced around fearfully, and noticed that Patty's flouncy blouse and polyester pants, so unbecoming on her person, were thrown haphazardly onto the floor.

Backing out of the room, the sisters conferred hastily. They had to decide what to do, and whom to contact. "One of us will have to stay outside the room and prevent anyone else coming in," said Bel. "I'll stay," said Bee. "Your Italian is better." She took up her stance grimly outside Patty's room while Bel hurried down the stairs to notify the B and B owners, who could call the *carbinieri*.

Within minutes, there was a flurry of activity. Sophia had called the police, and Roger relieved Bee from standing guard so that she and Bel were able to gather the rest of the tour group together. The *carabinieri* arrived, and the room was filled with police, the medical examiner, and ambulance crew. Bee and Bel were ushered into the sitting room to meet with the lead officer, who introduced himself as Lt. Vincenzo Monseglio.

Bee had gone to their room and retrieved all the official tour documents, including a copy of Patty's passport and her emergency contact information. She informed Monseglio that Patty's next of kin was on the tour, and a junior officer was dispatched to have James identify the body before it was removed to the morgue. Bel and Bee shuddered, knowing how disturbing the sight was. They hoped James had a strong stomach.

"*Signoras*, what do you know about the deceased?" The officer's large brown eyes looked at them speculatively. "How long have you known her?" Bel had to bite her tongue to keep from saying "too long!" It was no time for flippant answers. The sisters explained that Patty had contracted with their tour company, and they had only known her a few days. While they talked, he flipped through the pre-tour information packet Patty had filled out for them, scanning it silently but thoroughly.

"She had an allergy?" he asked, nodding toward the open page. "Yes--to peanuts," Bee answered quickly.

"She appears to have been a ……." the officer paused, searching for the discrete term, "a rather large lady. She was not limited in her diet?" It was Bel's turn to answer. "No. She was careful but enjoyed her meals." Here Bee coughed. Bel continued quickly. "She did check with restaurants to be sure there were no peanut products. She told us she nearly died after eating peanuts a long time ago, so she was pretty careful."

"I see. And what had she eaten last night at the restaurant?" There was a brief pause as Bee and Bel thought how to explain the previous evening. Bee sighed. "She didn't join us for dinner. There were unpleasantries exchanged, and the group preferred not to have her eat dinner with us. We all went out for dinner and she stayed here." She thought for a moment. "At least, I assume she did. I actually have no idea if she stayed here or went out." Monseglio looked at her, an eyebrow raised, waiting.

"We came back here for dessert." Bel picked up where Bee had left off. "Sophia and Roger--the owners--had promised us a wonderful dessert. We ate out on the terrace, all of us. While we were eating, we heard a door close, and then footsteps. We just assumed it was Patty spying on us."

Without changing his expression, the Lieutenant smoothly asked "And why, *Signora*, would you assume that?"

Bel and Bee exchanged glances. "Well, frankly..." Bel began. Bee interrupted her "Patty was a difficult traveling companion, and the group was tired of her. Everyone assumed that she was watching us because that's the sort of thing she did." She shrugged her shoulders. "There's no use trying to pretend any of us liked her."

The door opened, and an officer escorted James in. There were documents to be signed. The sisters got up to leave, but he shook his head, saying "Please stay. I don't speak or read Italian, and it would make me feel better to have you near." Bel sat back down, and Bee stood beside him. "That is, if it's ok?" He looked at the officer. "But of course. These are routine next of kin authorizations. I'm so sorry for your loss." Lieutenant Monseglio looked at James curiously. "Sl

"Yes." ˙   He corrected
himself. "Sl   . My aunt was
not a very n   as touched to
see tears in   ed on her. It
nearly killed   ake, I always
tried to rem   ok his head.
"He was muc   nager. Patty
was the child   mom quite
young. She wa   he time he
came home, s.   le flushed.
"I shouldn't sp

The office.   . We love
them even whe   ce them."
Bee nodded--sh   ... to like at times.

"What's ne   james asked. "Should I make funeral arrangements? I don't know if she wanted to be cremated. I only found out I was her heir a few weeks ago." At that, the Lieutenant's eyes widened slightly. James didn't notice, but Bee did. It made her stomach flip. Did the quiet Italian officer think there was a connection? Who could suspect James? She tried to brush off her thoughts, but they were uncomfortable, and wouldn't quite leave her mind.

The Lieutenant was speaking. "Perhaps you should be in touch with her lawyer to see if it is stipulated in her will. In the meantime there will be an investigation to determine cause of death. At that point, we will proceed as needed." James looked confused. "I don't have a clue who her lawyer is. And what does 'as needed' mean?" He looked at Bee and Bel for clarification, despite the perfect English with which the statement was made.

"I think," Bel said gently, "They have to be certain of the cause of death before they proceed. To be certain there was no foul play." James looked shocked. "Foul play?! No one in Italy knows her!"

"But you do, don't you?" said Lieutenant Monseglio as he rose from his chair. The color drained from James' face, and he stared at the officer. "Please don't leave the building. We'll be speaking with all the tour members in turn." With that, he left the room, and the three Americans sat in silence.

"Oh my God." James moaned. "I have to talk to Avery. I don't want her to hear of this from anyone else." His head jerked up. "What a mess. I have to call my cousin."

"Patty's daughter?" Bel asked. He nodded, miserable. "It's not that she'll miss her. It's just so damned complicated." He turned to the sisters, his face sad and anxious. "You see...Avery is not just our daughter. She's Patty's granddaughter." Bel sucked in her breath, remembering the tremendous resemblance Avery had to James--her mother's cousin.

"Oh, dear. Did Patty know?" Bee rubbed her forehead, knowing how much more difficult this revelation made things. James shook his head. "No, Patty disowned her daughter as soon as she discovered she was pregnant. Hasn't spoken to her since. Bill and I had been together for a couple of years, and took Vicky in. We didn't have much to do with Patty on a regular basis--you can imagine why--" he smiled grimly, "so keeping Vicky for the rest of her pregnancy wasn't as hard as it could have been. Once she had the baby, she left town. We paid her college tuition so she could start life over." He smiled, a real smile this time. "Vicky was happy to have us adopt Avery. She knew we wanted a family, and this way she knew Avery would be safe and loved. It was a wonderful solution to a difficult problem."

The smile faded as he continued. "I'm afraid it will all come out now, and I want to prepare Avery and Vicky. Will you excuse me?" He left the room, and Bee and Bel stared at each other.

"Damn." Bel spoke first.

"Agreed." said Bel.

Chapter Sixteen

Per the Lieutenant's request, Bee and Bel had gathered everyone in the dining room. The aroma of the delicious pastries, the espresso, and fresh fruit filled the room, but no one was eating. The room fell silent as the sisters entered. Sophia handed Bel a cup of coffee, and Bee a cup of tea. They nodded their thanks, and sat. All eyes were on them as they took a sip of their restorative caffeine--they hadn't realized how drained they were.

"Well," began Bel. "As you must already know, there has been a tragedy among our group. This morning Patty was found..." here Bel paused, searching for the proper respectful term. "She was found...unresponsive when the maid brought her coffee to her this morning." Bee noticed several eyebrows lifting--because Patty was dead, or because she had coffee delivered to her room, she wondered. She was a little ashamed of the thought--but there it was, and it seemed to her that no one else in the room but James looked stricken by the news.

"What happened?" Several voices spoke at once. Bee held up her hand, and the room went quiet again. She spoke, slowly. "Bel and I were awakened an hour or so ago by the maid. She had gone to Patty's room, as Bel mentioned. Patty didn't respond, so the maid let herself in, and realized immediately something was wrong." Bel continued as Bee took a sip of her coffee, her hands wrapped around the mug, instinctively seeking warmth. "The maid was very frightened and asked us to come check on Patty. We entered her room, and found her in bed." She gave an involuntary shiver, and Bee squeezed her sister's hand. "It was obvious that she was... gone. We had Sophia and Roger call the police, and we have been asked to remain here in the B and B until their preliminary investigation is completed. That's all we know. James, would you like to add anything?" All heads swiveled toward James. Bill's arm went around James, protectively.

James hesitated. "There's not much to add, I guess. Those are all the facts we know at the moment. But, yeah, I guess there is something to add. I can't pretend that I--we--" he looked at Bill, and smiled wanly, "--will be grieving for a lost loved one. I am sorry she went alone, and from what I saw, uncomfortably." He blanched, then took a breath and continued. "But. I am relieved, also. What was supposed to be a pleasure trip for all of you was pretty much ruined by her poisonous attitude and nasty mouth. Having lived with it all my life, I can't say enough how sorry I am that you were all exposed to her cruelty." He buried his head in Bill's shoulder, overcome by the 'guilt by association', and the years of petty, deliberate unpleasantness.

Caroline was the first to speak. "Everyone knows Patty and I did not get along. She made a point of trying to embarrass me publicly. But James, I am sorry for your loss. Family is family, and we are not responsible for the choices they make. We love them and live with it. I just want you to know I bear you no ill will--Patty's words were hers alone, and they're gone with her." She moved across the room, and enveloped the two men in a hug.

Charlie stood, and cleared his throat. "Mother and I thought about leaving the tour because of her. I'll be honest, I did not like that woman, and she seemed to have it in for us. But that was her, son, and you don't owe anybody an apology as far as I'm concerned." James stood, and reached out a hand to the tall Iowan. "Heck, no, boy. We're past that. Give me a hug." The two men embraced, and Mary jumped up to join them.

Lucy wiped her eyes. "I'm a lawyer, and we always have something to say. But I'll keep it simple, James. We're here for you." James swept the petite woman into a bear hug.

Margo sat, pale and still. As the only member of the tour yet to speak, heads turned her way, expectantly. She looked out the window, searching for words. "James..." She started, then stopped. "James, I'm so fond of you and Bill. I wish I could say I'm sorry for your loss. But that would be a lie. She was horrible, and I'm glad she won't hurt anyone anymore." There was a sharp intake of breath in the room. Margo continued, the words tumbling out. "She was awful to me, and awful to everyone in this room. I wish I were a better person, a stronger person, but I for one am glad she is gone. I'm sorry." She began to cry. James came to sit by her, and wrapped his arm around her. His simple gesture was the last straw, and Margo wept, huge wracking sobs--all her grief and loss and pain rising to the surface, and overflowing her fragile frame.

Bee and Bel let her cry, knowing that the only one who could comfort her was James--they were strangely bonded in the manner of victims who have a shared history that no one else can understand. Quietly, Bee and Bel each got up and began murmuring to the others. Obediently, everyone went to the buffet and began to fill their plates in a distracted manner.

"You'll need your strength. Eat some protein, have a cup of coffee." Bee guided James and Margo to the line. Like tired children, they followed directions. Bill quietly brought James to the table, and Lucy patted the chair beside her, and Margo gratefully slid into the seat.

Everyone was eating silently when the Lieutenant entered the room. Everyone stopped, and looked at him. "*Buongiorno.* My apologies for interrupting your meal. Please go on." No one moved. "My assistant will need to take a statement from each of you. Please, do not leave the dining room until she has had an opportunity to speak with you. All very routine, I assure you."

He nodded at Bee and Bel. "*Signora* Bee, we shall start with you, if it is convenient." Aware of all the eyes on her, Bee rose from the table. Of course her chair made a horrible screeching noise as it was pushed back. It was shocking in the silence, and she blushed. Why me?! she thought, and in the corner of her eye, saw Bel shaking her head in amusement. Not funny! she thought crossly.

Having already met, they got to business pretty quickly. "*Grazie, Signora.* Please give me your full name, address, and contact information for the record." Bee did so, including her home and cell numbers, as well as her work land line, work cell, and work, personal and tour emails. The clerk recording the data ran out of space and used the margins. "You keep busy." The Lieutenant had a dry sense of humor, Bee thought, as his words were accompanied by a small smile. "Please, tell me about last night. There was mention of unpleasantness." Bee sighed.

"Patty had been rude to all the other tour guests. She enjoyed making nasty, barbed comments, finding the little sensitive spots. Do you know what I mean?" The officer nodded, familiar with the type. "Humans are the same the world over. Some are kind, some are not. I think she was not?" He looked at Bee, expectantly.

"No, she was not. She seemed to enjoy upsetting everyone on the tour. It has gotten so bad that yesterday we--my sister and I--gave her an ultimatum."

"What sort of ultimatum?" He looked at her closely. "She had to apologize to everyone. If she deliberately upset anyone again, she was off the tour. We would refund her a prorated amount, but she would not be allowed in the vehicle and we would no longer cover her hotel expenses." Bee shook her head. "I guess we were naive to think we could actually expect her to change her behavior. Honestly, we've never had to deal with someone like this on a tour."

"What happened when you gave her the ultimatum?" The Lieutenant pressed on. Bee shrugged. "Just what you'd expect from someone like that. She blustered about calling her lawyer, then sulked, then agreed. And we went our separate ways--she to her room, us to ours."

"Did she have a roommate? Someone to verify her time in her room?"

Bee frowned. "She had a roommate originally. She paid for a double, and was paired with another guest. She made herself so unpleasant we had to book an additional room and give them both their own rooms."

"That must have added quite a bit to your expenses." It was a question, but framed as a sentence. Bee laughed. "Believe me, it was worth the extra money." He looked at her questioningly. "We had a choice of one of us rooming with her, or spending the extra money. There was no question." He nodded. "Let us get back to that evening. The apology?"

118

Bee made a face. "The worst night of all. Patty entered the room, announced that she had something to say, and launched immediately into a horrible little poem, denouncing everyone and taunting everyone with nasty innuendos."

The Lieutenant made a "go on" gesture, and Bee reluctantly continued. "After the initial shock, Bel said 'Enough', and moved toward her. Then Patty took a swing at her with the fireplace poker. Luckily, she was big and clumsy, and we all saw it coming. Everyone jumped up and grabbed her. She ended up on the floor, and no one was hurt. It was ugly. That's when we told her she was done. We terminated all association with her. She left the room--we told her to pack her things--and that's the last time I saw her. Except for this morning, when...." Bee was suddenly exhausted.

"She didn't speak with you again? No contact?" Monseglio pressed her. "Nope." Bee was firm. "Wait. We never saw or spoke to her again. But we heard her. At least we think we did...."

"Explain, please." The officer was patient. Details mattered, he knew.

"We were all on the terrace, eating a marvelous tiramisu that Sophia had made. It's a family specialty. Everyone was enjoying it--it was very quiet because we were all so, well, focused on the tiramisu." Bee felt foolish, but the Lieutenant nodded. He smiled, and said "I understand. My wife makes a fettucine alfredo that is almost holy. You feel reverent and blessed while eating it." Bee grinned at the kindred spirit sitting across from her. "Yes! It was so blissful to sit in that beautiful place, eating that heavenly food, that we were all quiet and happy."

"And then?" Back to business.

"We heard the door close, and heavy footsteps on the staircase. Since Sophia was in the kitchen with Roger, we just assumed it was Patty spying on us."

"Did that bother you?" he asked. Bee shook her head. "Oddly enough, it didn't bother any of us. In fact, we were rather pleased with ourselves in a very immature way. It was rather satisfying to know we were having such a nice time and she was excluded permanently. Are we bad people?" she asked, her conscience obviously stirring.

"I don't think so. I think you were very patient people relieved to be rid of what sounds like a rather annoying person." He smiled. "I wonder why you didn't banish her sooner?"

"Ah. Because we own a very small business that depends on good reviews from our customers. Believe me, one bad review could set us back years." Bee was serious as she thought about the forthcoming reviews for this trip. Oh my, she thought.

"Thank you, *Signora*. I think I have all the information from you that I need at the moment. Please do not hesitate to call me if you think of something--anything--that I should like to know." The Lieutenant bowed as she stood to leave the room. She paused at the door. "Our tour group has reservations for the Uffizi this afternoon. Will we be able to go?"

He looked at his watch. "Six more tour members to interview, your sister, and the driver. We should be finished in about two or so hours. After that, you are free to leave the building, but..." he smiled and shook his head. "I must ask you to remain in the city until after the autopsy is completed."

Bee nodded. "How long does that usually take?" dreading the answer. A classic Italian shrug was the response. "Cause of death is usually pretty clear. But why--now, that's another story."

Bee was startled. "Do you think someone killed her?!" She blurted out. "I thought she had a heart attack or something!"

"Now why would you think someone killed her?" He countered, not batting an eye. "I didn't'!" Bee retorted. "Not until you said something!" She was obviously upset. He led her back to the chair. "*Signora*, it's my job to be sure that nothing is overlooked. You understand that." She nodded, but her hands shook slightly. "Why did you think she had a heart attack?" His question was lightly put, but Bee sensed the depth behind it. She thought before she spoke. "Well. She was in her room, and the maid had to unlock it to get in. She was in bed. There was a used plate on the floor beside the bed. So she had eaten something. It was obvious she had thrashed around--the covers were all pulled up. I guess it looked like she had had a heart attack to me."

"Are you sure you aren't a detective?" He teased her gently. "You have a very good eye for detail." She stood, ready to leave the questions and the visions it brought forth. He continued, "I am sure it will be a medical problem, but it is my job to find out." He bowed, and this time, Bee slipped out the door.

Chapter Seventeen

As she entered the dining room, Bel was already being escorted out to meet with the Lieutenant. With a shock, Bee realized the timing was no accident--they wanted to be sure the two of them had no time to collaborate on their versions of the events. As she sat down at a table, she noticed her hands were shaking. She quickly folded them together, and put them in her lap.

Bel's interview went much the same way. She described the events of the evening before. Knowing what Bee had already told him, he was more interested in hearing about Patty and her relationships with the other tour guests. Bel shared the reason for Patty's single room, and her relationship with James. She mentioned nothing about Avery and her relationship to Patty--her knowledge of that was second hand, and added nothing to the scenario, she thought. Better to let James explain all that. Bel had questions of her own for James, and wanted a chance to think them through before mentioning anything to the Lieutenant. She had questions for him, too.

"Our group is supposed to be touring Florence this afternoon. We'll obviously miss our morning tour at the Accademia, but I'd like to salvage some of the day if possible." She looked at the officer, hoping he would provide good news. He smiled back at her. "You know, your sister said almost exactly the same thing. Do you two always think alike?"

Bel considered. "Yes...and no. We have very different husbands, and very different careers. I would hate her job, and she would hate mine. She couldn't imagine teaching history to half- awake college students who are bored, hoping to find the one student in the class who will be excited about the subject. I couldn't possibly sit behind a desk all day, editing cookbooks and thinking about recipes and authors, and how to improve both." She took a breath, and grinned. "But when you get down to it, we share the same world view--values, I guess you'd call it. We like the same sort of things, and the same things make us laugh or cry. When she needs help, it's always something I can do. And when I need help, she knows exactly what I need." She smiled at the thought. "I'm pretty lucky to have her as a sister. And you know what? She's damn lucky to have me!"

The Lieutenant struggled to keep from laughing, and said gravely, "I agree *Signora*, on both counts. Any more questions for me?"

"Of course." Bel looked at the officer, and wondered how much, exactly, to ask him. "I'm not sure what is acceptable to ask and what isn't. I don't want to ask anything you can't tell me." He nodded. "Thank you for your sensitivity. I will be happy to answer anything I can, and will tell you when I can't. What do you want to know?"

Encouraged, Bel thought through her questions. "I have no idea how an untimely death investigation runs in the US, and even less in Italy. How long does the process usually take? And are we free to roam around the city, and continue on with the tour? Should we cancel our reservations in Assisi? How does one arrange for the uh....remains to be shipped home? Should I call the American Embassy in Rome?"

Under the barrage of questions, the Lieutenant held up his hands. "One at a time, *Signora*. I am a simple policeman with limited English. Please slow down!" Simple policeman my foot, thought Bel. And his limited English was far better than that of half her student population.

"I will start with your last question first, since it's the only one I remember. The next of kin-- *Signore* James--will need to call the consulate. He will need a death certificate from our office. They will advise him on what to do next." He thought for a moment. "The remains can be shipped home--perhaps he should be in touch with a mortuary. I'm afraid I do not know much about that. Please, remind me of your other questions?"

"May we leave the city? And should I cancel our reservations in Assisi? And how long will the process take?"

"Ah, yes." He nodded. "No, I think not at the moment. Yes, perhaps that would be best. And I really couldn't say--so much depends on cause of death. Have I covered it all?" His large brown eyes looked at her quizzically.

"I think so. But I will probably think of more questions when everything quiets down." She suddenly felt old and tired.

"That is usually the way," he agreed. "The shock to the system makes it hard to organize one's thoughts." Bel recognized the truth of this, and closed her eyes for a moment, shutting out the world for a moment to try to focus.

"And now, a few questions for you. Fair enough?" Bel opened her eyes wearily and nodded.

"Tell me," he started "What did Patty think of her nephew James?"

Surprised, Bel looked at him quizzically. "James? Well, other than some nasty remarks about his being gay, I never noticed any antagonism. She paid for James and Bill to come on the tour, and they were pretty nice to her, considering her snide digs. Why do you ask?"

"Ah, now that is one of those questions I cannot answer, *Signora*. Do you know whether James had money issues? I understand he was informed that he was *Signora* Patty's heir just before the trip." Monseglio leaned forward, waiting. Bel shook her head. "I have no idea. Our information sheet asks only for site preferences, health concerns, and other social things. For example, I knew that Patty was allergic to peanuts before she arrived. We had no idea she was so...large..." Bel hesitated, trying to choose her words wisely. "It quickly became obvious that she was physically incapable of any strenuous walking or climbing, and we had to adjust our plans accordingly. We're used to having to be flexible when it comes to things like that. But as far as personal financial information--we don't ask anything like that about our guests." She frowned at the idea.

"Of course. I just wondered if anything had been said." the Lieutenant said. Bel shook her head again. "I'm afraid I'm not very helpful in that regard."

"Thank you, *Signora*, for your time. We will be in touch if there are any questions that come up about *Signora* Patty or the other tour guests. Please, you may contact me at any time if there is anything--anything at all--that comes to your mind." He handed her his business card and escorted her to the door.

Bel entered the dining room in time to see Caroline being escorted to her interview. Interesting, she thought. Patty's former roommate is the first one to be interviewed. Bee had a fresh cup of tea waiting for her, and she slid into the seat next to her sister gratefully. "What did you think of Lt. Monseglio?" Bee asked. "Did you get any information from him?" Bel thought for a minute. "I think he was very courteous, which makes it easy for him to get information. He puts you at ease, and relates to you as a person. It reminds me of Jack, in some ways." Bee nodded. "I thought of Jack right away! The same calm quality of conversation--not making a big deal out of something, but tucking away the thoughts to pull together later. He was very easy to talk to."

Bel continued. "I didn't get anything from him that I suspect you didn't get. I was pretty convinced that Patty had a heart attack, but I'm wondering about something." Bee looked at her sister, knowing that her mind worked methodically, filtering details to come to a solid conclusion. "What's tickling your brain?" she asked.

Bel closed her eyes, and reluctantly brought the image of Patty's room to mind. She mentally walked through the door, and looked around slowly, remembering the details. "It's the plate." She opened her eyes, and looked at Bee. "The plate," she repeated. "She must have snuck down to the kitchen to get something to eat." Bee looked thoughtful. "She wasn't with us for dinner. I wonder if she went out and got something, or if she just raided the fridge." Bel raised an eyebrow. "It's Patty we're talking about. My money is on her helping herself to whatever appealed to her in the fridge. And I'm betting it's the tiramisu. Remember the brown smears on her face?" They both shuddered at the mental image of the pale face, blue lips and staring eyes, and the brown smears around the mouth.

"By any chance, did you speak to Sophia while I was being questioned?" Bee hoped that Bel had filled in more details. "Nope. Too busy holding hands with the rest of the group. Everyone's nerves are a little raw."

Bee nodded. "Mine, too." She confessed. Bel reached out and patted her hand. "Me, too. But this is pretty straight forward, as far as I can tell. I'm pretty sure it was a heart attack, or maybe an allergy. Just depends on what was on that plate."

One by one, all the members of the group visited with the Lieutenant. Some came back with red rimmed eyes, others just looked exhausted. Mary, with her tender heart, had obviously been crying. Bee wondered if she was crying for Patty, or because the interview was so stressful for her. Perhaps a combination? Margo, the last person interviewed, returned looking tense, and poured herself a cup of coffee with shaking hands.

"Two more hours until we leave for the Uffizi Gallery," said Bel to the group. "Walk around a bit, photograph this lovely city--the architecture is stunning--and let's meet back here for a quick lunch." The group nodded solemnly, and began drifting off. Bee looked at her sister quizzically. "Why did you send them away?" she asked. Bel rolled her eyes at her. "Remember rule #2?" she said. "Oh, yeah-- 'When in doubt, just go out'," said Bee. That concept had saved a couple of tours in the past; when things weren't going as planned, the sisters retreated to rule #2, and having their participants become immersed in an exotic locale usually helped. At any rate, staying around a hotel where a death just occurred was not an ideal way to spend a vacation.

Bee and Bel waited until Patty's body was removed by the coroner's staff. They tried to avert their eyes from the sight of the sweating, straining men hauling her remains down the steep stairs. Bel and Bee knew just enough street Italian to blush as they heard the men complaining about the weight. Dead weight, thought Bel. She shuddered. "Bee," she said, "Do you believe that the Italian *carabinieri* will actually determine the cause of Patty's death?"

"Why do you ask?" responded Bee, instantly wary.

"I just have a strange feeling about this," said Bel. "I'm not sure this is as simple as it looks."

"Oh, for Heaven's sake, Bel! Here you go again, playing detective! Too many Nancy Drew books when we were kids!" Bee shook her head and turned away from her sister. It was a fact that Nancy Drew mysteries took up almost all of Bel's bookcase space when she was growing up. Since then, she had graduated to more sophisticated mystery writers, but the genre continued to fascinate her. She especially loved psychological thrillers, while Bee adored typical English mysteries. Both of them enjoyed problem solving, and had occasionally been accused of minding others' business. Unfairly, of course.

But. The nagging word stuck in Bee's mind. But. Bel was, as their Celtic grandmother had put it, "sensitive." When Bel had a feeling, it was wise to trust it. Bel had felt her universe rock the moment her grandfather had died, many miles away and long before the era of cell phones. And Bel was the one who had known "something" was going on a number of times before. Bee turned back to her sister, to find her staring out the window, looking troubled. "Ok, detective. If you've got a feeling, I'm listening."

Relieved, Bel came to sit beside her sister. "It's just that...it seems so neat and tidy."

"That room was anything but neat and tidy!" Bee exclaimed. "Piggy was Patty indeed! I mean, Patty was piggy indeed! Clothes tossed on the floor, her suitcase spilling over, dirty plates on the floor..." Bel interrupted her. "Not the room, silly. The assumptions. She's overweight and middle aged, so everyone assumes it was a heart attack. But...it just doesn't feel right."

"Oh, Bel. Please don't look for trouble. This tour has been enough trouble so far," Bee pleaded with her sister.

"Heck, no. I won't go looking for any trouble. I just get the feeling that trouble will come looking for us..." Bel frowned. "Let's go check on James. He may need help navigating the system on this." The sisters tidied up their table, and checked in with Sophia about lunch. She kindly agreed to provide a light lunch for the group, and apologized that there would be no tiramisu--it had all been eaten last night, apparently, but she assured them she would provide a simple meal, easy on nervous stomachs. They thanked her, and headed off to find James.

128

"No tiramisu? Hm." Bee said. "There was a whole one left when we finished last night. I doubt that Roger could eat a whole one, no matter how delicious it was!" Bel nodded. "I'm telling you, that was tiramisu on the plate in Patty's room!" "But a whole tiramisu?!" Bee looked doubtful. Bel snorted--not very lady-like, Bee noted--and said, "We're talking about Patty, here, and she didn't get any dinner..."

The conversation ended as they entered the hall where James and Bill were staying. Not for anything would they say something to add to James' distress. They knocked gently on the door, and waited. Bill opened the door, and relief washed over his face. "Thank God. Come in!" Puzzled, Bee and Bel obeyed, and entered the room. James was at the small table, his head in his hands. He lifted his head, and smiled grimly at them. "That was not a conversation I ever hoped to have." He gestured toward the phone. "My cousin was...abrupt. I know it's been a long, hard road between them. Or, rather, there's been no road between them. And I know it's a shock to get that phone call. Hell, it was a shock for me, too." Bill put his hand on James' shoulder, and James closed his eyes and rested his head on Bill's arm. Watching them, Bee felt a lump in her throat as tears filled her eyes. It was an intensely intimate moment, and she was conscious of a physical ache to feel Jack's hand on her shoulder. Much as she loved getting away from it all, she missed him, and, she realized, missed the quiet support he always provided.

"What did you tell Avery?" Bee asked, gently. Bill answered. "Just that Patty had passed away in the night. There's really nothing more to tell, at this point. Unless Vicky decides that she wants Avery to know the rest, we'll respect the privacy we promised her when she gave up Avery for adoption. Avery took it pretty well--she's never been very fond of Patty, and we've limited her exposure to her, for obvious reasons."

"I'm glad that's over for you. Did Lt. Monseglio walk you through the next steps?" Bel inquired. "We came to see if you needed any help with the details." James shook his head. "I've already informed the US Consulate. They need me to provide a death certificate. I'm trying to locate Patty's attorney at home, and it's hit or miss. She was so angry at her husband's attorney when he passed away that she found a new one for herself. Of course, she didn't tell me who it was--and I would never have thought to ask." He took Bill's arm, and shook it. "I'm trying to convince Bill to go with you to tour the Uffizi this afternoon. Tell him to go with you! There's no need for him to stay here while I make phone calls to all the attorneys in small town Connecticut!" It was obvious from the look on Bill's face that there was no point in arguing with him. Instead, Bee sided with him.

"That's silly," she said flatly. "Bill has no interest in looking at art when you're here, coping with this mess. We couldn't--and wouldn't--try to talk him out of it. He needs to know you're ok, and help in any way he can. You could use the help, and the shoulder to rely on. I know I would."

Bel nodded, and added, "It's the best part of having a partner--they're there to lean on when you need them." Bill folded his arms across his chest, and glared at James. "See?!" he said fiercely. "I'm not going anywhere." James reached up, took Bill's arms, and wrapped them around himself. "Thanks, guys. I was trying to be noble. But I'm grateful that you were here to talk sense into me." Bill rolled his eyes, and Bee and Bel giggled. The tension in the room eased, and Bill excused himself to run down to the dining room and grab a coffee. He offered to bring some back for the sisters as well, but they declined, knowing well the effects of too many cups of caffeine before leading a tour.

As the door shut behind Bill, James looked at the two women, searching their faces. Bel, ever attuned to subtle nuances, looked at him and said "What is it? What's bothering you?"

"It's just..." he hesitated. "I mean...do you think?" He was having trouble putting his thoughts together. Bee leaned forward and took his hands. "James. You're worrying about something you haven't mentioned to Bill. What's going on?"

His shoulders drooped. "How did you know?"

"Never mind that. What's up?" Bee prompted, knowing Bill would soon return with the coffee.

James took a deep breath. "It's something Lt. Monseglio said. It's been bothering me. Do you think she was....well, do you think it wasn't a natural

130

death? Monseglio implied that I was the only one who knew her, who was related to her...Do you think he thinks I did something to her?" The words came out in a rush, and he looked from face to face.

Bee was the first to speak. "I don't have any indication that he thinks it was anything but a natural death. Remember, the room was locked when the maid went in this morning. From what we saw..." here she hesitated, and Bel continued. "From what we saw, it looked very much like she had had a heart attack, or perhaps an anaphylactic episode. Her color was very bad, and her lips were..." It was Bel's turn to hesitate, not wanting to be too graphic.

James picked up the line of thought. "Yes, I saw her face. They had put her on the gurney, and all I saw was her face. But her lips were blue." He turned his face away as if trying to avoid the distressing image. "But Monseglio...he seemed to say that he was looking for something else, and in my interview with him, he told me not to leave the city. Does he consider me a suspect or something?" His hands began to shake, and he smoothed back his hair, trying to get them under control.

"It's his job to consider all the possibilities. He has to be sure that no one just assumes she had a heart attack and doesn't bother to examine all the evidence. I don't think you're any more suspect than any one of us on the tour." Bel spoke as she would to a student who had just gotten a poor grade on a paper. Calm, matter of fact, and reassuring. James visibly relaxed.

"Thanks. I think my nerves were getting the better of me." His hands were no longer shaking. Bill came through the door, carrying a tray laden with coffee, sandwiches, and fruit. "Here's the deal. You need to eat, and I'm taking away the computer until I see at least half a sandwich disappear. You haven't had anything to eat yet today, and it's lunch time. Got it?" Bill issued his commands like the high school teacher he was; Bee and Bel knew there would be no argument allowed. It was the perfect opportunity to leave them, and they went out the door promising to check in later.

"What do you think?" Bee said, when they were back in their room. Bel shook her head slowly. "I don't think we have the full story yet. There's still something he's holding back, and I get the feeling it's ugly."

"I think you're right," Bee agreed, "but what?" Bel stood at the window, looking down at the crowded street below. From the window, she could see the Ponte Vecchio; beyond that, the Galileo museum, and the tower of the ancient Duomo. "I'm not sure. But I think it has something to do with Avery. I think there's more to that story. Seems crazy that she knows her aunt and great aunt--but has no idea they're her mother and grandmother."

"Sounds like a Dr. Phil episode to me." Bee was struck by a thought. "You don't think Patty had any idea, do you? That she would threaten to tell Avery?" Bel considered. "No....I don't think so. I wouldn't put it past her, but you know how she made those nasty little rhymes when she 'apologized'? I think those barbs were the tip of the iceberg. Do you remember what she said about James and Bill?" Bel turned to her sister, whose memory for words she knew was legion, despite the Words with Friends rivalry.

Bee closed her eyes and thought. "'roses are red, violets are blue... stole from your boss!' That's what she said! She implied that James stole something!" She looked at Bel, her heart sinking. "Do you know what that is?" she whispered. Bel just looked at her, waiting. "It's motive, Bel. It's a motive for murder."

Ashen faced, the two looked at each other. "Bee, we don't even know if this is an untimely death!" whispered Bel. "True, Bel, but what if..? I mean, James just inherited a fortune from his aunt..." The women pondered for a moment, but before they could continue their line of thought, there was a timid knock at the door.

Mary stood-- or rather, cowered-- in the doorway. "May I please come in?" She raised tear-filled eyes to them. The sisters ushered her into the room, and offered her the only chair. Mary sat quietly, twisting her hands and biting her lip. "I'm so sorry to bother you," she said meekly, "but I don't know where to turn. You see, Patty knew something about Charlie and me...well...that I wouldn't want Lt. Monseglio to know about. Charlie doesn't know I'm here, but I really need to tell someone. Even though she threatened to tell the group about us, we didn't hurt Patty! In fact, Charlie was with me almost every minute of last night-- except for when he snuck off to the kitchen for a bite at midnight!" Mary's anguish was plain to see, but Bel and Bee exchanged puzzled glances. "Mary, what are you trying to tell us?" asked Bel. "It's the little rhyme she made up that night," Mary sighed. "She must know what we did, and I think she was going to spill the beans. We came on the tour to get away from all the...talk." Mary's hands trembled, but she looked them square in the eyes. "Anyway, we were in our room almost all night, so Lt. Monseglio will have to look elsewhere to put the blame."

Quietly, Bee said, "Mary, as far as we all know, Patty died a natural death. I don't think the Lieutenant suspects anyone of foul play." Pushing herself out of the chair, Mary crossed the room, turning back to say, "I hope it stays that way!" She slipped out the door and was gone.

Bel gave Bee The Look. It had been invented by their mother and perfected by them. it meant: Holy Hannah, what now??? "Okay, Bee, you of the prodigious memory, I bow to your intellect. Remind me of Patty's nasty poem about Mary and Charlie." Bee said, "I will if you actually bow. Yes, physically bow." Bel knew better than to argue, so she did just that, her middle fingers raised at the same time. "Ooh, naughty!" Bee laughed and screwed up her eyes, bringing the poisonous poem up in her memory. "Hmmmm....it referenced selling out to Mallmart. What do you think it means?" Bel said, "I think I remember reading a story in The Atlantic Monthly about small towns that suffer when Mallmart or any of the big box stores move in. Everybody has heard that, of course, but this one had a little twist. It talked about the people in those towns who actually profit by selling their land or businesses to the mega companies, and how their neighbors reacted. Do you suppose Charlie and Mary sold their store and upset the community?"

"Seems probable," agreed Bel, "But unlikely to cause enough of a disturbance to make Charlie and Mary afraid they'll be accused of murder!" Bel thought for a minute. "I wonder..." she mused. "Did you notice that every time Charlie lost his temper Mary kept reminding him 'remember what happened last time?' She said it a couple of times."

Bee nodded. "You know, I did notice, but it always happened at a time when we were worrying about something more important, so I didn't spend a lot of thought on it. What do you think?"

Bel shrugged. "I think there's been a problem in the past--what, I don't know--but I'm pretty sure Charlie's temper may have gotten him into trouble. Maybe over the business buyout?"

It was time to meet the group for a quick lunch and their afternoon tour. The dynamics would certainly be different--with no Patty to worry about, they could even relax and enjoy the visit to the Uffizi themselves. It would be just the thing for soul-weary folks--a chance to submerge themselves in great art, timeless beauty, connecting people across the generations. Bel loved the Uffizi, and couldn't wait to see her favorites again.

Chapter Eighteen

The group was already gathered when Bee and Bel arrived in the dining room. Sophia had laid out a wonderful assortment of breads, meats, and cheeses to make sandwiches. Olives glistened in a glass bowl, and there were fresh sliced tomatoes. Simple, but hearty enough to hold everyone through hours on their feet. Bottles of sparkling water stood at hand, lemon slices ready to slip into glasses. Red wine, of course, was open and breathing on the side board. The group had courteously awaited their arrival to begin, and Bee and Bel suddenly realized they were hungry. They helped themselves to the rich, creamy cheese slices, and piled the spicy salami onto the focaccia, creating open faced sandwiches. Bee hoped no one would notice the liberal drizzle of olive oil she added, but the lovely green pool of shimmering oil on her plate betrayed her. "Oh, that's a great idea!" Caroline eyed Bee's plate, and copied her. Bee felt Bel's eyes on her, and refused to make eye contact.

During lunch, they were gratified to learn that Rule #2 had done its job. The room was filled with eager exchanges of information--Margo and Lucy had visited Dante's "house", quick to explain that the Casa di' Dante was never actually his residence, but a marvelous example of a nobleman's home in the 13th century. Caroline had gone with Paolo to the Ponte Vecchio, and explored the second story of the famed goldsmith's bridge. Charlie and Mary had gone to the beautiful Duomo, and marveled at the amazing painted ceiling, and enjoyed the peace and quiet. Mary had found a charming little shop beside the Duomo that sold exquisite soaps, and passed some around for everyone to admire. Bee made a mental note to visit the shop, as the soaps not only smelled fabulous, but each was stunningly packaged with simple but dramatic graphics.

Sophia slipped into the room quietly, and laid out a stunning fruit platter. There was a fresh pitcher of coffee, and a teapot, much appreciated by Bel. Bel was secretly pleased to note the plate of luscious chocolates--it might not be tiramisu, but it would do!

When everyone had completed their meal, Bel stood. "I'd like to give a brief introduction to the Uffizi while we are here," she began. "The galleries get very crowded, and it can sometimes be hard for a group to hear when there are many visitors. So I thought we could give you some basic information--things to look for--that might otherwise get lost." Bee piped up, "One reason we like to visit Florence in the springtime is because the Uffizi gets very crowded in the summer--people wait up to five hours in line during high season!"

"Not us!" Bel assured them. "Not only is it a quieter season, but we have advance tickets. We'll be able to go right in, with a minimal wait." She continued her introduction. "The Uffizi was begun in 1560 as offices for Florentine magistrates. That's what Uffizi means--offices! Cosimo de Medici arranged to have some of the family collection displayed there, and it was noted that Leonardo da Vinci and Michelangelo, along with other artists, would gather there for inspiration and relaxation! One of Europe's oldest art galleries, it opened officially to the public in 1765. There are 45 halls--but we'll only hit the highlights with you, and then give you time to wander about and discover things on your own."

Bee was pleased to see how eager their faces looked. Not like Patty, she thought, she would have been complaining about walking through the galleries! Bee was a bit ashamed of her unkind thoughts; but, she reflected, they were pretty accurate.

"As we walk through the main corridor, be sure to look up!" Bel was enthusiastic about the subject, and it was obvious that her eager anticipation was contagious. "Look up, and admire the incredible frescoes on the ceiling. I'll point up when we get there!"

Bel briefly outlined the route they would take through the museum. "Our entry tickets are for 2 o'clock; we'll guide you for about two hours, depending on the crowds. After that, I would strongly urge you to visit the rooftop cafe. Your feet and all your senses will need a break, and you will be glad to sit down." The group laughed, ruefully acknowledging the truth of Bel's observation. It was part of what made her such a good professor. She knew that the brain could only absorb what the feet and the backside could endure. "After that, feel free to wander about the museum. We'll meet at the exit at six, and head back here to the B and B."

Bee was quick to interject, "There's a marvelous gift shop, as well, if you're looking for some beautiful things to bring home. We also wanted to let you know that we are trying--" she paused for emphasis, "--trying to arrange a tour at the Accademia tomorrow, in place of the one we missed this morning." There was an awkward silence, the group torn by the hope of seeing the famous statue of David, one of the most iconic works of art in the world, and the reminder of what had happened that morning. Caroline asked quietly, "Will James and Bill be joining us this afternoon?"

"No, unfortunately not. James is trying to locate his aunt's attorney so he can begin the paperwork necessary for funeral arrangements." Bel replied.

"I have a suggestion, then." Caroline turned to face her fellow travelers. "Would any of you like to go in with me to buy them a book at the Uffizi? I'd like to DO something for them, under the circumstances, and since they won't get to see the gallery..." her voice trailed off, uncertain of the response. Her green eyes sparkled when there was a spontaneous round of applause, and eager murmurs of assent. It was decided that Bee would purchase the book while Bel led the tour. Bee was delighted--extra time in the gift shop, spending other people's money! In Italy, no less. It doesn't get much better than this, she thought, and then remembered that there had been a tragedy less than 24 hours earlier in their little group. Guiltily, she looked at Bel, to find her shaking her head. How did she always know? Bee thought. How does she DO that??

The little group left the B and B for the Uffizi. Although they were relatively close to the museum--just on the other side of the River Arno--they had Paolo drive them. Bee and Bel had worried that no one would feel comfortable taking 'Patty's seat', and had decided one of them would sit up front with Paolo. When they got to the little bus, however, Caroline hopped into the front seat, and grinned at Paolo. He said something under his breath, and Caroline smiled, then frowned and shook her head at him. Bee suspected he had alluded to his pleasure in the change of passengers next to him.

Paolo left them in the piazza in front of the long gallery. Bel shepherded the group to the main entrance, tickets in hand. She was relieved to see that the line of tourists waiting for entrance was relatively short--that meant the gallery wasn't packed to the gills, and they would be able to actually stand before the works of art to explain them. She quickly and politely greeted the guard in Italian, and remarked that it was a pleasant surprise to see a short line. He smiled wearily, and replied in Italian-- commenting that while the line might be short, so were tempers and some of the visitors were less than pleasant. Indeed, during their short conversation, a sweaty man barged up to the rope where Bel and the guard were conversing.

"Excuse me! EXCUSE ME!" His loud, demanding voice was, unfortunately, American. Bel winced. "I have tickets for 2 pm. I have reserved tickets." His insistent voice grew louder. The guard excused himself to Bel, and turned to the red-faced tourist. "Excuse ME." The pointed comment was lost on the man. New Jersey, Bel thought. I bet he's from New Jersey. The guard continued. "You have reserved tickets for 2 pm?" The man thrust the tickets at the guard. "So do all those people. You may get in line after them." The guard's sweeping gesture toward the line of tourists waiting patiently astonished the man. With a courtly bow, and a wink unseen by anyone but Bel, he gestured to her. "*Signora*, please take your group through." Grateful, Bel smiled and whispered "*Grazie!*" as she hurried her little group past the man, whose family were arguing with him, urging him to show the guard the tickets again.

138

Inside, the little group gathered after passing through security. After conferring quickly, Bee headed off to the gift store to find a beautiful book of Uffizi works for James and Bill. And, she thought, a little Christmas shopping! She would rejoin the group when finished, checking some of the major paintings for the antenna with the purple scarf. She knew, from past tours, where Bel was most likely to stop to discuss her favorite works.

Bel led the five tour guests into the main corridor, and pointed upwards. They were delighted to have the chance to see the frescoes, and amazed by the number of visitors who passed through the corridor, unaware of the beauty above them. Bel headed first to the portraits of the Duke and Duchess of Urbino--a wonderful work by Piero Della Francesca. To the casual eye, it was a simple piece, and not necessarily a flattering one. The profiles of the Duke and Duchess were severe, and they would win no beauty contests. Bel explained that the Duke was painted in profile, as he had lost his right eye in a tournament. She pointed out the many subtle symbols in the painting, and noted that the work also had another painting on the reverse side. The group was delighted to learn the human elements behind the famous faces.

The hallways were busy, but not packed, as the group moved from masterpiece to masterpiece. Many of the guides with larger groups had microphones that transmitted directly to their guests' headsets. Bel preferred talking directly to her groups, feeling that she was better able to address their interests if she spoke to individuals, rather than an anonymous group. There was a fine art to being able to speak loudly enough that all of your group could hear you, without imposing your dialogue on other visitors. A case in point was the tour group ahead of them. The lithe guide was able to hold her group's' attention, but not disturb other visitors. Unlike the tour right behind them, she thought irritably. She could hear the leader droning on, loud enough that everyone in the gallery could hear him. Bel decided to change her route, so the inconsiderate guide wouldn't be on their heels all afternoon. She reversed course, and entered one of the side chambers. She was startled as she entered the room--an Asian group was exiting, and there, she could have sworn, was "Assogot"! Damn, she thought. Bee isn't here to chase him down, and I can't leave the group! She hoped their paths would cross again in the large buildings.

Bel led Margo, Lucy, Caroline, Charlie and Mary to another of her favorite paintings, pointing out several major works as they passed by. There was simply no way to "see" everything in one tour, and choices had to be made. Bel hoped the group would appreciate the paintings she chose. They stopped to discuss the wonderful "Bacchus" by Caravaggio, an extraordinary piece for the time. Unlike the other masters before him, Caravaggio had chosen to work with his subject alone, doing away with the landscapes that contained such intense symbolism. He decided instead to focus on the humanity of his subject. His Bacchus was the most important feature in the scene, and Caravaggio had used a series of mirrors to create what was, essentially, a primitive "photographic" view of the subject. Painted in 1596, it was a dramatic breakthrough in technique. Bel loved the lazy, sensuous Bacchus, and was enchanted to discover that the image reflected in the wine bottle--newly discovered after restorative cleaning--was thought to be Caravaggio's self portrait. Bel's listeners craned their heads to see the image, and Bel stepped back to give them a clearer view. As she moved to the side, she heard Charlie's voice, just ahead of her. In a harsh whisper, he muttered to Mary, "What did you tell them?!" It wasn't a pleasant conversation, by the tone of his voice. They moved forward with the group, and Bel didn't hear her reply. Hmm, she thought. There's more there than Mary told us, I'm sure of it now. She filed away the thought to discuss with Bee later.

Where was Bee? She thought crossly. The gallery wasn't that crowded. Surely she could have picked up a book, paid for it, and joined the group by now. If only she had been here, they could have caught up with "Assogot" and asked him a few questions. Her grumpy train of thought was quickly set aside, as another group was gathering, waiting for their turn to examine Bacchus.

"Let's head to the Botticellis," she suggested. "These are very popular works, so there may be a crowd there. If there is, we'll just enjoy looking around until we have a chance to move close to the pieces." Excited, they followed her obediently down the magnificent hallway, like good little ducklings. She smiled at the image, and her mood lifted. Bel didn't stay cross for long.

They were in luck--the previous tour group moved away from "The Birth of Venus" just as they entered the gallery. She quickly positioned herself in front of the canvas, and began to point out the details. "'Venus' is based on Ovid's Metamorphosis," she began. "Take a look at the incredible detail in the painting. Everything in the painting conveys a message, and art patrons of the time would have been able to 'read' the painting. For example, the lovely violets symbolize love--as does Venus herself." She went on, highlighting the different images and their meanings. Bel enthusiastically shared her love of the classic painting, and her energy was transmitted to the group. They eagerly listened, Bel was a natural-born teacher, and it showed. They continued to "La Primavera", another Botticelli, and here, Bel used the Socratic method--asking her group to tell her what they knew about the painting, based on what they had just learned. It was a wonderful method of getting everyone engaged, and they enjoyed the process tremendously--no dry droning on of random facts about the painting or the artist.

In the gift shop, Bee had found just the perfect volume immediately. It was a lush, oversize "coffee table" book with amazing photos of the major works, with quirky information about the artists, their lives and their subjects. Bee just knew James and Bill would appreciate it. She tucked the book under her arm, and began her hunt for gifts to purchase for family and friends, and...if something special appeared, for herself. She deserved it, she rationalized to herself--it had been a very stressful tour. She giggled out loud, causing a few heads to turn, when she realized she was rationalizing a purchase of an item she had yet to see or even want! She was absolutely thrilled when she discovered a gorgeous silk scarf in a display case--royal blue, with golden bees scattered across it. Since it was in a case, she knew the price was going to be high. But it was beautiful--ha! she thought-- BEEutiful and she would keep it forever, not like the "pashminas" sold in the streets by the vendors who insisted they were really silk....

She asked the shop assistant to show her the scarf, drawing in her breath when the fine silk was draped over her hand. "It's lovely!" she whispered. "*Bella*! Please, can you tell me how many Euros?" The three figures made her gulp. She thanked the girl, and regretfully shook her head. She wandered over to the jewelry case, and was delighted to find earrings that her daughter would love--reproductions from one of the masterpieces on display. In the same case was a tiny sterling spoon, this one based on a piece illustrated in a still life. And check! thought Bee. There it is! The perfect Christmas gift for Bel! She felt very virtuous, giving up the lovely scarf and choosing instead the sweet little spoon--not much difference in price, either, she knew, but banished the unworthy thought and cheerfully pointed out the spoon and earrings to the same shop assistant.

As she went to meet her at the cash register on the other side of the counter, Bee casually looked in the next case. And there....there was the perfect necklace. A tiny gold bee, alone on a delicate gold chain. Bee stared at it, entranced. The assistant turned back to her, impatient. "How much?" Bee pointed. "It is on sale. Forty Euros." The young lady obviously did not work on commission, as she made no effort to encourage Bee. "I'll take it!" Bee breathed, thrilled. Her day was made. She hurriedly paid for the book and her treasures, now eager to join the group and tell Bel of her find. She frowned at the thought. Bel was likely to give her the eyebrow for spending time shopping for herself during 'working' hours. Well, she would see what type of mood Bel was in when she caught up with the group, and decide then whether to share her shopping goodies, or wait until another time. Distracted, Bee was looking down at her shopping bag as she made her way out of the shop and into the gallery. She inadvertently bumped into a shopper entering the store. "*Mi scuse!*" she said automatically, looking up to apologize. "Hey!" she said. "Hey!" but "Assogot" was gone, and a German couple behind her were propelling her forward.

She stepped aside once outside the door, but was stalled in re-entering by a large unruly tour group, lead by an exasperated guide. "Please!" he kept saying "Please! We need to board the bus in five minutes!" Bee knew from experience how frustrated he was, and smiled at him sympathetically.

She--and he--knew full well the bus would not be fully loaded for at least half an hour. They made eye contact, and he recognized by her photo ID that she was also a tour guide. He shook his head and shrugged, the universal "what're you gonna do?" gesture. Bee was glad that early on they had decided they would never lead tours of more than ten people--so much easier to work with! Not this time, though, she thought grimly. She turned swiftly, following the wake of the large group, and began to search the shop for "Assogot".

The swirling, chattering group of tourists broke into twos and threes as they searched for souvenirs. Bee was far too short to see over the heads of the tall Scandinavians--Swedes, Bee thought briefly--to see "Assogot", who, like Bee, was on the short side. Exasperated, she circled the shop again. As she passed the glass window, the tour guide outside raised her umbrella. Bee stopped, her attention caught. There, on the other side of the pane of glass, was "Assogot". She waved her hand to get his attention. Startled, he looked at her, his iPad in hand. His group moved forward, and he hesitated. Bee waved more urgently, beckoning to him. He raised the iPad, took her picture, smiled, bowed, and walked on.

Damn! Thought Bee. Double Damn! She headed out to find Bel to tell her how close she had come to actually meeting him.

She caught up with Bel and the group in gallery 35, standing before the only Michelangelo in the gallery. The "Doni Tondo", painted in 1508, was a lovely representation of the Holy Family. Michelangelo painted it there in Florence, and it was considered one of the masterpieces of 16th century art. Bel loved it because the little family looked like a real family--not accompanied by cherubs, saints, or other heavenly creatures--just Mary, Joseph, and what looked to be a two year old Jesus, sitting on his father's knee, playing with his mother's hair. It was truly a sweet image. Bel also got a real kick out of the line of nudes in the background, symbolizing ignorant pagans. They looked like they were having fun. The beautiful frame had been carved by Michelangelo himself--was there anything the man couldn't do? Bel wondered briefly. She saw Bee rushing up to the group, carrying a large gift shop bag. She looked agitated. Bel stepped away from the painting, to allow the group a closer look. It also gave Bee the opportunity to grab her and hiss in her ear.

"You're never going to believe what just happened!" Bee whispered.

"You saw "Assogot." It wasn't a question, it was a statement. Bee stared at her in amazement. How did she do that?!

"How do you know?!" She demanded. Bel laughed. "His group was going out as ours was going in. I was really cross that you weren't here to chase him down."

Bee stomped her foot. "Damn! I actually bumped into him, but the crowds pushed us both along in opposite directions. I tried to go back into the shop to talk to him but there were these Swedes…" Bel looked at her, puzzled. "Did you ever try looking for a 5 foot 5 man in a room full of Swedes??" Bee was frustrated all over again. Bel laughed. "I see your problem. Did you ever find him again? No, obviously not." She looked at her sister. "If you had, you'd have told me that first. What happened?"

"It was weird," Bee said. "I walked around the shop twice, looking for him, but never saw him. As I was standing at the window, a tour group went by. And there he was! I waved, and he actually saw me!" She took a deep breath. "And here's the weird part. He took a picture of me. Somewhere back in his country, his friends will be looking at me waving frantically at him. They're going to think I'm nuts." "Well…." said Bel. Bee didn't dignify the remark with a response.

There were one or two more paintings Bel wanted to highlight, and the group moved on. Bee tagged along behind, lost in thought.

Bel suggested that the group retire to the gallery cafe. Situated on a terrace, the remarkable view was limited by stone walls, probably built to prevent tipsy tourists from toppling over into the cobbled street below. Huge planters ringed the seating area, flush with seasonal flowers and greenery. The little tour group elected to sit outside, and most ordered coffee. Mary, however, eyes red-rimmed, said that she didn't want any more caffeine. "I feel too jumpy already," she confessed. Bee looked at Mary with concern. Bee was very sensitive to others' feelings; years of watching and judging Bel's famous fits of impatience had honed her people skills to a fine point. Yes, Bee thought, Bel got the brains, but I got the social intelligence. Maybe now would be a good time to share her latest self-indulgence in the gift shop. Rustling her bag, she glanced up to see Bel frowning at her. "What did you buy there? " Bel asked. "Did you at least manage to get the book for the guys?" Bee huffed. "Well, of course I did!" she muttered, stung by Bel's abruptness. "Do you want to look at it now, or wait until we get back to the hotel?"

"Sorry, Bee, I guess I let the stress get to me," said Bel. She put a gentle hand on Bee's shoulder. "Let's show the group your find!" With that encouragement, Bee removed the gorgeous book from her shopping bag and opened it on the table. Gesturing for the tour group to join her, she carefully turned a few pages so that they could appreciate the quality of the reproductions.

"Perfect!" breathed Caroline. "I'm sure James and Bill will love this book! Thank you for choosing it for us, Bee." Bee smiled modestly. "It was nothing," she said.

"What else do you have in that bag? " Bel asked suspiciously.

"Damn, I should have bought myself that scarf after all," Bee thought.

Bel looked at her sister and frowned. Once again, Bee had let her self-indulgent nature tempt her. Her big sister was a wonderful human being, she thought, but sometimes she didn't keep her focus on priorities. She sighed. Bee was worth it, though--she smiled at her sister, shook her head, and waited expectantly for Bee to reveal the treasure that was so obviously delighting her. Whatever it was, it had driven all thought of the tour right from her mind until it was hers.

While Bee was sharing her beautiful new necklace with the group, Bel wandered over to the edge of the terrace. It was roped off a few feet from the walls--no doubt to protect tourists from themselves, Bel thought--and she stared out over the high crenulated walls at the tower ahead of them. There it had stood for centuries, she thought. How many thousands of people had passed below that tower, she wondered idly. How many lives had played out in the shadow of that tower? The thought brought Patty to mind, and Bel shivered. She turned away from the tower, trying to shake the ghastly vision of Patty, eyes open and lips blue. Bee was there.

"I'm sorry." Bee reached out to touch her sister's arm. "I shouldn't have been shopping and left you with the group. I got stung by a bee." She gestured at her necklace, now around her neck. Bel laughed. "It's gorgeous. I'm glad you found something special. It wasn't a problem. With this small a group, it's easy to keep track of them. Not like…." She stopped, feeling a little cruel for thinking unkind thoughts about Patty. Bee finished her sentence.

"Not like when Patty was always lagging behind, sitting where she shouldn't, and upsetting everyone. I know. It's such a relief, and it makes me feel so guilty." They looked at each other, knowing it was both true, and honest. Patty was a pain. Being dead hadn't changed the truth of that.

"What next?" Bee asked. "Is everyone going back to the hotel with Paolo? Or are they strolling back and shopping?"

"Frankly, I think everyone is exhausted. This tour was a great diversion, but I think the emotional stress has caught up with everyone. Margo looks like she's going to faint, and Mary is looking weepy. What say we round them up and head back, and suggest a nap for everyone?"

Bee agreed rapidly, and went off to make the suggestion. Bel could see the heads nodding in agreement. She proceeded to the counter, and settled the bill for the group. When she returned to the table, everyone had their wallets out and ready. "Put those away, guys. It's our treat."

"Why, Bel--thank you!" It was more than worth it to see smiles return to the weary faces of the travelers. Bel hoped the little gesture would brighten what had started as a very grim day.

"Paolo will be waiting for us in the square in one hour. That will give you time to walk slowly through the gallery to the gift shop, browse for a bit, and meet us outside." Bee announced the plans to the group, and within minutes the chairs were pushed back and the group was moving to the exit. Bee and Bel headed out, and the group dutifully followed. Like lambs to the slaughter, Bel thought--then grimaced, the analogy being horribly appropriate. She was sorry the group was so ready to leave--there was so much to explore still in the fabulous museum. She knew, though, they had probably had all the art their feet and their brains could absorb for the day.

Arriving in the gift shop, the group perked up a bit, and drifted off to explore the delights of the museum-quality merchandise--no tacky "David" boxers here. Bee dragged Bel over to look at the beautiful scarf. "What do you think? Should I get it?" She held her breath, hoping Bel would talk her into it.

Bel peeked at the price tag. "Yikes! Walk away, sister, and be grateful for your beautiful necklace." Bee pouted. Bel laughed, and moved on to explore the jewelry case. Bee trailed behind her.

"This is where I spotted Assogot. He was right there!" Bee pointed at the window. Bel shook her head. "What do you think the odds are that we keep running into the same guy all along our tour route?"

"Do you think it's as weird for him as it is for us?" Bee asked, musing. "I wonder what he's going to tell everyone when he gets home?" They laughed, thinking of the story that their mystery man would tell.

They found postcards for their collection--one from every tour stop since they began leading tours--and made their way over to the cashier. Mary and Charlie were ahead of them in line, and didn't see them behind them. Charlie was bent over Mary, and they were "exchanging words", as Bee and Bel's mother would so delicately put it. The sisters couldn't hear what they were discussing, but it was evident by the tone of their voices that it wasn't the beautiful art work they had seen that day.

When Lucy tapped Bee on the shoulder, she jumped. She flushed, thinking she had been caught eavesdropping. Lucy didn't notice, confused by prices on the shelf below the book she wanted to purchase. Bee hastily offered to help her sort it out, and handed her postcards to Bel to purchase for her. As Bel stepped to the counter, she used her best Italian to tell the haughty salesgirl to ring up the scarf with the bees--pronto. Impressed, the clerk moved quickly to bring the scarf to the register to show Bel. Bel waved her hand, indicating it was fine, and told her to wrap it quickly. Another item off the Christmas list, she thought, and smiled. She would make sure Bee opened it when they were together, so she could enjoy the look on her face.

The group met up again in the square outside. The sun was setting, and the plaza was slowly emptying. Tourists were wandering off to cafes, school groups heading home, and a cool breeze had sprung up. The little group chatted quietly together, talking over dinner plans, waiting for Paolo to arrive. The Mercedes bus was a welcome sight, and Paolo's smiling face cheered them all. Caroline hopped into the front seat, and he reached out and squeezed her hand. The drive back to the hotel was quiet--the bus was warm, and everyone was tired. As they pulled up in front of the hotel, Caroline turned to look back at Bee and Bel.

"What's the plan for the rest of the tour? It's not that I'm insensitive to what happened, but I'd kind of like to know what's next." There were murmurs of agreement from the other passengers.

Bee and Bel looked at each other. "To be honest, we're not quite sure ourselves." Bee nodded, and Bel continued. "The police have asked that we stay in the city temporarily, at least until they have a tentative cause of death." She took a breath, the words drying up her mouth. Bee took up the conversation. "We're expecting to hear from the Lieutenant sometime tomorrow, if we're lucky. Bel and I have arranged two optional tours for everyone for tomorrow--one to the Accademia in the morning, and in the afternoon, a walking tour of Dante's Florence. We know it's hard to have to adjust to changes, but we have no control over the time table."

"Will we still get to Assisi?" Mary spoke plaintively. "I really wanted to see where St. Francis came from." Lucy and Margo nodded in agreement.

"I really don't know." Bel shook her head regretfully. "Until we have permission to leave Florence, we have to take it day by day."

"Why?" demanded Charlie. The harshness of his voice startled everyone in the bus. "I mean, do they think we killed her or something?" The suggestion was shocking, spoken aloud. "Well?" he demanded.

"There's been no such suggestion." Bee spoke soothingly. "It's simply protocol. We're the only people in the city who knew her, and they are trying to determine her last movements so they can pinpoint the cause of death."

"She died of mean." Charlie's voice was low and harsh.

"Charles!" Mary sounded appalled.

The bus pulled up in front of the hotel, and everyone got out in shocked silence. The sisters were the last ones out, having occupied the least desirable rear seats.

"Ladies." Charlie was waiting for them. "My apologies. I shouldn't have been so rude. It isn't becoming to speak ill of the dead, no matter how much she deserved it." Without waiting for a reply, he bowed slightly, and turned and strode off to catch up with Mary.

"Well." said Bel. "Well, indeed." answered Bee.

Paolo closed the door behind them. "That Charlie." Paolo shook his head. "It may not have been polite, but it was accurate." He hurried off to join Caroline, waiting for him on the steps.

Bel stared at Bee. "Well, well."

"Indeed." said Bee, and they walked into the brightly lit hotel.

Chapter Nineteen

ee and Bel were grateful to see that Sophia and Roger had placed bottles of red wine on the sideboard, and a platter of cheese and sausage beside it. They helped themselves to a glass each, and sank into the comfortable couch situated in front of the huge marble fireplace. Bee put her feet up on the table in front of them. Bel frowned at her, and pointedly looked at her feet and raised that damned eyebrow. Bee ignored her, and took a long sniff of the wine, closed her eyes, and sipped deeply. When she opened her eyes, Roger and Sophia were standing in front of them. Guilty, she jerked her feet off the table, and spilled her wine on her blouse. Bel rolled her eyes. Sophia quietly left the room and returned with a damp towel to blot the wine.

Graciously ignoring Bee and her efforts to make herself presentable again, Roger handed Bel a note. "Lieutenant Monseglio came by this afternoon. He asked me to give this to you." Bel held the note in her hand, studying it.

"Did he have more questions for you?" She asked. Sophia snorted. "Questions? No, not too many more questions. But he took everything that was in the refrigerator. And the plates in the dishwasher. And the trash. I don't mind about the trash, but that he took our dinner for tonight!" Her eyes snapped. Roger looked at her, his admiration for her spirit obvious. He smiled, and kissed her hand. "I will take you out for dinner tonight. It won't be as delicious as your cooking, but I won't have you cook twice." She smiled at him, the tension leaving her body.

Tears came to Bel's eyes. The visible affection between the couple made her emotional. She was surprised at how much she missed Nate right at that moment. She stole a glance at Bee, and discovered that instead of wiping her blouse, she was wiping her eyes with the wine-soaked cloth. She was missing Jack, just as much as Bel longed for the comfort of Nate's calming presence. She had also managed to smear red wine around the delicate skin of her left eye. Bel decided not to mention the stain; Bee would only overreact and blame her for the mess. And besides- there was the time when she had walked through a busy restaurant with soy sauce on the back of her pink dress- in a very prominent and suspicious place- and Bee had neglected to mention it until they reached the sidewalk. Where Bee had collapsed in sputtering laughter.

She quickly opened the note, and read: "*Signoras*, Thank you for meeting with me today. Please excuse me, my writing of English is not as good as my poor speaking of English. I be sorry to miss you this evening. Please you call me to confer when you return. Yours, Lt. Monseglio the officer."

Bel looked at Bee. Bee smiled, and commented, "I wonder if that's how we sound when we speak Italian?" Bel grimaced. "I'm not sure we sound that good."

"What do you think he wants to speak with us about?" Bee wondered.

Bel, her brow furrowed, answered. "I don't know. But I think it's time we did some homework of our own before we call him back. Let's do a little digging."

Bee groaned. She had seen that look on Bel's face before. It reminded her of the look on her neighbor's terrier when he spotted a squirrel. There would be no rest, no dinner, no more lovely red wine until Bel was satisfied. Resistance was futile, she thought, then smiled wistfully, thinking of her Star Trek-loving geek husband. It would be nice to hear his impressions of the horrible events hanging over this tour.

That reminded her-- "Bel!" Her voice startled Bel, who was deep in thought as they headed to their room. "Hey. What was Nate about to say this morning?! You said he sounded excited about something." That stopped Bel's determined striding down the hall. She turned and stared at Bee. "Bless your memory for words, Buzzy!" She squeezed Bee's shoulder. Bee hadn't heard the childhood nickname used in years. Bee's eyes watered again--remembering their mother calling her "her little buzzy bee"--undoubtedly where the two of them inherited their love of wordplay. Why am I so emotional today? She wondered, as she swiped her eyes AGAIN. Bel grimaced; the red smears on Bee's eye were getting harder to ignore.

"I'll get Nate on the phone, and you start some research on our guests. Methinks there is more beneath the surface than we know." Bel was focused on the tasks before them.

"It's the middle of the day at home!" Bee protested, but only half-heartedly. Nate had known Bel for many years, and wouldn't be surprised by the call. In any case, nothing would get her off track now, Bee knew.

They were to meet the group for *aperitivo* in an hour or so; computer research, a phone call to Nate, and a call to Monseglio all to be accomplished before rejoining the tour guests meant no chatter, no putting feet up and no gloating over the treasures Bee had found today. Bel was already on the phone with Nate by the time Bee was headed into the bathroom. Of course, she had brought her phone in with her. Just a few minutes of Words with Friends would clear her brain, she thought. There was no time for that, though--shortly after Bee entered the bathroom, Bel was pounding on the door.

"Put that phone away and get out here!" Dang it, thought Bee. How does she DO that? She hastily flushed the toilet, and stuffed her phone in her waistband, hoping to hide the evidence and retain her dignity. She carefully washed her hands, allowing the water to run longer to make her point. She calmly exited the bathroom, and frostily said "Whatever are you implying?!" The moment was spoiled when her phone slid out of the bottom of her pants onto the floor.

She couldn't help herself. She giggled. Bel took advantage of the moment and scooped up her phone. "Aha! Now I have a hostage! You won't get this baby back until you finish your research!" She danced around the room, holding the phone high above Bee's head, waving it in her face. In a vain attempt to recapture any pride she had, Bee ignored her sister, and seated herself at the tiny table by the window and opened her laptop.

Bel joined her, instantly sober. "Nate was furious. He knew something major was up when I hung up in such a hurry, and he's been fretting all day. He called Jack, by the way, so you'll have some of the same type of texts, too."

Bee nodded, barely acknowledging the comment, as she typed in Patty's name. "What did he have to say?"

"Lots. Don't bother with Patty--he found enough information to confirm exactly what we already knew intuitively. She was a snake--manipulating people, using obscure regulations to push people to her advantage, blah, blah, blah. Nobody liked her, and the community will be much happier with her gone. So let's move forward. Look up her husband and let's get the name of the company he worked for. I have a feeling."

Bee typed furiously. "Ok, I've got it. Now what?"

"Check and see if there is any list of employees, recent changes, anything you can get that may hint at internal issues. Go back a year or two."

Bee trusted Bel, but she had no idea what she was supposed to be looking for. "A little clarification, please!"

Bel looked over her shoulder. "Just put James' name in the company search engine. I think he worked there. That's got to be what Patty was referring to in her delightful little rhyme."

"Bingo!" Bel grinned. "James left the company about six months before Patty's husband died. Here's a picture of him at the going away party." They high fived, feeling like they had found an important piece of a giant puzzle. They were interrupted by a soft knock at the door. Bee quickly closed her computer as Bel answered the door.

She looked into the hall, and saw Caroline backing away. "Caroline? Did you knock?"

The redhead was flustered. "Yes. But. I think…" She faltered, and looked at Bel, and then down the hall, as if trying to escape.

154

"Come on in." Bel spoke low and soothingly. She reached out a hand, and gently pulled Caroline into the room. She followed Bel in and slumped into the offered chair. The sisters were taken aback when she began to cry. They stood quietly, letting the racking sobs abate. They weren't tears of grief, Bee thought. Those were angry tears. As Caroline calmed herself, Bee offered her a tissue. Silently, Caroline took it, and wiped her eyes and blew her nose.

"I'm sorry. I shouldn't have come." She took another tissue and pressed it to her eyes.

"Caroline." Bel was using her professor voice now--strong, deliberate, commanding. Caroline's head jerked up, and she met Bel's eyes.

"Talk to us." Bee marveled at how Bel knew the right thing to say. Soft, sympathetic tones would have driven Caroline out of the room. The matter-of-fact Texan needed to know that they, too, could be practical and not distracted by emotion.

Caroline sighed, and shook her head ruefully. "This trip was my new beginning. My chance to leave the old stuff behind, clear my head, get some perspective, and move forward. My life got turned upside down last year, and it wasn't pretty. When I got back to Texas, I was moving to another city. Starting over where no one knew me." She pressed the tissue to her eyes again, determined not to cry.

"There's no easy way to tell this, so I won't bother trying to pretty it up." She took a breath and began. "You know Patty's lovely little rhymes? Well, it wasn't Paolo she was referring to, I don't think." Here the sisters looked taken aback. Caroline gave a short laugh. "No, no, I don't mean I was sleeping with anyone else on the trip!"

"Whew." Bel muttered. "The only other option was Charlie...." Bee frowned at her.

Caroline continued. "It's pretty obvious to me that Patty did some very extensive research on me. She apparently found out that I was hauled before the state review board for..." here she hesitated, searching for the words. She plowed on, determined to get through. "I was brought up because some of my therapeutic techniques with one particular client were....borderline. I really don't want to say more about that." She defiantly looked at each woman in turn, searching their faces. Finding no judgement there, she relaxed and continued. "It was a difficult few months, and there were times when I thought I would be charged with prostitution, disbarred and have my license revoked. But I was found to have complied with all the professional regulations--barely. Legal, perhaps, but maybe not as ethical as it should have been." She frowned at the distasteful memory. "But my reputation in the town was ruined. No one would dare come to my practice, and it was obvious that my social life as well as my professional life was over. I needed to get out of town. So I took my savings, and booked an obscure tour far away--" Here the sisters exchanged indignant glances, "--that no one else in Texas would even consider. They are barbarians for the most part." Caroline said, scornfully. That placated Bee and Bel a bit.

"But my point is this. If the police here find out about all this, they're going to think I killed her to keep her quiet." Caroline's strong voice quavered, and she started to cry again. This time, it was soft, gentle weeping. This was grief, not anger. She looked up. "And you know what the worst part is? I think I love Paolo, and if he knew it wasn't him Patty was referring to, he might never speak to me again."

Bee looked at the weeping woman, and put her arms around her. Now was the time for sympathy. Caroline buried her head in Bee's ample bosom and had a good cry while Bee stroked her head.

Hmmm, thought Bel. Is she more concerned about being accused of murder, or losing her summer romance?

When Caroline pulled herself together, the sisters sat down beside her. "So we have two issues here." Bel was in professor mode again. "One, you are concerned that the police will determine there is a motive for murder. Two, you are concerned that Paolo will leave you."

Caroline nodded. Her green eyes were vibrant against her flushed cheeks.

"We can't speak for the police." It was Bee's turn to think out loud. "But we've worked with Paolo for the past few years, and we know him pretty well. He's a very intelligent man, and isn't easily shocked. He's Italian, after

156

all. Have you two talked about extending your relationship past the tour? Because that's really the question. If you haven't, it will resolve itself in just a few days. If you have…" Bee paused, expectantly.

For the first time, Caroline smiled. "We've talked about it. We're talking about whether it would be better for me to stay here, or him to come to the US." Her eyes lit up.

"Wow!" Bel blurted out. Caroline blushed. "I mean, congratulations!"

Bee ignored her sister, and continued. "Caroline, if you mean to have a long term relationship with Paolo, I think you already know what you need to do. I DON'T think you need to explain to him that she was referring to someone else, just that she was letting you know that she intended to expose your trouble with the board of review. It certainly would put you in a different light with your fellow guests, and that was her goal, apparently." Bee mentioned nothing of the implied blackmailing that James had inferred was Patty's specialty.

"But what about the police here?" Caroline's face lost its hopeful glow.

Bel answered. "As far as we're concerned, the nasty little poem was meant to expose your relationship with Paolo, which we already knew about. I don't think the rest has any bearing on the case, do you?" She looked at Bee. Bee shook her head. "I can't see any reason why it would have to come up."

Caroline got to her feet and hugged them both. "Paolo is waiting for me. I told him I had to check on the tour details. He kept insisting he would know soonest, as you would let him know where we were going first! I better get back there and talk to him." She teared up again. "I've never been so happy as when I'm with him. I know I look like a cougar. But he is so much older than his years. His soul…" She sighed. "Wish me luck. And Bee-- what on earth happened to your eye?" "Huh?" Bee said. She raced to the bathroom mirror, wailing, "Why didn't you say anything, Bel?" "Oh, it was a little matter of soy sauce…" Bel murmured. The sisters shared a snicker and Bee cleaned her face.

With the door closed quietly behind Caroline, they looked at each other. "Oh. My. God." Bee moaned. "Who ARE these people on our tour?!"

Bel laughed. "Remember when we used to go to the mall and make up stories about the people walking past?"

"Yes! We'd create a whole life for them, based on their clothes, their shopping bags…" Bee smiled. "I bet we were far closer to the truth than we realized! Apparently everyone on this tour has a backstory worth hearing!" Bel looked at her speculatively. "You never did tell me what happened that summer you spent in Idaho. Well?!"

Bee just looked serene. "I was a minor. The records are sealed."

A pillow flew across the room in response.

Chapter Twenty

Bel claimed the bathroom first as the sisters prepared for dinner. She threatened to take Bee's phone in with her. Well used to her tactics, Bee had quietly slipped Bel's phone into her pocket when Bel escorted Caroline to the door. When Bel stood and waved the phone at Bee, she smiled--and waved Bel's phone right back at her. "You sneaky thing, you!" Bel was impressed. "Truce?"

"Hmmm. I'll think about it. I just might like a peek at your...." Bel reached out a hand, the hostage phone free at last. "C'mon. You win."

"That's what I wanted to hear!" Bee handed her sister the phone. "Don't mess with the best, grasshopper!"

"Don't mix metaphors--you're an editor, you know that!" Bel retorted as she swirled away.

Bee turned back to her computer. She decided to research Caroline's story a little further. She pulled up Caroline's home town on the computer, and entered her name.

Multiple references popped up. Bee picked one and opened it. Oh, my, Bee thought. No wonder she wanted to get out of town. If that was what made it into the papers, Bee could only imagine what the gossip had been like. Caroline really did have a past she'd rather leave behind. Patty would have enjoyed exploiting that. Bee shuddered. What awful, sad secrets had Patty ferreted out in her community? How relieved would everyone be to hear of her passing? What an awful legacy, Bee mused. When their mom had died, they had gotten so many cards and notes, describing her influence across so many lives. Well, Patty had been an influence too--just not a positive one. Bee felt a rush of gratitude for her mother and how lucky they had been. Imagine Patty as a mother?!

Her reverie was interrupted when Bel reappeared, looking refreshed and elegant. "Did you call Monseglio?" Bee looked guilty. "Your Italian is so much better than mine..." she began. Bel looked at her, "He speaks perfect English, Bee."

"Right. Well, silly me. But now that you're out of the bathroom, I'll just scoot in while you speak to him!" Bee jumped up and ran to the bathroom. The sound of chicken clucks followed her across the room.

Bel snorted, and picked up the Lieutenant's business card to call him. The phone rang once, and his deep voice answered *"Pronto. Monseglio".*

"Buongiorno, Lieutenant. It's *Signora* Bel," she started. He took command of the conversation immediately. *"Signora. Grazia.* You had a lovely afternoon at the Uffizi?" It seemed like more of a statement than a question, but Bel replied in kind. *"Si,* Lieutenant. Inspiring, as ever." "And your guests, did they all attend?" Bel wondered where this conversation was headed. "No, Lieutenant. James and Bill stayed behind to try to find Patty's attorney and make the necessary phone calls to the family. The rest of the guests joined us, though."

There was a delicate pause. "And your guests. Was there much.... conversation about the unfortunate start to the day?"

"But of course!" Bel exclaimed. "It deserves conversation when a traveling companion suddenly dies, and the police become involved. They are concerned about the remaining travel, and unfamiliar with the legal procedures required and therefore very curious."

"Of course." Monseglio's voice was bland and unrevealing. "It is natural to be concerned. After all, a friend has died."

Bel considered. Bee had slipped into the room and given her The Look--Bel lowered the phone and put it on speaker. "Lieutenant, my sister has joined us. I do need to make one thing clear, though-- Patty was no one's friend on this tour. She had made herself unpleasant to all."

The voice on the other end of the phone chuckled. "So I had been told. Allow me to correct myself. A traveling companion, then--shall we say that instead?" Bee snorted, and Bel's hand shot out to cover the speaker.

"Ah, *Signore* Bee. *Buon giorno.*" Bee thought she detected a hint of a smile in the otherwise very correct greeting. "Good evening, Lieutenant. Have you any progress to report?"

"I love Americans!" He exclaimed. "Straight to the point. No wasting time on niceties that all parties know are simply a prelude to the real conversation."

Bee looked at Bel, alarmed that she may have offended him. Bel shrugged her shoulders, and spoke. "Our guests are curious, as are we. We've never (here she looked at Bee and crossed her fingers) dealt with the police before regarding a homicide, and we don't have any basis on which to offer information." She looked at Bee, who was busy writing something on a scrap of paper. Bee held it up, and Bel clamped a hand to her mouth. It read "AT LEAST NOT IN ITALY!"

"And that is why I thought I would check in with you." The smooth, professional voice had returned. "Shall we meet at your hotel in the morning? Nine?" The earliness of the hour surprised them. Italians were not known for convening important meetings so early in the day.

"Of course!" The sisters spoke at once. "Stereo!" the deep male voice chuckled. "I shall look forward to it." And with that, he rang off.

Monseglio put down the phone, and returned to the appetizers his wife had set out on the patio where he sat. Thoughtful, he looked at his glass of wine, and swirled it. The coroner's preliminary report lay on the table in an envelope. He pulled it out, and looked at the photos again, shuffling through the pages, shaking his head. "Something just doesn't smell right," he muttered, just as his wife came through the door. "Well, thank you very much!" She spun on her heel and went back indoors. "Francesca!" He jumped up and followed her in, anxious to explain.

Chapter Twenty-One

There was a sharp rap at the bedroom door. Both women jumped, and Bee stuffed the note into her pocket. Bel opened the door to find Sophia, holding a tray with a bottle of red wine and three glasses. "May I come in?" Her lovely accented English held a note of hesitation.

"Anyone carrying a tray of wine and cheese is always welcome," said Bel, cheerfully. Sophia entered the little room, now filled with evening light, and looked around fondly. "This is my favorite room in the place," she announced. "Roger and I had our honeymoon here--this was our room!" She proceeded to tell Bee and Bel how they had met, fallen in love, and were married, all in the course of six months. Roger had returned home to England only to sell his home there, and when he returned, they used the proceeds from that sale to buy their honeymoon haven. She had been happy to get out from under the constant scrutiny of her brothers, who were none too happy with her choices.

"We have been here for four years now. I love our place, our life." She sighed. "But can I tell you something?" The sisters nodded over the rims of their wine glasses, wondering where the conversation was headed.

"I am worried. I have family connections…." She stopped, and looked at them. Bel spoke first. "Family that would not appreciate being tied to something that led to further investigation."

Sophia nodded, and turned to look out the window at the street below. "Italy is a small country. For all we can appear so charming to tourists, dark things happen here. There is much that tourists never see…" Bee interrupted her. "Sophia, there isn't a hint of involvement from the police."

"The police are corrupt." She almost spat the words out. "At least in Sicily I know who is on the payroll. Here, I do not know. And so I am afraid."

"Why would you be afraid?" Bel was surprised. Sophia gave the classic Italian shrug--a gesture conveying impatience and resignation in one move. "It's not me that would be the target. It is my family. If I am implicated in something, it gives...others...how shall I say it? Leverage?"

Bee said slowly, thinking as she spoke, "So, if you are linked to a crime, your family--history--" she struggled for discreet phrasing, "could become a bargaining point?" Sophia smiled, but it was a thin, unhappy smile. "Something like that. In any case, I'm considering leaving Florence for a bit. To visit my nonna."

"Sophia, no!" Bel shook her head firmly. "That's just inviting trouble. If you leave after being told not to, it will stir things up and give the police--and anyone else who is interested--a good reason to look closely."

"Bel's right. We may not be Italian, but we're pretty well versed in human nature. Stay put, stay calm, and it will all work out." Bee urged.

Sophia's eyes filled with tears. "Roger and I want to start a family. And I am haunted by my family. How can I bring a baby into a world where I am always watching, waiting, worrying that because of my family, everything important to me could be a pawn for power?" It was a question with no answer. They could only listen. Sophia stood, and wiped her eyes with the back of her hand. "Ah then. I shall stay and smile at the policeman. I shall pour him coffee, and stay in the background. It was a bad day for me when Patty arrived. I love you two--you are always welcome--but never again with one like that, eh?" She shrugged, lifted the tray and let herself out of the room.

"Well damn." Bel swore softly. "Our first encounter with--"

"Don't say it!" Bee pleaded. "If you don't say it, we can pretend we didn't have any idea what she was talking about, and you know I can't play poker!"

They contemplated their glasses in silence. Bel spoke first. "I guess it puts having weird old Uncle Bert in perspective." Bee choked on her wine. "That's too bizarre! I was just thinking about him!"

Bel mused, swirling the remaining sip of wine in her glass. "I wonder if he really did get abducted by aliens." She drained her glass. "In any case, it's a lesson in perspective. We were so embarrassed by him as kids. We didn't have 'FAMILY' (here she made air quotes) that threatened to destroy our lives."

"To Uncle Bert!" Bee raised her glass, and drank. Bel followed suit.

Chapter Twenty-Two

*Y*awning, Bee rose and suggested they prepare for dinner. "Where do you want to eat tonight?' she asked Bel. "Frankly, any place that can get us in and out quickly-- I am exhausted," said Bel. "Well, then, how about..." Bee was about to finish her suggestion when a timid knock on their door startled both women. "Oh, Lord, what now?" wondered Bel. Bee hustled to the door and saw that Charles and Mary were waiting. She asked them in and offered a seat to the couple. Mary was twisting her hands anxiously, while Charles stood with his legs aggressively open, hands behind his back. "To what do we owe the pleasure?" asked Bel brusquely.

Mary's eyes were reddened, and her whole demeanor was that of a worried and perhaps even frightened woman. More gently, Bel said, "Mary, you look as though something is on your mind. How can we help?" Mary took a deep breath, and her look at Charles was one of entreaty. She took a second and said, "We just wondered what the Lieutenant was saying about Patty's death. Have you heard anything?" "Not yet," said Bee, "but we know that the trash, contents of the refrigerator, and all the other food was removed by the police today." Bel shot her sister a warning glare, but Bee sailed on, oblivious. "It looks to me as though her death might have been food related."

Mary sighed deeply. "Charles has something to say," she said softly. "Yes, well, I just wanted to know if Patty said anything to you about-- uh-- our history. And also. I am sorry I said those things about Patty. She was a horrible person, but I shouldn't have called her names. Say, have you had a look at her computer?" asked Charles.

"No, but the police took that, too," Bee replied. Charles paled. Bel interjected, "Why don't you tell us what this is really about, Charles?"

Charles paced the little room while Mary bit her lip, and Bee noticed that her eyes were filling. "It's just that we don't want to be suspected of any wrongdoing in Patty's death. How long would we be kept here if the police thought we were guilty of hurting her?" asked Charles. "Why would anyone think you had harmed her?" asked Bee. Charles hesitated, and Mary cried, "Oh, just tell them, Charles! It will probably come out anyway!"

Charles looked at his wife, then at the sisters. Finally, he took a seat. He put his head in his hands, then looked up and told them the story. "Years ago," began Charles, "we had a nice little pharmacy in our small town. Everyone knew us, and people trusted us to fill their prescriptions accurately. We certainly weren't rich, but I made enough with the business that Mary could spend most days at home, working in her garden, cooking our meals, and looking after Charles Jr. I had friends in town, a hardware store owner, a garden center owner, a guy who owned a tire shop. None of us was making it hand over fist, but we all had what we thought was enough. We got together to play cards, and everything was going well. Then, one of our friends was diagnosed with cancer. He didn't have the best health insurance--none of us did--and the hardware store was all that was keeping his family afloat. I began to worry about what would happen to us if one of us got really sick. Mary and I have been together for 34 years, and the three of us are all we have for family. I started worrying about money." He took a breath and continued.

"Then Mallmart came to town, wanting to build one of their superstores. Our friends were dead set against it; they were scared that their businesses would fold once the big box store came in. We banded together, talking to people in the area, telling them to vote "no" in the town referendum. I even had posters made saying "No big box stores!" and hung them in the pharmacy. The executives at Mallmart, however, asked me for a meeting. It seemed that the land they wanted was adjacent to my shop. They made me an offer I couldn't refuse, and I sold out to them, without saying anything to my friends." He hung his head, and turned away from the three women in the room. "Then…." he winced, "my friend who had cancer shot himself. No insurance money for his family because it was suicide. They were ruined." His voice thickened and he couldn't go on. He moaned. "There's more. At his funeral, people started to talk. They said what they really felt about me--about us. I was so upset; I lost my friend, lost my store, lost my self respect. I went a little crazy." The silence filled the room.

"Go on." Mary's voice trembled. His voice was so low they could barely hear him.

"When the Father began to preach about loving your neighbor, someone hissed. At us! It wasn't our fault! But I went a little….crazy, I guess." Bee and Bel could hardly breathe, it was so tense in the room. "The usher was stopping at every pew, inviting people to Communion. But he skipped us. Just walked right past as though we weren't there. I could hardly think straight. I thought he was overcome with grief and just missed us, so we stood up to go for Communion. But when we got to the altar, the priest shook his head." Bee could hear the grief in his voice, but the anger resonated still. "I don't know what come over me. But, and I'm not proud of this, something just exploded inside. And I hauled off and punched that priest. Took three guys to pull me off, they said. Broke his nose and his cheekbone. You know I'm going to a special sort of hell." And he began to cry.

"So," Mary whispered, stroking his big hand, "we can't really go home again. Thank God Charlie Jr. was away at school. Nobody will talk to us. Money we have, but all our friends are gone. We're lucky the priest didn't press charges, and the sheriff is--was--" the sadness echoed in her voice, "--an old friend who told us to get out of town or he'd be forced to arrest Charlie. We closed up the house, and went to visit Charlie Jr. and left straight from there for the tour. "

Bel shook her head. People never failed to astound her. "I don't understand what this has to do with Patty's death," she said.

Mary caught Bel's hand. "Don't you see? Now it's on record that Charlie hurt someone--badly--when he was angry. We're…looking for a new place to settle down. If Patty had chosen to share the information she'd found, no place would welcome us. Don't you think that sounds like a motive?!" Her voice was shrill, and she was almost hysterical. Charlie moved to her, and folded her into his arms. They clung together, a little island of isolation and grief.

With a glance at her sister, Bee moved forward and put a hand on their shoulders. "How can we help?"

"I don't know!" Charlie sighed. "But you've been so kind and resourceful, we just wanted to come clean and let you know, just in case some ugly questions come up. The worst of it is going to be explaining it to Charles Jr. I dread that." The big man's shoulders sagged.

Bel spoke briskly. "Tell him exactly what you told us. He's young, he's been away from the community for a while, but he'll know soon enough, if he doesn't already, and he should hear it from you." Charlie nodded sadly.

"Your friend's tragic decision isn't your fault, you know. But perhaps the three of you could come up with a way to help the family out. The sheriff sounds like a decent guy. Maybe he'd help you figure out a way to help the family without your name being attached to it, so they'll accept it." Bee thought of Mary--her father had committed suicide, too. A little anonymous help might have made a big difference in her sad childhood.

Mary spoke first. "I'll write him. I'll ask if he can create a benevolent fund or something. We went to prom together, so I've known him a long time." There was a glimmer of hope in her eyes, and her shoulders and back straightened for the first time on the trip. She no longer looked like a little mouse.

"Thank you." Charlie's voice, still low, was full of emotion. "I thought we could get away from our troubles, but they followed us here. Truth is, the trouble was in me. It isn't going to be pretty when we go home. I doubt we'll stay any longer than we have to in order to sell the house, but...well, we'll face that when we get there. I just don't want to delay that by sitting in an Italian jail as a suspect!"

The sisters could only repeat that, as far as they knew, Patty's death was health-related, but promised to keep them informed. The couple hugged each sister in turn, and slowly left the room.

"Sister!" commanded Bel.

"Yes?!" Bee waited.

"Let's get the hell out of this room before someone else knocks on the door!" They grabbed their purses, and ran.

Chapter Twenty-Three

They found a quiet restaurant, far from the tourist path, where they could sit and be undisturbed for an hour. They ordered a bottle of red wine, and a margherita pizza to start. Bee couldn't wait for it cool off, and burned the roof of her mouth. "Ow! Damn it. Perfect end to this day." Bee swore. Bel looked thoughtful. "I'm not so sure it's the end yet."

Distracted from her burn, Bee looked up. "What on earth do you mean? What else could we possibly add to this day?"

Bel laughed. "Oh, don't tempt fate! I just meant I have a feeling we'll have more visitors…"

It was Bee's turn to look thoughtful. "Hmm. So far we've had James and Bill, Caroline, Charlie and Mary. That leaves Lucy and Margo. Shall we place bets on who we think will be the next one through the door?"

"Bee, that's tacky. And I'm betting it's Lucy."

"Done. I say Margo. What are the stakes?"

They considered for a moment. "Loser has the second shower the rest of the tour?" Bee suggested. "Nah, that's a reward for you--you'd get 15 minutes of extra sleep!" Bel grinned at her sister. "How about…loser buys the wine for the remainder of this ghastly 'vacation'?" "Done!" shouted Bee.

She was unaware that Bel knew every homemade wine shop in the cities they planned to visit; shops where wine was siphoned into soda bottles for under two Euros. Bel chuckled to herself. She knew that Bee would fuss and try to wiggle out of the bet if she lost. She had been doing just that since she was four years old. Bel felt a little guilty--she had been baiting her sister like this for years.

"Ha!" thought Bee. She's a champion. She'll have figured out some way to turn this to her advantage. We'll see what she's cooking up!

"Isabella!" hissed Bee. "Turn around, quick!" Bel tried, but as she twisted her torso, a cramp caught her right across the middle of her chest. Wincing, she waved her hand at Bee and said, "Just tell me--what's up?" She remembered anew the yoga class that she kept meaning to join.

"It's Assogot-- and there he goes!" Bee jumped up but overturned her chair, causing the other diners to look up and frown. "Ugly Americans!" said one fellow, apparently needing a bit more wine to be sociable. Bee, her face burning, righted her chair and dashed to the door. In a minute she returned. "I guess I just missed him," she said. "There wasn't anyone out there but a couple of tourists looking lost. But I really wonder why he keeps turning up where we are. Do you think he's following us?"

"What did you actually see?" Bel quizzed her sister as she resumed her dinner.

"There was a big group of people walking by. I noticed they were all Asian, and they were pointing at the sausages hanging in the window. Some of them were taking pictures of them. I thought that was interesting, and while I was looking at them, one of them lowered his camera. And I SWEAR it was Assogot!"

Bel gently stroked her chin. Oh God, she thought, time to deal with the chin hairs again. Distracted, Bel tried to still her fingers, but it was a losing battle. Usually, Bee turned her gimlet gaze on Bel's face, finding and pulling out offending facial hairs. In all the recent excitement, though, Bel assumed that Bee had too much on her mind. Maybe tonight I can talk her into taking care of that...

"Bel!" her sister's voice brought her back.

"Bee, let's not jump to conclusions-- although, I must say, I really do not believe in coincidence," noted Bel. The two were pleased to see their pasta dish arriving at the table.

"Good thing we walk so much on our tours," murmured Bee.

"Walk?" squawked Bel. "Is that what you call riding with Paolo?" Changing the subject, Bee deftly said, "Speaking of Paolo," Bee said,

"I wonder how he and Caroline are doing after their talk?" Bel rolled her eyes, and took a bite of her dinner, refusing to rise to the bait.

Bee watched Bel close her eyes, enjoying a blissful mouthful of fettuccine. Bel was startled when she opened her eyes and saw Bee observing her. "You look like you're enjoying that." With great dignity, Bel replied "It's a gift to be able to appreciate the subtle flavors--as a cookbook editor, you know that." Bee laughed. "Oh, indeed. It's just nice to see you both enjoying it and wearing it." There was a small blob of alfredo sauce that had landed dead center on Bel's blouse. She frowned. "I hate to waste a bite of that sauce." The two of them burst into laughter, again drawing stares. Bee lifted her glass in *salute*, and the two of them drank deeply, unconcerned by the raised eyebrows and shaking heads. "You know, Beatrice, you're not such a rotten sister." Bee smiled, and replied "You're not too bad yourself, Isabella. If I have to be stuck in the middle of a murder, I can't think of anyone I'd rather be stuck with!"

"Speaking of that…" Bel turned business like quickly. "Wonder why Monseglio wants to meet with us tomorrow. You don't think he has the coroner's report yet, do you?"

Bee shook her head. "It doesn't seem likely, does it? I mean, it only happened this morning."

"Incredible. Seems like forever ago, doesn't it? No wonder I'm exhausted." Bel suddenly looked weary. "Let's head back to the hotel. I'd like to get some rest tonight, and if I'm right and we're going to have more visitors, I'd rather get it over with early."

Bee agreed. "I still think Margo will be first." Bel smiled. "I can taste the wine now…." They summoned their waiter and asked politely for their bill. Bel, using her best Italian, quietly asked the waiter for the tab of the offended diner who had made the rude remark. She paid both bills, and wrote a note on the receipt. "We may be ugly, but at least we're generous. Come visit us in America some day!" She winked at the waiter, and he grinned at her, pleased to be her co-conspirator.

After so graciously settling their tab, they headed out into the soft spring evening. They walked past the magnificent Duomo, where young people and tourists had gathered, sitting on the steps enjoying the cool night air. Street vendors were persistently but politely offering their goods for sale, keeping one eye out for customers and another for the *carabinieri*, who routinely swept the square clean of the illegal salesmen. As soon as the *carabieneri* moved on to another square, however, the hardworking vendors emerged from the shadows and began their trolling again. The sisters were almost to the hotel when they heard their names being called.

"Bee! Bel!" It came from a sidewalk cafe. They were surprised to find James and Bill beckoning to them. "Does this count?" Bee asked. "Not a chance." Bel knew immediately what she was referring to. "It doesn't count unless they knock on our door."

They joined the couple at their small table. "I'm so glad to see you out. How are you coping?" Bee asked. James raised his glass. "Bill insisted we would feel better. As usual, he was right." They touched glasses, and tossed back the last of their drinks. "Would you ladies care to join us in a nightcap?" Bee hesitated, but Bel answered first. "Of course. And will you fill us in on what you've learned?"

They settled themselves at the table, and James nodded to the waiter. Four glasses of limoncello appeared. The sweet beverage was just the right end note. Icy cold, it had intense lemon flavor and the heat of alcohol--a pleasing set of contradictory sensations. James lifted his glass. "I feel the need to drink to Patty. For all she made everyone miserable, her actions gave us--" here he squeezed Bill's hand, "the greatest gift of our lives: our beautiful daughter. For that, I owe her a toast." Bill raised his glass. "To Patty. Perhaps fate will look kindly on her because in her cruelty she really did make us very happy." The sisters raised their glasses, and the four companions drank.

"Mind you," said James "she was still a bitch and I'm not sorry to say so." Bel, still sipping her drink, began to choke and cough. "I know, I know. Not very nice of me, I know. But I've spent the whole damn day trying to figure out what to do now. A nasty business."

"Did you find her attorney?" Bel asked. Hartford, while a small city by national standards, still had its fill of attorneys. James rolled his eyes. "What

176

a nightmare that was. When I get home, I'm putting everything in a binder labeled 'IMPORTANT STUFF' just in case anybody needs information!" Sounding exasperated, he continued, "I finally figured out how to get past the receptionists and the blather. Took me hours, but I found her attorney. Can't say he sounded particularly saddened by the news. But I did get him to fax me a copy of her will."

"But tell them the news!" Bill urged. James looked thoughtful. "Seems old Patty had a soft side after all." The sisters looked at him quizzically. "She left ten thousand dollars--wait for it--to her cat. Or, specifically, for the care and feeding of her cat." They stared at him, astonished. "Uh huh. Nothing to her daughter, but 10K to her cat." He shook his head ruefully. "And the rest, for the most part, to me. And another 5K to the hospital where she had her operation so long ago. What's that about?!" He turned sober. "The good news is, her estate will let us make sure Avery can finish school with no debt, and make our lives a little easier. The bad news is, we're talking about enough money that it looks like a motive for murder." The little group was quiet while they absorbed the news.

Bel spoke first. "You just can't worry about that now. Don't go looking for trouble, our mother used to say."

Adopting their mother's classic pose with an imaginary scotch in one hand, and a cigarette in the other, Bee quoted, "It'll find you soon enough." The sentence was punctuated by Bee miming a smoke ring being blown. They all laughed, and the tension dissipated.

"But what about her...preferences... Did you learn what she preferred for burial?" Bel tried to phrase it delicately.

"That's perhaps the only easy part of all this. Patty wanted to be cremated, so we can have that done here, rather than shipping her back. Ugh. Sounds rather cold, but I am glad I can carry out her wishes in that respect without it being a huge hassle." James shuddered. "I dread the idea of a funeral. I don't know too many people who would show up, other than those who might just want proof that she's actually gone."

Ever-practical Bee spoke. "So don't have one. There's no rule saying you have to. Just put 'services were held privately' in her obituary. Save yourself the energy." Bel looked a little shocked, but Bee continued. "You know how the community feels about her. If anyone wants to be kind, they know how to reach you. Let it go--let her go. You, Bill, Avery, her daughter--you're the only ones that matter. Save the money it would cost you and give it to a home for pregnant teens. Or contribute to a social services group that helps the homeless. Whatever works for you, to turn this legacy of grief into something positive that will let all of you feel like her passing made the world a better place--no, wait! That doesn't sound nice and that's not what I meant!"

James hugged her, and gratefully reassured her, "No, don't worry, I get it. She can finally do some real good in this world, to balance off all the other stuff. I like it. What do you think, Bill?"

Bill grinned. "I'd love to see some of the money donated to help pregnant teens, but I'd REALLY love to see a donation made to help kids who are struggling with their sexuality, so all of Patty's homophobic comments disappear and some kid somewhere finds a community that accepts him or her, just the way they are. You're the accountant--time to balance the karmic account!"

"Brilliant!" said Bel. "Somewhere along the line, way back when, a little girl named Patty got off on the wrong foot with the world, for whatever reason. It's a sad story, really. How nice that she can finally get some attention for doing something positive!"

"Done." James looked relieved of a tremendous burden. "I have to say, inheriting money from her made me feel like a hypocrite. Now I have some great ideas that will make spending her money a pleasure! Thank you, ladies." He stood, and offered his arm to Bee, and Bill followed suit, offering his to Bel. "May we escort you home?"

Chapter Twenty-Four

B ack in their room, the sisters discussed whether to get into their pajamas. They were both of the opinion that nightwear was strictly for comfort, and as such wasn't presentable for company. Bel still insisted that she "had a feeling" that they would have more company that night. Bee wanted very much to get out of her street clothes and into something comfy, but Bel shook her head. "Don't do it. You know I'm right." Bee contented herself with kicking off her shoes and changing into sweats. They settled down on their beds, checking email. They had multiple emails from spouses and children, demanding to know precisely what the hell was going on. Those at home were well used to getting cryptic emails about bizarre events while the two of them were together, but death was a bit rarer--not unheard of, unfortunately, but not the usual. They were busy reassuring everyone when the long debated knock was heard at the door. Triumphant, Bel shot her sister a look as she headed to the door. "Lucy!" she hissed. "Margo!" Bee hissed back.

"Paolo!" Bel exclaimed. "What are you doing here?" The surprise in her voice was evident. "Please. May I?" He sounded exhausted. Wordlessly, Bel beckoned him in, and shut the door behind him. As she followed him into the room, she and Bee shared the "Holy Hannah" look. Paolo didn't notice, as he paced back and forth in the small space. "Sit!" Bee commanded. He was making her nervous.

He sat. He twisted his hands in his lap, and looked from one to the other. They waited. "Please. I need advice." He stopped. "Paolo, what's bothering you?" Bee spoke more softly.

"It's *Bella* Caroline. I…" Bel's eyebrows drew together, ready to angrily defend the green- eyed Texan. No double standard would be allowed. Oblivious to his potential tongue lashing, he continued. "We have decided. I will go to the United States with her." Without realizing it, Bee and Bel had been holding their breath. Their exhalation was audible. "Congratulations!" They both spoke at the same time. "But what seems to be the problem?" Bee looked at him curiously. "I need a sponsor. I cannot stay in the US without a sponsor, and she has quit her job. Because she has no income, she cannot be my sponsor. I want so much to be with her, but I can only go as a tourist, or wait until she has a new job. And some other man will try to steal her from me, I am sure of it!" They would have laughed out loud, if he hadn't been so obviously distressed. "So I come to ask you. Do I stay and wait, knowing all those men will be desiring her? Or do I go, and only spend a few months and have to leave when my tourist visa expires?"

"Or," Bel proposed another alternative. "You could ask your employer to sponsor you."

"But I do not have an employer in the US!" he almost sounded ready to cry.

"Paolo?" Bee poked him. "Think about it. Who pays you for this tour?" "*Signoras.*" He looked at her, still not comprehending. She went on. "Paolo, where are we from?"

Suddenly, he understood. "You?! You would sponsor me?!" His face broke into a wide grin. "I will do anything! You do not have to pay me for this tour!" He leaped up and hugged them both, sending Bee's reading glasses tumbling to the floor. Bel grabbed hers protectively, and laughed at his glee. "We'll work it out, Paolo. Stop worrying. We can talk about it later." He fairly danced out of the room.

Bel turned to Bee. "Wow. Didn't see that one coming!"

"Our bet is null and void, then. Neither of us won!" Bee had a satisfied grin. "You were going to drag me into all those cheap wine shops to fill up your soda bottle, weren't you?"

Bel stared. How did she know?!

Bee smiled. "Don't play poker, kid. And don't try to pull one over on your sister when wine is involved."

Checking their watches, they discovered it was long past the time when any reasonable person would come knocking on their door. They agreed, though, that it hadn't been a reasonable sort of day, so to expect reasonableness would be foolish. Despite that, they did decide to slip into their pajamas, and put their feet up. Within minutes, there was gentle snoring from both sides of the room.

Bel, the lighter sleeper of the two, rustled in her sleep. Something had tugged at her consciousness, but the dark room and her sisters' rhythmic breathing settled her and she never fully awoke. In the hall, a figure crouched in the dim light in front of their room, and slid a folded piece of paper through the small gap between the door and the marble tile.

Chapter Twenty-Five

Next morning, Bel was up bright and early, as usual. Bee was snoring softly, but Bel could hear a subtle change in the sound; she knew that Bee was beginning to awaken. Now was the time to pounce. Creeping across the room, she inched closer to the mound that was Bee. Suddenly, she grabbed one of Bee's toes, gave it a little pinch, and shouted, "wakey, wakey!" Bee wrenched herself upright, blinking, and frowned at her. "Who are you, the Pink Panther?" she grumbled. "It's too damn early for games. I need coffee!"

"Then get your lazy butt out of bed!" grinned Bel." Let's go find out what this day has in store for us!" "Do you think we will be able to resume the tour?" asked Bee. "Not that there's any dearth of interesting sights in Florence, but..."

"We have to wait and see, Bee," Bel said. "Cross your fingers!"

After dressing, the two opened the door and headed out to the dining room. It was a lovely day, and they knew they would be served breakfast on the patio, ringed with ancient stone, and even this early in the spring, blooming with new life. Neither of them saw the little slip of paper on the floor of their room.

As they had hoped, breakfast was *al fresco*--the tables simply laid, and the aroma of fresh coffee mingling with the delicate scent of early blooms. The teapot was at the ready, Bel noticed gratefully. Breads, cheeses, and fresh yoghurt with berries stood on a side table. The warm sun came through the young leaves, dappling the tables with soft light. Bel and Bee sank gratefully into the inviting chairs--what a wonderful way to start the day, Bel thought. Bee wrapped her hands around the steaming mug she had poured, and leaned back, soaking up the sun. Her eyes closed, she took a deep breath. "What time are we supposed to meet Lt. Monseglio?" "Oh, don't!" Bel sighed. "This was so lovely. Now we have to think about Patty. Thanks a lot." Bee opened her eyes, and fixed her gaze on her sister. "We need to focus, Bel. He's going to have more questions, and as of last night, we now know way more than we should about a motive for murder."

Bel nodded. "You're right. I just wanted to enjoy breakfast without thinking about it!"

Bee sipped her tea thoughtfully. "As far as we know, Patty didn't know anything about the others. The nasty little rhymes could just have been generic, couldn't they?" Her voice sounded pleading. "Well, we may not know that Patty knew, but we know because they each told us." Bel sounded matter of fact. "You do know that sentence made no sense at all, don't you?" Bee the editor glared at her sister. "Exactly." Bel smiled. "We need to be sure that what we say doesn't make enough sense to pursue. "

Bee raised her mug to her sister. "You know you're a devious one, don't you?" Bel smiled modestly. "Why, thank you!" she murmured, with a naughty gleam in her eye.

They finished their breakfast quickly--knowing they were to get together with Monseglio soon. They decided to go back to their room before meeting with him, returning to the front room via the hallway where Patty's room was still cordoned off. They hurried through the hall, anxious to have a few minutes to possibly peek at the room before they met the Lieutenant. Opening the door, Bel pushed in first, needing the ladies room in a hurry. Bee laughed as her sister slammed the door. She stood, pounding on it as Bel hushed her. Turning back to the room, she spotted the folded note on the floor. She stooped over, and unfolded the plain white sheet of paper. Her face went still and sober. "Bel." Her tone was completely different. Even through the door, Bel could hear the change. "What's wrong?"

She hurried out of the bathroom. Bee handed her the note with a shake of her head. Bel looked at her quizzically and opened it. The only thing written on it was "The Hartford Herald, Sept. 17, 1984". Bel looked at Bee, who answered the unspoken question.

"It was on the floor, just inside the door. It was there when we came in, but I have no idea when it was shoved under the door. Remember, we didn't turn on the hall light when we went out this morning."

"We don't have time to research this now. We're supposed to meet Monseglio in ten minutes." Bel folded the note carefully. Bee took her turn in the bathroom before they left. Bel sat on the bed, waiting, thinking, the note tucked into her pocket.

"Who do you think...." Bee started when she joined her sister again. "I don't even want to speculate." Bel spoke firmly. "If we go any further with this, we'll be ethically bound to mention it to Monseglio."

They quietly left the room, and headed down the hall toward Patty's room. They knew they had a better chance to get a look at the room if they didn't announce their presence before they arrived. As they turned the corner, light spilled out of Patty's door--someone was already there and busy. Bee turned to Bel, a finger to her lips. Bel smiled and nodded. Bee could be so dramatic. They crept forward, and stopped just before the door, craning their heads to look. A crew of officers was working, carefully lifting bedclothes, soiled clothes, and anything else that covered an unexposed surface. The man bending over the bed spoke rapidly and excitedly in Italian--so quickly neither of the women could catch the words. The rest of the officers in the room turned sharply to look at what the man was holding. He cradled a small, white box in his gloved hands. Another officer approached him with a large plastic bag, and the box was gently slid in.

Bel grabbed Bee's arm, and pulled her backward. They moved quickly to retrace their steps. From the opposite direction, they heard Monseglio's deep voice approaching. They froze, and then Bee quickly whirled back the direction they had just come from. Puzzled, Bel followed. In a slightly louder than normal voice, Bee said calmly, "Let's walk past Patty's room and see if Lieutenant Monseglio is here yet."

The Lieutenant stepped out from Patty's doorway, his large frame blocking the doorway. "*Buongiorno, Signora*" he said, with a slight bow.

"Good morning!" they echoed.

"Ah! Stereo again! Do you practice that, or is that something twins do?" He asked.

Bee bristled. "We're not twins! She's much older than I am!" Bel snorted. "Much?! Not that much, little sister!" She emphasized the 'little'.

Monseglio put his hand to his heart. "My apologies!" with that, he put a hand on each, and deftly moved them away from the door. "You do know this is an active police investigation site, and you must not interfere?" he said gravely. "Oh, my!" Bee looked shocked. "We had no intention of interfering!" She sounded so taken aback, that even Bel was convinced. The Italian shook his head.

"I seem to be apologizing to you both regularly. Forgive me. One must be suspicious first in this business." Bel thought the corners of his mouth were struggling not to smile. Bee looked slightly mollified. "Popular literature is full of meddling ladies of a certain age, is it not?" he said gravely. This time Bel reacted. "Excuse me? A certain age? Achieving middle age is not an excuse to accuse us of obstructing justice!" Bee wasn't sure if she was acting or actually insulted--either way, she certainly looked insulted. This time, Monseglio looked genuinely exasperated.

"It appears I cannot speak to women without insulting them since this case began. Yesterday I made a comment to myself and my wife thought it was a comment about her cooking. Now I have upset you ladies. Shall we pour ourselves a cup of coffee and begin again?" They had made their way to the attractive family room where Sophia had thoughtfully put out a tray with coffee, tea, and fruit. Bee looked at the fireplace where just two days ago Patty had spouted her poisonous "apologies". She shuddered and turned away, the vision of Patty lunging for Bel still fresh and disturbing.

Bel saw Bee's face, and reached out a hand to her sister. "I'm fine. Stop thinking about it." Bee's eyes filled. The idea of someone hurting her sister was too awful. With a look of complete understanding, Bel handed her sister a cup and saucer. She took a gulp of the proffered coffee. She wiped her nose, and smiled at her aggravating, precious sister. Damn it, she thought. She forgot the sugar.

Monseglio stood while the sisters settled themselves into the comfortable chairs. "Good morning!" They looked at him questioningly. "I'm starting fresh!" He explained. They smiled, and responded "Good morning, Lieutenant. Do you have news for us?"

"I do, in fact. But first…" He waved the envelope he was holding, then deliberately put it down on the table beside him. "First, I'd like to hear if you have any news for me?" He looked from face to face.

"No, not really." Bel began. "We met James and Bill last night, and James has found Patty's lawyer after a great deal of trouble. He had no idea who her lawyer was, so it involved a lot of phone calls." Monseglio nodded, encouraging her to continue. Bee spoke next. "He was able to determine that Patty preferred to be cremated, so we were hoping you could help us with what the policy is here, so we can let James know how to proceed."

"And did he tell you details of her will?" He probed. They looked uncomfortable, and he waved his hand. "Of course we can subpoena the information if needed." Bel shrugged. "He told us that he inherited almost her whole estate. She left $10,000 to her cat--or, more precisely, for the care of her cat, and an additional small bequest to an area hospital." Monseglio was obviously trying to keep the surprise out of his voice. "Excuse me. Is it my poor English, or did I hear that she left $10,000 to her cat?"

Bee nodded. "Her cat."

He scratched his head. "Is this typical in the US?"

Bel snorted, and felt Bee's elbow in her ribs. She changed it to a cough, while Bee continued. "No! But then, I don't think Patty could have been described as typical." He looked at her, waiting. "I mean, she was… rather…." Bee's voice faltered. Bel finished the sentence. "Mean. Even in the US, she would have been considered atypical. She alienated so many people, apparently, and I guess that in the end, James and her cat were the only ones still kind to her."

He gave a brief nod. "So she was not…typical. And now, the members of your group. Did they know each other before the trip?"

"We sent around everyone's email addresses shortly before we left. They all met at the hotel the first night in Rome, except for Patty and James and Bill. They came from all over the country." Bee nodded as Bel finished.

"Our turn, Lieutenant; what news do you have for us?" Bel was using the professor voice--the one that made its listeners straighten up and focus. Bee was amused to see Monseglio shift and stand at attention. He reached for the envelope.

"There is a preliminary cause of death." It was the sisters' turn to straighten up, with a quick intake of breath. They were surprised at the speed at which results were obtained.

"It appears she died of respiratory failure." Bee turned her head away, surprised at the sting the words brought. Monseglio continued. "The coroner will continue his examination, but it appears to have been precipitated by either a major asthma attack, or perhaps anaphylaxis."

Distracted, Bel wondered briefly at the amazing command of English the Lieutenant had. His grasp of language was far beyond what she would have expected, she thought. What's his backstory? She heard Bee talking, and turned her attention back to the conversation.

"How awful for her. How tragic that her unpleasant behavior to Caroline resulted in her having a single room. Had Caroline still been rooming with her, she would have noticed and gotten some help for her." Bee sounded sad.

The Lieutenant eyed her. "Perhaps. It happened very quickly, from the report I have. That would be a blessing."

Bel said simply "Now what? What does this mean for the tour? May we head to Assisi?"

Monseglio spread his big hands. "Regrettably, no. We have established a preliminary" --he emphasized the 'preliminary'--"cause of death, but we have not yet established WHAT precipitated the respiratory failure. Soon." He saw the disappointment in their faces. "We are working very quickly to resolve this. We have had a call from the American Embassy, requesting a "timely" release of the body." He looked at them, and noted their shock. He was surprised to discover himself relieved to know they were not the ones pressuring the department to wrap the case up quickly. He liked the two sisters, and had been nettled to think they had gone above and around him. It was obvious they had not.

"I trust you will find plenty in Florence to entertain your guests. We should be finished soon." He spoke reassuringly, with the practise of one used to conveying bad news in comforting tones.

Understanding that they had been dismissed, the two women rose, and shook his hand in turn. "Thank you, Lieutenant. We appreciate you keeping us in the loop." He looked puzzled by the phrase. "Informed!" Bee smiled. "We'll call the hotel in Assisi and cancel." Bel sounded resigned. "May we give them your name to confirm that it was out of our control? We would prefer not to be billed for the night we won't be spending there."

"But of course." He added "Please keep me looped!" Monseglio looked pleased with his use of his new vocabulary.

Chapter Twenty-Six

They headed back to their room, trying to maintain a normal pace. They spoke quickly to each other, planning out the next hour.

Quietly, they discussed the tasks ahead. Bel, with her better command of Italian, would phone the hotel in Assisi, and cancel the reservation. If there was any question of them being charged, she would use Monseglio's name. Bee would meet the guests as planned and announce the changes required by the police. She would have Caroline present the book to James. Bel would try to make reservations for the group at some of the other museums, as well as try to put together another cooking lesson or vineyard tour. They needed something special to make up for missing Assisi. Despite Patty's death, there were still other paying customers to consider. Their research on the cryptic note would have to wait until the other issues were resolved.

They met Sophia in the hallway. "Sophia! Just the person we need to see!" She looked behind her, then moved in closer. "What is it?" She looked so worried, Bel was tempted to laugh, but didn't.

"We've just met with Lt. Monseglio. Thank you so much for putting out the coffee and tea. You're so thoughtful." Bel could see her face relax a bit. "You're welcome, of course." The statement was an unspoken question.

Bee spoke in a conversational tone. "The investigation isn't quite finished. It seems Patty may have had an asthma attack." Sophia's body relaxed further. "How awful." The statement contrasted completely with the relieved tone of her voice.

"But." Bel continued. "The police don't want us to leave just yet. So we'll need to cancel our stay in Assisi. Will you please, please, be able to put up with us for another night or two?' Bee crossed her fingers, dreading a move to another hotel. Guests can only be discombobulated so much before they reach critical mass as a group.

Sophia smiled. "Of course. We had blocked off the next few days as a holiday for us, so we have no guests arriving. And Monseglio has informed us that we too shouldn't leave the city, so we aren't going to see my *nonna* after all." Here she gave a rueful smile. "What will you do with the extra days here?" she asked, curiously.

"We're trying to figure that out. It has to be something pretty interesting to make up for having to give up Assisi." Their relief at not having to move hotels was short lived; anxiety about the next few days took hold again.

"I have a suggestion." Sophia's eyes sparkled. They waited, curious.

She continued. "My cousin is in Firenze. She is the lead in the opera "Lucrezia Borgia" being performed at the Teatro dell'Opera di Firenze this season. Have you seen the new Opera House? It's amazing!"

"And?" Bel prompted, trying to get her back on track.

Sophia smiled. "There is a huge crowd scene for a ball at the palace. They use many non-singing extras to stroll through the scene to make it more..." she searched for the word in English. "Impressing?"

"Impressive!" Bee nodded, curious as to where the conversation was going. Sophia continued. "Yes! And if you'd like, I can get my cousin to arrange for your guests to be in the opera tomorrow night. They would get to meet the cast, dress in beautiful clothes, appear in the ball scene, and hear the opera from back stage. Do you think they would like it?" Her eyes fairly danced. "Roger and I were planning on doing it. My cousin had already made the arrangements. It should be like a giant costume ball!"

The two sisters shared a glance. "Are you kidding?" blurted Bel. "What an amazing experience that would be!"

"Us too?!" pleaded Bee.

"But of course! said Sophia. "It should be an exciting experience for all!" She gave them a brief hug before heading back to the kitchen.

The sisters hustled away, eager to tell the tour group the news. This was a unique opportunity that all the money in Italy could not have purchased, and the sisters knew their group-- and knew they would all enjoy the experience. Indeed, it was an evening that they would treasure, and love telling their friends about.

While Bel phoned the hotel in Assisi, Bee met with the group, and told them of the new plans. As expected, the group were excited and thrilled about the opportunity to join the opera for a night. Bee told them that they were awaiting permission to leave the city, but needed to stay in Florence at least one more day to accommodate Lt. Monseglio. "Well, it could be worse," said Caroline. "We could be stuck in Houston!" "Or Hartford!" added Lucy. Everyone agreed that they were looking forward to some of the myriad of delights still to be sampled in Florence.

Caroline left the room and returned carrying the beautifully wrapped art book. "James, we wanted to give you and Bill something to share with you some of the treasures we enjoyed in the Uffizi. We hope you like this." With a flourish, Caroline handed James the book that Bee chose for them in the Uffizi gift shop. James was overwhelmed. "You people are the best!" he exclaimed.

"I don't know how you feel, but Bill and I were talking. We would like to host all of the group this time next year, for a reunion. Perhaps somewhere warm? At any rate, Patty's money would be put to good use that way. What do you think?" Heads nodded, with smiles all around, and it was apparent that a post-Patty get together would be welcomed by all. James unwrapped the art book with care. "This is lovely!" he said, "and it will always remind me of you. This tour took a tragic turn, but I consider you all to be new friends. Your kindness to Bill and me went a long way in saving the vacation from being all misery. Thank you so much! I so look forward to seeing the statue of David at the Accademia today."

Caroline led the group in enthusiastic applause. Bee could feel her eyes fill; this camaraderie and kindness was rare on a short tour, but all the more precious for that. She reflected on the fact that, even knowing the secrets the participants had entrusted to her and Bel, she cared deeply for all of them. Despite the cheerful chatter surrounding her, she was troubled. It was possible there might be one person in the group who held an even more ominous secret. For, as Lt. Monseglio told them, they still were not sure whether Patty's death was a tragic accident, or a vicious act of purpose. Bee shivered, and put that thought aside.

Bel entered the room, and made her way through the happy group to her sister's side. She gave a thumbs up, to Bee's vast relief.

"I worked it out. They will be happy to hold our deposit for the next tour, and released us from the two nights we had booked in Assisi. Apparently with the Pope taking the name Francis, business is booming and they have more requests than they can handle."

Bee smiled. "Looks like the Catholic church has helped us out of this mess. Guess we better light a candle at the next cathedral we visit!" Bel shook her head. "I won't be a hypocrite for just two nights lodging!" Bel's views on organized religion were well known.

"Anything else lined up?" Bee asked hopefully.

"Yes!" Bel was obviously pleased with herself. "The Accademia had a tour group cancel this morning that had booked a private tour with a curator. They were happy to slide us into that spot. That means we'll get to have a mini private lecture at David's feet! And even better, no waiting in line."

"That's fabulous. How much is it going to cost?" Ever-practical Bee wanted to know.

"At this point, does it matter?" Bel questioned.

"Touche. Let's just try to finish this out on a good note and move on. Maybe we can deduct this from our taxes as a loss." She thought out loud, and Bel raised her eyes to heaven.

Bel moved to the center of the room to make her announcements about the day. A happy hum filled the room. Bee stood watching the group, and smiled, relieved to see harmony and pleasure. Watching the effect her words had on the group, Bel stuck her hands in her pocket, and was jolted to discover the folded piece of paper she had put in there earlier. What kind of time bomb is this, she wondered. Who left this for us?

When everyone settled down, she elaborated a bit about the opera experience, and made sure to give Sophia credit for the arrangements. A little good publicity for Roger and Sophia would go a long way to offset the problems created by having a guest die in their hotel, Bel thought ruefully. She also announced the semi-private tour of the Accademia; there was an excited buzz, and Bel was thrilled to see the expressions on everyone's faces. As awful as the last day had been, the final days of the tour looked to be interesting and unique enough to leave their participants with good feelings.

"We all read The Inferno by Dan Brown, and we will discuss it at dinner tonight. In the meantime, would anyone like to visit the Galileo Museum? It's an easy walk from the Accademia, and has his original telescope." asked Bel. The tour group agreed enthusiastically. As it was a small museum, there was time for a visit between their tour of the Accademia, and the pre-dinner wine hour. "Let's take half an hour to rest and change into comfortable shoes," said Bel, "then meet back here." Bee could tell by the intense look her sister sent her that they had private business to conduct in their room.

Once upstairs, Bel pulled the note out of her pocket. "Now?" wailed Bee. "Now," said Bel "Let's get this underway. Let's look up September 17, 1984 in the Hartford Herald," she said firmly. Bee sighed, and pulled out the computer.

"Ok. Let me pull it up. " Her brow furrowed, she concentrated on her keyboard. "Here it is. Oh dear." She went silent, and pointed at her screen.

"Prominent local anesthesiologist found dead." Bel read the headline out loud.

"Dr. Edward Hansen, formerly associated with Hartford Mercy Hospital, was found dead yesterday, an apparent suicide. Dr. Hansen resigned from his position as Head of Anesthesiology last year after the hospital was threatened with a malpractice suit by a patient, Ms. Patricia Graves, after a near-death experience. Ms. Graves alleged that Dr. Hansen improperly managed her pre-op anesthesia, resulting in 'extreme medical and psychological distress.' As part of an out- of- court settlement,

Dr. Hansen agreed to resign from the hospital. Dr. Graves leaves his wife Meredith, of the home, and a daughter Margo, 14."

They sat in stunned silence. "Shit." The normally very proper Bel didn't swear often, but in this case, it seemed appropriate. "Oh my." Bee was stunned. "I am SO glad we didn't know this before we talked to Monseglio this morning." She looked unhappy. "Do you think we should tell him?"

Bel looked thoughtful. "Somebody wanted us to have this information. I wonder who, and what for?"

Bee knew better than to interrupt the train of thought, although a tiny voice inside her itched to inform Bel that the proper phrase was "...and for what?" But Bel could get irritable when her laser-like focus was trained on an idea and someone dared disrupt her. She waited. Finally, Bel spoke again. "The only people who haven't visited us to pour out their fears are Margo and Lucy. I think one of them must have left it. But why?"

Bee countered the assumption. "But it could have been James, couldn't it? He knew Patty's history, and could have put it together."

Bel shook her head decisively. "No. My gut says it was Margo or Lucy, wanting us to be aware that Margo could be considered as having a motive." She looked at her watch. "That's all the time we have to chew on this. We've got to get the group to the Accademia." Reluctantly, the two closed the computer, changed into their trusty walking shoes, and headed to the lobby.

Chapter Twenty-Seven

The curator was delighted to have a small group of well-read Americans. His originally scheduled group had been a large group of boys from an English prep school. As many museum educators agreed, adolescents were not their easiest audiences, especially when discussing the magnificent, and naked, David. This group would be less likely to comment on the size of David's testicles, and more interested in the miracle of proportion and artistry accomplished by Michelangelo.

The group hung on every word, silently taking in all that he said. He explained the presence of the masking tape on David's beautifully sculpted ankles, monitoring the tiny cracks that had appeared in the magnificent piece. After about twenty minutes, one of the museum guards discreetly coughed. His attention was drawn to the large group of visitors waiting behind the velvet rope that had cordoned off the area for his talk. "Please, follow me. It is time to share David with the others who are waiting." The group followed him off to another wing, and the crowds surged toward the statue. Bee searched through the crowd, half expecting to see Assogot. She laughed at herself, and caught sight of Bel, also scanning the faces of the tourists pouring past them. They made eye contact and smiled.

The little group followed the curator through the building. He grew ever more enthusiastic, enjoying the rapt attention. Bee looked at Bel, and discreetly gestured to her watch. Bel nodded, and gracefully eased herself forward. When the curator paused for breath, she quickly moved to his side.

"Can you please join me for a round of thanks for Dottore Vincenzo? He has been so gracious to share his time and his knowledge with us today." He beamed, and bowed repeatedly as the group applauded discretely. He cheerfully shook hands with everyone, concluding with Bee and Bel. "*Signoras*, it was a pleasure. I cannot tell you how much I enjoyed your group. What a relief for me that 35 adolescent boys are stuck on a broken-down bus in Verona, and I had the privilege--delight, even--of speaking to your guests. You have made my day."

Ever alert to future tour potential, the sisters asked for, and received, his business card, and gave him theirs. Bee made a mental note to write him a very nice thank you note that evening.

It was time to get off their feet and refuel. Tourists needed regular feeding and rests, much like preschoolers. Bel smiled at the image in her head of them all as giant toddlers. Thank goodness no one had the terrible twos. The image of an obese, cranky Patty as a baby rose to her mind. She quickly turned her thoughts to finding a quiet cafe on the way to the Galileo Museum.

Once there, the group relaxed and chatted quietly in small groups. Bel and Bee took a table with Bill and James; Charlie, Mary, Margo and Lucy sat together, while Caroline sat with Paolo, holding hands and gazing at each other.

"I don't want to spoil the lovely morning," James began, "but I wanted to let you know I saw Monseglio this morning." The sisters nodded, feeling a bit guilty that they hadn't sought him out first. "They have established a preliminary cause of death." He stopped, waiting until the server placed steaming plates of pasta before them.

"Yes." Bee said gently. "We saw him early this morning too, but didn't have a chance to speak privately with you before now." Bel was grateful to see him nod. "Good. I don't have to explain." The relief on his face was obvious. It was a distasteful subject. "I'm sorry to miss the Galileo Museum, but I have an appointment with an undertaker this afternoon to make the arrangements." They nodded, regretting the unpleasant task that lay before him. He read the sympathy on their faces. "It's ok. Now that the shock is over, and I'm clear on her wishes, I can do this." Bill reached out and patted his arm. "WE can do this." He corrected James. "WE can do this." James repeated, and smiled at his partner. They all dug into the delicious pasta-- delicately sauced with cheese and fresh sage. Conversation stopped as they concentrated on the simple but delectable dish. They finished by wiping up the sauce with pieces of rustic bread. After draining their glasses, the two men signaled the waiter and asked for their check. "So we will meet you tonight for drinks and the book discussion."

"*Ciao!*" Bel and Bee waved as the two men headed out. They stood, and visited the other two tables in turn. Bel suggested to everyone that they meet at the museum in an hour, giving everyone the chance to do a little shopping before the tour. The suggestion was happily received, and the two sisters were glad to have an hour to themselves. Much as they wanted to go shopping, too, they felt the need to talk through the odd twist the day had taken. Bee reflected that one small square of paper had the potential to do so much damage… She and Bel were the last to leave the small cafe, and headed out to find a quiet spot in which to sit; more importantly, where they would not be overheard. They found a bench in a small park nearby, and sat--Bee on the sunny end, Bel in the shade.

"You shouldn't sit in the sun, Bee. It's bad for your skin." The fairer Bel took great precautions to protect her skin. Bee turned her face to the sun. "My moisturizer has sunscreen. I need the vitamin D."

"Ha!" Bel snorted. "You just want to show off a Tuscan tan when you get home." Bee smiled serenely, and waited for her sister to continue. "We've got less than an hour. Let's get to it." Bel was instantly businesslike. "Let's play "What do we know?" Bel reached into her purse and drew out her ever-present notebook. "Take notes."

Bel began the list. "Ok, let's start with people with a motive." Bee just looked at her. "Seriously? We'd do better listing people WITHOUT a motive to save time!"

"Just write it down!" Bel said snappishly. Oh, boy, thought Bee. She's on the hunt. She took up her pen and wrote "Motives".

"James, of course, because he stands to inherit. Plus it appears that Patty was threatening to expose something--theft of some kind." Bel was using her fingers to count off the names. "Bill, as James' partner, was tired of the harassment. Plus, their daughter was Patty's granddaughter--maybe they didn't want her to know and have it blow their family apart." A bit of a stretch, thought Bee, but dutifully wrote it down.

Bel continued. "Caroline. She had what seems to be an inappropriate liaison with a client, and was nearly ruined because of it. And Paolo, too, because they are now a couple, and Patty exposing Caroline threatened their livelihood and his emigration."

She was on a roll. "Roger and Sophia, because Patty was holding them hostage with the promise of awful reviews on travel sites if they didn't cater to her whims. Sophia has--shall we say, family connections--that make an in-depth investigation potentially dangerous."

Bee interjected. "Charlie and Mary. They have a nasty mess to go home to. And Charlie has a problem with his temper. And his fists, apparently."

"US!" Bel added. Bee looked up, startled. "Well, it's true. Not that we would, but, if we're being fair and listing everyone with a motive, we should be included. Patty was obviously very angry with us after giving her the ultimatum. She could have ruined our business with the same kind of tactics she threatened Sophia and Roger with." Bee grimly wrote down their names as well. Next to their names, she wrote: "with which she threatened Sophia and Roger." Bee couldn't quite suppress a gleeful snort. It was so rare to catch Bel in a grammatical error that she would savor these corrections for years. And possibly trot them out at the next family gathering...

"Margo." Bel sounded regretful. "Perhaps Margo most of all." They sat silently, thinking of the headline they had read. "How awful." Bee murmured, thinking of 14- year-old Margo.

"You know what? I do believe you're right after all." Bel spoke slowly. Bee nodded. "Margo. She's the only one not on the list."

"Does that strike you as odd?" Bel asked. Wearily, Bee shook her head. "Maybe it would have before we met Patty. I mean, what is the probability that EVERYONE on one of our tours would have a motive for murder? Now it's just kind of a relief to know that ONE person on our tour isn't harboring a deep, dark secret."

Bel was not convinced. "Of course, we don't know who sent us the note. It could have been Lucy. She's the only one on the tour who would know enough of Margo's history to even put together the 'coincidence' of Patty's story and Margo's."

Playing devil's advocate, Bee argued, "But it COULD have been Margo, letting us know that she was in danger of being a suspect, but just didn't have the nerve to do it in person." They sat and thought, turning over the information in their minds.

"New category!" Bel commanded. Bee obediently turned the page, pen poised. "Cause of Death." Bee looked at her questioningly.

"We KNOW it was respiratory failure. But what caused it? Make two columns, please." The professorial tone was coming out. "On one side, Asthma. On the other, Allergies." Bee drew a line down the middle of the page.

"What causes an asthma attack?" Bel asked, thinking aloud. "Compromised airways, stress, allergies, fear, infection. Lots of things contribute." Bee wrote quickly, trying to fit it all in. "Which of these symptoms applies to Patty? She seemed to be in decent health, other than her weight, at least as far as I could tell. She wasn't coughing or wheezing or sneezing." Bee desperately wanted to list the other dwarfs, but knew now wasn't the time. Bel continued. "We would have noticed symptoms of a cold or infection on the bus. It's too small not to hear every little sniffle."

Bee crossed off 'infection' and 'compromised airways'. She thought out loud. "Well, she was under stress, I guess. Although while she was reciting her evil poems, she certainly looked like she was having fun. Her piggy little eyes just gleamed, didn't they?"

"All right. So let's list allergies. Her only known allergy was to peanuts. But she seemed very careful about what she ate. How and where would she have gotten peanuts?"

Bee spoke slowly, thinking through the events of the night before, searching her memory. "She was the last one down to the meeting that night. We had been drinking wine, and having appetizers. But she didn't have either, just launched right in with her horrid verses. So it couldn't have been then. We all went out for dinner, and she didn't join us." Bel nodded, encouraging her to go on. "We all came back to the hotel for dessert. Sophia made that incredible tiramisu with chopped hazelnuts. Remember, we heard footsteps on the stairs?"

"Yes!" Bel jumped in. "We knew--or at least we thought we knew-- that it was Patty, because the front door hadn't been opened. It clangs shut because it's so heavy. And the footsteps were going up, not down. At least, we thought they were because no one came through the doorway."

It was Bee's turn to interrupt. "Yes! So she had either gone out, and had come in just before us, or was sneaking up the stairs after lurking there and waiting to listen in."

"And!" Bel added triumphantly. "And she couldn't have been out, because Sophia was in the kitchen and would have heard her, and told us about it." She beamed, thrilled with the deduction.

"But." Bee sounded unhappy. "But what?!" Bel snapped, piqued that her brilliant detective work was being questioned. Bee ignored her and continued. "But if that's the case...then IF Patty ate peanuts, either she got them from the food she stole from the kitchen and it was an accident, or...."

"Or somebody put the peanuts in whatever it was she ate." Bel was instantly sober.

"Remember the white box the police found in her room this morning?" Bee closed her eyes, visualizing it. "And remember the brown smears on her face and on the plate?" Bel looked at her, horrified.

"Tiramisu!" she whispered. "But whose? If the box had tiramisu, then it wouldn't be Sophia or Roger--would it?"

"They could have purchased a slice somewhere else, and added the peanuts to it." Bee's voice sank.

"Anybody could have done that." Bel shook her head.

They looked at each other unhappily. The possibility of murder seemed even more likely.

It was time to meet the group at the Galileo Museum, beside the River Arno. They walked briskly through the streets, valiantly ignoring all the leather shops along the way. They continued their discussion until a block from the museum. Bee stopped by a trash can, and pulled out her pad. She tore the pages out, and ripped them into little bits before depositing them in the bin. Bel, eyebrow raised, waited for an explanation.

"I'd prefer not to take a chance on anyone--and I mean anyone--seeing what we have been thinking about. It's much harder to deny anything found in print." The editor in Bee was cautious about committing anything to print without being very, very sure of the source. She was also very aware that any suggestion of guilt reflecting on their customers could easily be misconstrued.

Chapter Twenty-Eight

At the Galileo Museum, the sisters met the tour participants, and gathered them to summarize what they would see inside. Bel was in her element. "Before we go in, take a look at where we're standing." Heads swiveled, puzzled. "Look down!" she advised. The signs of the zodiac were imbedded in the street before the museum. They took turns photographing each other on "their" signs. Bel then began her introduction to the Museum. "After the visual arts declined in the 1600's, Galileo and other scientists rose to prominence. Inside, we will see a wonderful collection of clocks, gadgets, telescopes, and other scientific tools. You can follow the history of inventions here. Although the Uffizi is always crowded, this museum tends to be under-visited. Enjoy your time here, and be sure to see the case that holds Galileo's fingers!" This pronouncement had the expected effect. Mary gasped, wide-eyed; Charlie shook his head and chuckled; Margo shot Bel a suspicious look, and Lucy paled. "No, it's true," said Bel. "Go see for yourselves."

The two sisters took up their usual positions, one at the head of the group, another at the rear. The group fractured into smaller groups, depending on their individual interests. Most of the group concentrated on the second floor, where Galileo's instruments--and his fingers--were displayed. Caroline was mesmerized by the map-making instruments. Charlie was excited about the microscopes, and Galileo's telescope. Bee and Bel met up at Galileo's fingers, and posed for pictures with the incredibly long digits.

At the agreed upon time, the group met again at the entrance to the museum. Bee noticed that the participants were beginning to have a glazed look in their eyes. Too much of a good thing, thought Bee. She turned to Bel and whispered, "Time for a change. Gelato? Please?" "Oh, Bee," said Bel. "Stomach again? I wanted to discuss the museum visit with the group, to reinforce their learning." Bee sighed. "I really think their ability to absorb new knowledge has peaked. Look at the faces!" Bel had to admit she was right. Sometimes she was accused of being insensitive; she really wasn't, but often missed subtle cues from others. "Okay, you win. Let's walk a little bit and then settle them in a cafe. I know--let's visit that fabulous beaded jewelry shop that we discovered last time-- after they refresh themselves." Bee brightened, and peeled off to let the group know the plan.

After a short walk, they came to a bar-cum-cafe. The tour group settled themselves happily, some ordering beer, most ordering tea. Bee wanted gelato. Bel had to admit--the refreshments did the trick; in a short time, they were ready to move on to the bead shop. Charlie propped himself up against the wall outside the shop. "Now, Mother," he muttered, "don't go spending too much here. You know we have to be careful." Bee raised her eyebrow and looked at Bel, who seemed oblivious to the interchange. What did Charlie mean by that? Hadn't they made a lot of money when they sold out to Mallmart? She put the thought aside and entered the tiny shop.

Already, the clerk had put aside little wicker baskets for the shoppers' choices. They were amazed by the variety of necklaces, earrings, and rings, all made of tiny beads. Every color imaginable was represented here, from pastels to jewel colors to metallics. Modest prices and excellent quality lead everyone to make purchases. The clerk was graciously wrapping up an elaborate plum-colored necklace for Caroline. "He'll love it!" she confided to Bel. Bel figured that Paolo would appreciate anything that Caroline wore--most of all, if she wore nothing else--Bel blushed a little. It had been too long away from home, and all the delights therein.

Mary had picked out an elaborate pink necklace, many strands woven together with baby blue highlights. For under 15 Euros, it was a deal, and Mary was glowing. Bee had noticed that Mary had previously declined to buy anything for herself. In all the museum shops, which were arguably the best in the world, Mary had browsed, but not made a purchase. She was glad to see that the woman was treating herself at last.

Chapter Twenty-Nine

T he group happily climbed aboard the little bus. How Paolo always managed to pull up so quickly after they phoned him to let them know they were ready to go was a mystery. Bee's mind leapt to the next mystery--what would their *aperitivo* be tonight? Sophia had promised them a tasty surprise to fortify themselves before dinner. It was no wonder their clothes were getting tighter, thought Bee. So much delicious food to enjoy! She sighed, content. Delicious food and another book discussion-- two of her favorite things. They had certainly earned an evening of spirited book talk and a fine Italian meal. The vehicle was filled with the contented hum of kindred spirits sharing the highlights of their day. So different, Bee thought, from when Patty had belligerently occupied the front seat. How could one person be so toxic, she wondered? Her thoughts went instantly to the toxicology report that was coming. What would it show? She was so busy thinking about it, she didn't hear the question from the back seat.

"Bee!" Bel's voice was raised. "What time shall we meet everyone?" On automatic pilot again, Bee answered quickly. "We'll meet everyone in the family room in an hour. Feel free to bring your books or maps for reference for our discussion." The bus pulled up to the entrance, and everyone jumped out and headed off to their rooms to freshen up. Bee suspected that almost everyone would lie down and put their feet up, after a long day of museum floors. She was glad to have the time to do just that herself. Really, she thought, museums could make a ton of money if they would install a foot massage stand about halfway through their exhibits. I'd pay for that! She wondered if she could talk Bel into rubbing her feet if she promised to brush Bel's hair later tonight. She snickered. She had a running game of seeing how many brush strokes it took before Bel began to snore. The record was four.

Alone in their room, they went over the information they had put together in the park that afternoon. "Let's just wait and see, Bel. There's no need to get ahead of ourselves on this. If Monseglio says they've declared it respiratory failure, we just let it go." Bee pleaded to no avail. Bel shook her head and stopped rubbing. "It's the white box, Bee. If he has any brains at all, the white box will bother him. Where did it come from? Did Patty bring it in, or did someone leave it for her? That's pretty much the question."

"Rub!" Bee commanded. "I thought the question was to be or not two Bees?" A pillow flew across the bed, signalling Bel's disapproval of the pun. "You, Bee, should be ashamed of that joke. This is serious stuff!" Her sister sounded stern, but Bee saw the twinkle in her eye.

"Sorry!" Bee said. She didn't sound the least bit sorry.

Bel continued with her thoughts despite the interruption. "I mean it. If Monseglio doesn't say anything about the box, where does that leave us?"

Bee turned serious. "It leaves us saying goodbye to all of them and hoping to never see any of them again, even with James' nice offer of a reunion. I'm not sure we should dig any further than where we are now, Bel."

Bel sighed. "I know. But…" She stood up, dropping Bee's feet onto the bed. "Ouch!" Bee groused. "That wasn't long enough." Bel laughed. "Long enough to earn me enough hair brushing to fall asleep!"

They took the rest of the hour to review for the evening discussion, and changed into different clothes. Bee looked at her sneakers longingly, but with a sigh, slipped on her Ferragamo flats. She was very proud of those sleek designer shoes, having spotted them in a thrift shop last time they had a shopping expedition, while Bel was at the counter looking at spoons. It was always a thrill to find a treasure like that, and the two of them enjoyed gloating over their finds at the end of a long day of shopping.

210

Bel had a great eye for spotting the "good stuff", so Bee was very pleased to have found the beautiful shoes first.

The group assembled promptly in the family room, drawn by the delicious aroma coming from Sophia's kitchen. Red wine and slices of crusty bread were already laid out. Roger was pouring, and the guests milled happily around him. Sophia entered the room, carrying a beautiful bowl of caponata to be spooned over the bread. The eggplant, tomato, and caper dish was delicious, and everyone heaped spoonfuls onto their plate to spread over the rustic bread.

The room was silent, as everyone was enjoying the dish. Sophia had thoughtfully provided gluten-free crackers for Margo, so she could enjoy it too. "While everyone is quiet, I thought I'd fill you in on tomorrow night's preparations." All eyes were on Sophia, but no one stopped eating. "The opera is delighted to welcome you. They request that everyone come to the opera house in the morning, where you will be fitted with a costume and placed in the scene." There was an excited buzz in the room. "You may not be placed with your partner." Here, she glanced anxiously at Mary and Charlie, and James and Bill. Everyone laughed, and all shrugged good-naturedly. "The set designer will decide who will escort whom in the Grand Parade--the scene in which we will all appear." The buzz was louder this time. "There is a mandatory rehearsal in the afternoon at 3, and call time is 7 pm for the opera. I'm sorry your afternoon may be a bit disjointed." She looked around at the group. "It would be a good day to eat like a traditional Italian--your main meal early in the day, and just a light snack later that afternoon to tide you over, and then a late dinner after the opera."

There was plenty to discuss, and Bee used the opportunity to ease back to the bowl of caponata. It was so healthy, she rationalized, that a second helping wasn't a bad thing at all. Bel appeared at her elbow. "Don't even try to justify it." Bee tried to look indignant at the suggestion. "Just help yourself and pass me the spoon. This stuff is amazing." Bee laughed, and handed over the spoon. Bel heaped up her plate, too.

When the group settled a bit, Sophia was able to escape back to the kitchen, flushed with pleasure at the success her announcement, and her *aperitivo*, had been. Bee stood, and posed a question. "Normally, we would go ahead with our book discussion. Tonight's scheduled talk is about Dante's <u>Inferno</u>. Have you all read it?" Heads nodded, eyes intent on Bee. "Coincidentally, that's where my name came from!" She bowed in response to their applause.

"I wonder, though, if it wouldn't be an even better idea to have the chance to talk about the opera we're going to be in tomorrow?" Bee asked.

There was a chorus of agreement, and Bel stepped forward with her laptop. "Neither of us was familiar with the work, so we researched it earlier today. Written by Donizetti and first performed in 1833 at La Scala, it's based on Lucrezia Borgia, of whom I'm sure all of you have heard." Bel had slipped into professor mode, and had them all paying rapt attention.

"Like many operas, the plot can be a little convoluted." Here Bee snorted, and rolled her eyes. Bel ignored her and continued. "The short version is this: traveling companions are on their way to visit the Duke of Ferrara, and his wife Lucrezia Borgia. Along the way, Gennaro hears the story of the dangerous Borgia family. Bored with the tale, he wanders away and falls asleep. A beautiful masked woman arrives in a gondola and finds him asleep. She kisses his hand, and he awakens and is instantly smitten. He sings of his love for her, and tells of his childhood as an orphan. His friends return and recognize the infamous Lucrezia, and tell him of her horrible crimes." Bel took a sip of wine, and Bee continued.

"Of course the Duke assumes the young man to be his wife's lover, and arranges to have him murdered. The young man expresses his disdain for the family by tampering with the Borgia coat of arms, leaving it to read "orgia"--orgy--instead. Long story not quite short, the young man is accused of the crime of defaming the family, while Lucrezia is accused of infidelity. The Duke demands she choose the manner of Gennaro's execution, but meanwhile secretly poisons him. In triumph, the Duke leaves and Lucrezia rushes to his side and administers the antidote, pleading with him to flee." It was Bee's turn to pause for a sip, and Bel took up the story.

"Instead of leaving like a sensible young man, he refuses to abandon his companions, and returns to the party--which, incidentally, is our scene--and they drink together. Lucrezia, thinking the young man has left, announces that in revenge she has poisoned their wine, not knowing that Gennaro--the young man--is with them. As his friends die, he steps forward and announces that she has killed him, too. He then tries to stab her, but is stopped when Lucrezia reveals that he is, in fact, her son. She begs him to drink the antidote, but he refuses, preferring to die with his friends. Lucrezia then dies, too. Just your typical opera!"

Bel then used her laptop to play some of the more notable pieces from the opera. The group eagerly gathered around to listen. Bee noticed that James hung back, a pained expression on his face. She quietly moved around the group, and took his arm. She gently pulled him away from the group. "Are you ok?"

His eyes met hers, troubled. "It's just a little close to home at the moment. Nasty, powerful woman, illegitimate child, tragic death unloved…. " Bee nodded, and put her arm around him and squeezed. "I know. I wondered who would get that."

James sighed. "They all will, when they're not so excited about the idea of dressing up. I don't think it would have bothered me except for the part when she realizes he's her son, and she dies of heartbreak when he prefers to die with his friends than be with her. I mean, what if Patty realized when she was dying…." His voice thickened, and he struggled to regain his composure. Bee hesitated, but plunged in. "You know, James, I think the point isn't whether Patty realized anything in her last moments. Rather, the point is that even people who seem pretty…" she searched for a socially acceptable word, but James interjected "awful!" She smiled at him reprovingly and said, "difficult! Can still have redeeming characteristics. Patty left money to you, her cat, and the hospital. She ultimately wanted some good to come from her...demise. And I would try to focus on that." She patted his arm.

James enfolded her in a bear hug. "Thanks, Bee. It feels good to have something positive about Patty noticed. Even though I didn't like her--heaven knows I've said enough rotten things about her to feel guilty about--she was family, and it seems such a pity for a family member to die and everyone be glad, frankly." His husky voice was grateful.

Bee nodded, her head tilted to one side as she looked up at his handsome face. "I can see why Patty left everything to you. She may not have been a very kind person, but she certainly recognized it in you."

James' eyes welled up. "Damn it! Just when I thought I had it pulled together, Bee!"

She laughed, and linking arms, they rejoined the group, now busy chattering about the experience before them.

Chapter Thirty

The happy group dispersed, off to their own dinner plans. Charlie and Mary declared themselves too full and too excited to go out, and went off to bed. James and Bill were kidnapped by Margo and Lucy, despite pleading that they were tired. Bee noted the happy look on James' face, and was secretly very pleased that Margo and Lucy had reached out to him. Caroline and Paolo went off together, hand in hand.

Bel turned to her sister and with a quizzical look asked "Well? Feet or stomach?"

"Stomach!" Bee answered promptly. "But with a nod to the feet! Let's stay close to the hotel, so the feet don't feel abused."

"Good call." Bel approved. "What about the little cafe around the corner?" It was an innocent question, but Bee was alert to the sound of an ulterior motive. "Bel. What are you thinking about?"

Bel tried to assume an innocent expression, but failed. She could tell by the look on Bee's face that she wasn't going to be able to put one over on her--this time. "I want to check out the take-out containers around here." She avoided looking at her sister, examining her nails instead.

"You're messing about in something, Bel. We should stay out of this until we know what Monseglio says!" Bee shot her the fierce look her mother had used on them when they were up to no good.

Bel stood up. "It's no use arguing with me, little sister. I'm going to check it out, and you can come with me and help, or you can stay here and worry about me. Your choice!"

"Dang it, Bel. You've turned dinner into danger." Bee frowned. "I guess the upside is we can order tiramisu at lots of different places, right?" She grinned at her sister.

"I like the way you think, little sis!" They went out into the night, hunting for tiramisu.

As they strolled, they mapped out their strategy. They would have a glass of wine at the first place they came to, just to the right of the hotel. They would order a tiramisu to go, then retrace their steps, and order dinner at the first place they came to, just to the left of the hotel.

Bel explained her strategy. "If it was Patty who brought the tiramisu in to the hotel, you can bet she didn't go very far. And if it wasn't Patty…." She stopped, looking at the cafe before them. "Well, if it wasn't Patty, whoever it was probably wouldn't want to spend much time walking around with the container--the less time visible, the better." The waiter in his traditional long black apron waved them in, and the ladies took a seat facing the street. A glass of red wine each was quickly delivered. They sipped in silence, contemplating the street scene before them.

Bel broke the companionable silence. "I have a feeling." She stopped, and Bee waited. She trusted Bel's feelings. "I don't think we know everything yet." Bee was tempted to say "duh," but held her tongue. "There's something James is holding back. He still has a bit of the haunted look to him. As though he's afraid of something," she spoke meditatively, and Bel knew that thoughts were swirling in her sister's head. "Bee!" she commanded suddenly. Bee, startled, nearly spilled her wine. "What!" she glared at her sister, who was oblivious to everything but her own thoughts. "You looked up James and the company Patty's husband worked for. Tell me what the article said, tell me what the picture looked like."

While Bel had the 'feelings', Bee had the memory. She closed her eyes, and visualized the article. She sat silently, as though in a trance, and began to speak. "James is shaking hands with someone. His mouth is smiling, but his eyes are not. He weighs about 10 or 15 pounds less than he does now. He has stress lines at his eyes and mouth." Bel sat silent, knowing there was more to come. "The article talks about James leaving the company to take another position in town. He was hired by Patty's husband and trained under him, and would be very much missed." She opened her eyes. "That's pretty much the gist of it." Bel tapped her glass, now empty. "But why? Why would he leave?" She signaled to the waiter, who was hovering nearby. In beautiful Italian, she sweetly asked for the bill, and a tiramisu to go. She told the waiter it was her sister's' favorite dessert, but that her poor little sister was too tired to stay out any later. He bowed, and winked at Bee. "Hah!" thought Bee. He didn't believe that for a minute, no matter how good her Italian was. She found that strangely satisfying.

The bill, and a small styrofoam plate wrapped in plastic wrap arrived shortly. The tiramisu looked delicious, even all wrapped up. They settled the bill and took their dessert with them.

"It's not from here," Bel stated the obvious. "We can still eat it, though, right?" Bee was hopeful, and hungry. "Later! Will it fit in your purse? We don't want to order another one with this one sitting on the table."

Bee balanced it gingerly inside her purse. She always carried a big bag, large enough to hold all her necessary items, with room to spare for bottles of water, recent purchases, and a camera, and always in Italy, a corkscrew. No wonder her back hurt at the end of the day, she thought, as she hefted the purse onto her shoulder.

They walked along, passing the hotel, till they arrived at the next cafe. They found a seat, and looked through the menus. Bee was delighted to find a veal stew on the menu, served over pasta. Bel ordered pasta with fennel and sausage. They ate warm bread, dipped into olive oil liberally sprinkled with herbs and parmesan, while they waited for their meal to arrive.

"When was that article written?" Bel returned to her pursuit of information. Bee answered promptly, "Just about 20 years ago. Why?"

"It's tickling me." Bee recognized the term--it's what Bel said anytime information was just out of reach in her mind--there, but not yet recognizable. "Why would he leave his uncle at such an awful time, just when his daughter left too? James is a real loyal family man. Something significant must have happened to make him leave his uncle." The dinner plates arrived, and there was quiet as they ate. Automatically, they traded plates after a bite or two--they would always share if they got something new or different. Bee made a note to try to talk her editor into a new cookbook, featuring Mediterranean vegetables. The artichokes in her veal dish were the perfect compliment to the lemon and pimento--such an unusual combination! And Bel's fennel was sweet, earthy, and paired perfectly with the spicy sausage. She could envision a beautiful cookbook, with lovely illustrations of each dish...

"Bee!" Bel called her back to reality. "You can dream about cookbooks tonight!" Bee looked at her. How did she do that?!

"Think! What was significant in James' life 20 years ago?" Bel demanded, impatient now, hot on the trail of the elusive thoughts. "Avery was born." Bee was gratified to see the look of admiration on Bel's face. "You're brilliant!" Bel exclaimed. "That has to be the tipping point. Avery is born, and James has to be away from the firm to be sure that Patty doesn't see the baby and recognize her and kick up a fuss."

Bee licked her fork, and put it down regretfully. The plate was empty. "But," Bel, absorbed in soaking up the last of her sauce with a bread crust, looked up. "That's not enough to leave him anxious and worried. He'd be excited to have the baby, and keeping her away from Patty would be pretty easy, since Patty didn't work there. It may be a factor, but I don't think that's it." Bee frowned. Bel's logic was sound. The waiter returned to remove their empty plates, and this time, Bee requested dessert to go.

She politely asked for the bill, and added, "My sister," with a gracious nod to Bel, "needs to be back at home before her medication wears off. May we have a tiramisu to go?" Alarmed, the waiter backed away quickly, nodding anxiously. Bel started to laugh, and choked on the glass of wine she was finishing. Bee calmly thumped her on the back. Bel snorted, and the coughing began again. The waiter hurried over with the bill and a small white container, anxious to have them out of the restaurant before some other horrible symptoms appeared. Bel gathered her dignity, grabbed the dessert, and banged into the chair, scraping her shin. She moaned, and grabbed her leg, glaring at Bee. She straightened up and limped away.

218

Bee shook her head, shrugged sympathetically at the waiters, and followed her out.

She caught up with her sister in the street. "Payback is hell." Bel hissed at her.

"Whatever are you talking about?" Bee smiled blandly at her sister.

"My medication?!" Bel demanded. "Why, yes--your allergy medication. What were you thinking of?" Bee couldn't quite carry it off without giggling.

"He thinks I'm demented!" Bel fussed.

"Well," said Bee, "you looked a little crazy when you tried to snort your wine, and then confirmed it when you slammed into the chair." She looked thoughtful. "Actually, you didn't look all that crazy. But when your napkin was stuck into your pants when you stood up, you did look a little funny." Bel moaned. "Why? Why don't you tell me these things BEFORE I walk away?" She looked down, and the large white napkin was still tucked into her pants. She snatched it away, and shoved it into her purse, her face crimson.

"Why?" Bee answered sweetly. "Because someone pours cold water into the shower. Because someone pinches my toes before the sun comes up. Because someone--and by someone, I mean YOU--tries to pull a fast one on me every chance she gets. That's why!" She laughed, and tucked her arm into her sister's. "Admit it. You've earned it, sis."

"Hmph." Bel wouldn't look at her sister, but didn't pull her arm away. They arrived at the door to the hotel, and stepped into the marbled entryway. "Look at the container!" Despite the interruption, Bel was back on the hunt. "I think it's the same as the one Monseglio took away!" Bel held it gingerly out in front of her, as though it was a snake. "Now what?" said Bee.

"Now we eat the tiramisu!" Bel was practical, and not about to waste the rich desserts. They tiptoed into the kitchen to get forks for themselves. On a whim, they opened the refrigerator, looking for cream to top their cake. Giggling like naughty children, they helped themselves to a bit of whipped cream and started to sneak up the back stairs. In their room, they kicked off their shoes, divided the two pieces into four smaller ones, and each took a slice of the two different cakes. They stretched out on their beds, and devoured the pastries, comparing them critically one to the other, and to Sophia's masterpiece. They were agreed that the tiramisu from the second cafe was the better of the two, but nowhere near as good as Sophia's.

"If it had that amazing hazelnut topping, it would almost be as good!" Bel licked her spoon. Then put it down, a troubled expression on her face. "Bee. What if….what if someone put nuts on tiramisu to make it LOOK like Sophia's? And what if they weren't hazelnuts, but peanuts?" She looked at her plate, smeared with chocolate. Bee put her plate down, and looked at her. "Patty was so greedy. You know how she shoveled in anything she thought was tasty." Bee saw no point in mincing words between the two of them.

"She would have had two or three forkfuls in before she even tasted the nuts, if she even tasted them at all. She might not have realized it was peanuts!" Bee's voice sank to a whisper. They sat in silence, horrified. The knock at the door startled them both. Guilty, they grabbed the dishes and shoved them under the bed. Bee went to the door. "Margo!" she hissed as she went past the bed. "Lucy!" Bel hissed back.

James was at the door. Bee invited him in, and he joined them in the small room. He took the one chair by the window, and Bel nudged the dishes further under the bed with her foot, hoping they didn't show. He sat, gazing out the window, exactly as he had before.

"Déjà vu?" thought Bee. She really did think it would be Margo. James had already spilled his guts to them. The metaphor gave Bee the shivers, thinking of Patty and the tiramisu, and she willed the thought away. James turned to them, and sighed.

"I need to talk to you." He began, and stopped. Drawing a breath, he began again. "I want to talk to you. You've been so kind, and I really value your help and support. And I don't know what to do." They looked at him quizzically. "What's the matter?" Bee asked gently.

"I'm frightened." The words were simple, but the emotion behind them was palpable. He looked at them, beseeching. "I think I'm in trouble.

220

Or, rather," he corrected himself "I'm afraid I could be in trouble." The words began to tumble out.

"I told you Avery is Patty's granddaughter." They nodded, silent, to let him continue. "Vicky didn't have any insurance. She refused to see her parent's doctors, and she had no money to pay for her obstetric bills. When she was ready to deliver, we took her to a hospital in Massachusetts, and Avery was born there. It wasn't an easy birth, and there was follow up care needed. She was just a kid…." James' eyes reddened. "We told her we would pay the medical bills, so she wouldn't be traced through a billing system. We had no idea how expensive it would be. We couldn't pay it off, and it kept gathering interest. Late payments, dunning letters, all kinds of nasty phone calls at work." He shuddered, remembering. "Avery was the light of our lives from the moment we held her. We couldn't let anything compromise our adoption. So I found a way to pay for it." He stopped, his voice cracking. He cleared his throat, determined to get through it.

"I had been working for my uncle for a few years. He was so proud to have a "son" follow him into the business. He trusted me." James' voice grew thick, but he continued. "I handled the invoices. It was surprisingly easy to slip additional invoices into the system. I siphoned off just enough money to pay off the hospital and get the bill collectors off our backs." He sighed. "It was fine until the annual audit was due. We did it in house--my uncle was responsible for it. He picked up the discrepancies. He was…." he searched for words, and the pain in his voice was awful to hear. "He was devastated. He called me in at the end of the day, when just about everyone was gone. My invoices were on his desk. I thought I was going to faint. And all he said was "Why?". I told him as much as I could--that we paid for the baby, the hospital bills, and to help the mother start a new life. I just couldn't tell him the whole truth--that the daughter he was distraught about had delivered a baby he was never to know as his grandchild--because that was the promise we had made." He buried his head in his hands. "So there I was, a liar and a thief, still lying to the man who had given me a career, was my own flesh and blood, and the grandfather of the child I adored. He could have fired me right then and there--worse, he could have had me arrested.

But he didn't. He compromised himself. He wrote new invoices, crediting the company back for all the bogus bills, and he paid for it himself. He was a man of incredible integrity, and I made him a liar, too." James began to sob--fierce, ragged sobs. He gulped, and went on. "Every time he looked at me, his face would change. I couldn't stand being such a disappointment to him, so I found another job. I went in to tell him I had resigned, and he began to cry. I still don't know if it was relief, or grief. I was too much of a coward to ask him. He died about six months later. I really do think losing Vicky, discovering I was a thief, and then, my letting him down by leaving is what killed him." He stopped, and wiped his face.

"James, it was a long time ago. Why bring this up now?" Bel asked. His face hardened. "Patty. I'm pretty sure she guessed something was up. She kept a pretty tight rein on the family finances, and would have wondered why he was reimbursing the company. I don't think he told her anything, but....she has made nasty allusions to stealing and theft for the last 20 years, hoping to get a rise out of me. That charming little poem of hers the other night....well, if Monseglio decides it was murder, then I'm the prime suspect."

Bee and Bel glanced at each other, and Bel shook her head infinitesimally. Bee spoke.

"James, as far as we know, there isn't any hint of murder. You know what Monseglio said--respiratory failure. Let's just see what the morning brings. If Monseglio wants to question you further, be honest with him. And perhaps have Lucy sit in with you, just for your own protection."

He stood. "I just want to put that behind us. Saying it out loud was a big relief to me. I've never actually told anyone before--not even Bill. He knew my uncle had taken care of it, but I couldn't bring myself to say out loud what damage I had done." He tossed his head, and his voice was bitter. "I don't mind payback--karma has been waiting to catch up with me. But I just can't stand the idea that SHE may have laid a trap for me from beyond the grave." His face had changed, Bee thought, looking at him. He had truly looked frightened when he had entered their room. Now, he looked stronger; a bit angry, yes, but stronger and more resolute. His long arms reached out for them, and they moved in for a group hug. He kissed each of them in turn on their foreheads, and headed back to his room.

The door closed behind him, and the two sisters looked at each other. Bee bowed. "Grandmother was right. You do have the Sight." Bel just looked drained. "You know what still bothers me? And this has nothing to do with feelings." She looked unhappy.

Bee answered promptly. "He never said he didn't kill her, and he never said he was sorry."

"Exactly!" Bel nodded vigorously. "Are we being set up as character witnesses? Was it a pity party to make sure we wouldn't point the finger at him? Are we being used?"

Bee countered. "Or is he so absorbed in his own historic guilt that it doesn't even occur to him to deny what just happened? Either way, it makes him a prime suspect if Monseglio is looking."

The discussion went back and forth, point and counterpoint, with each sister switching position as new thoughts occurred to them. They ranged from sympathetic to suspicious, and both of them were exhausted when they realized how late it was.

"I'm too tired to even play Words with Friends. You want the bathroom first?" A weary Bel dragged her arm across her face. "Sure. I'm too tired too." Bee shuffled across the room, stopping to pick up her toiletry case. She quietly and unobtrusively slipped her phone into the case while her back was turned. She hummed gently as she headed into the bathroom and closed the door. As soon as the door was closed, Bel reached under her pillow and pulled out her phone. "We'll see who's too tired!" She cackled to herself. Just then, her phone trilled--sending her the message that Bee had just scored on a triple word.

Chapter Thirty-One

I t was a relief to not have any early morning tours scheduled. Everyone, it seemed, needed a day to sleep in a bit. The normally busy breakfast room was quiet when Bee and Bel wandered down just before eight. The coffee was ready, and as usual, Sophia had a tea pot just waiting to be filled with boiling water. Sophia and Roger were at a window table, enjoying the warm spring sunshine, and both jumped up when they entered.

"Sit!" Bel commanded, waving her hands at them. "We're perfectly happy to help ourselves and pour our own coffee. Relax!"

Ignoring her completely, the hosts cleared the table and in an instant had it re-set and ready for the sisters. By the time Bel had chosen her tea for the morning, Roger was bustling in from the kitchen with a hot kettle. "It's a pleasure to make a pot of tea for someone who really appreciates it!" He grinned at Bel. "Not like those heathens who wave the tea bag over the mug and call it good."

"You're in a good mood this morning!" Bee smiled at him and his beaming face. He bowed, acknowledging the compliment. Sophia, carrying in a tray laden with pastries, cheeses, and breads, laughed at him. She locked eyes with him, and the two smiled at each other, oblivious to the rest of the world. He took the tray from her, and carefully set it on the table, and waltzed her around the room. Bee and Bel, sitting in the window, nodded thoughtfully at each other. Bel raised her coffee mug in salute, and Bee raised her tea cup. They silently mouthed the word 'pregnant' at the same time. "Bet? I call October." Bee frowned. "Ok. I say late September. Loser has to skip a turn in Words with Friends." They touched mug and cup, and drank. Sophia and Roger came to their table, faces flushed from waltzing around the warm room.

"We have good news!" Roger blurted.

"Please tell us!" Bee didn't want to deny them the pleasure of sharing their joy.

"We got the bank loan!"

Bee didn't miss a beat. "Congratulations! That's wonderful news! We're so pleased for you." Her face didn't even flinch when Bel kicked her under the table. Roger practically skipped into the kitchen to prepare for the arrival of the other guests. Sophia took the seat offered.

"Such wonderful news!" Bel reached out and patted Sophia's hand. She grinned, and leaned forward conspiratorially. "And--I'm pregnant!" She laughed at the expressions on their faces, a mix of pleasure, triumph, and surprise. This time, the congratulations were even more enthusiastic. "Roger heard you mention months. He thought maybe you had guessed, so he wanted to tease you a little. We really did get the bank loan, but we're more excited about this!" Her face glowed.

"Well? Bee demanded. "When are you due?"

"November! It's early, but we're so excited. We're not telling most people yet, but we had an idea that you would figure things out. And now, the kitchen awaits!" She headed back to her morning duties, leaving them staring after her.

"So it always seems to go." Bel swirled the last sip of coffee in her mug. "One life ends, another begins."

"That's macabre. Don't tie this baby to Patty in any way!" Bee scolded her sister.

In the hallway, the phone rang, and they heard Roger answer with the classic Italian "*Pronto.*" They heard the sounds of his footsteps coming toward them. The happy look was gone from his face, and he spoke soberly. "It's Lieutenant Monseglio. He'd like to speak to either one of you."

They looked at each other. Bel quickly interjected "Deciding Factor!" Bee glared at her, but rose from the table and followed Roger to the phone.

She decided to stick to English, to be sure there were no miscommunications. She'd had enough adventures mixing up tenses in other languages to know she didn't want to do it again when dealing with serious matters. "Good morning, Lieutenant. This is Bee. How can I help you this morning?" She waited, her heart beating faster, but she had no idea why.

"*Buon giorno*! Thank you for taking my call, *Signora* Bee. I trust you are well this morning. I am calling to keep you looped." He sounded very proud of his use of the vernacular, and Bee decided not to correct him.

"We appreciate that very much, Lieutenant. Is there anything new to report?" She crossed her fingers, hoping to hear nothing of interest.

"I am calling to say I will be there in fifteen minutes. May we meet then?" It was definitely not a question, and it was clear he was not going to provide any information over the phone. Bee repressed a sigh, and said "Of course. We shall meet you in the family room then. *Ciao*!" She hung up the phone and returned to the breakfast room, now full of other guests helping themselves to coffee and breakfast.

"He'll be here in fifteen." Bee answered Bel's question, communicated through her upraised eyebrow. "Wouldn't say anything more."

"Hmmm." Bel mused. "Could be anything, I guess. Did he ask to see anyone else?" Bee, a large bite of pastry in her mouth, shook her head.

Sophia made her way to the center of the room, and clapped her hands. All heads swiveled in her direction. "*Buongiorno*, good morning. I just want to let everyone know that my cousin called this morning. You are all expected at the Opera House at 10:30 for costuming. Please wear under-clothes that you will be comfortable in for standing in front of the costumer. There is no place for modesty in the theatre!" Voices rose in excited chatter, as the idea sunk in. Clearly, they would be expected to strip to their skivvies in full view. Mary looked shocked, and Caroline laughed at her sympathetically. "Mary, don't worry. You'll be wearing more than what most people wear on the beach!"

Mary's cheeks were pink. "Oh my. I'm a little nervous now!" Caroline hugged the little woman. "Tell you what. I have a brand new camisole with me I haven't worn yet. Would you like to borrow it? That might make you more comfortable." Mary gratefully accepted, and Charlie squeezed her hand.

Bee turned to Bel. "Oh boy. Do we have any decent underwear on this trip?" Bel rolled her eyes. "You run up to the room and pull out your best stuff. I'll wait for Monseglio, and then we'll switch. We can use a hair dryer to dry undies if we need to." Bee jumped up and shot out of the room. She knew that both she and Bel tended to pack old underwear, planning to discard it before heading home. She was thrilled to remember that she had brought along a pair of bike shorts, just in case the urge to exercise had come over her. It hadn't, but just in case...She could wear that under her pants, and the matching sports bra would serve to keep her decent and prevent her underwire bra from being shared with the public. She laid them out on the bed, and pulled open Bel's drawer. Her things were just as randomly piled in there as in her own suitcase, and Bee was secretly relieved. She flipped through the clothes, and found a lacy top that could be a decent cover up. She knew Bel had no desire to show off her extra pounds, either. Tucked into the bottom of the drawer was a cute pair of pajama bottoms, little short shorts. That will do, thought Bee triumphantly. They could go to the ball without showing off the tiramisu, the fettuccine, and cheeses they had enjoyed! She snorted, amused at herself. Her little bike shorts wouldn't make the pounds disappear--there was no point in kidding herself.

The thought of the tiramisu suddenly brought Bee up short, and she reached under the bed to find the dirty dishes. She really didn't want those discovered under there. She rinsed them off in the bathroom, not wanting to carry the dirty dishes through the halls. Bee headed to the breakfast room, hoping to leave the plates on a table, and not have to confess their midnight raid in the kitchen. Roger had just bussed some tables, and while his back was turned, Bee quickly placed the dishes on an uncleared table and hurried from the room.

When she reached the parlor, she paused, hearing voices. She smoothed her hair, and walked in. Monseglio was standing by the fireplace,

228

a cup of coffee in his hand. Bel was comfortably seated, her face bland. Bee came and sat next to her after exchanging pleasantries with the Lieutenant.

"My wife thanks you for the beautiful flowers." He spoke gravely, but there was a reassuring glint in his eye. "I'm afraid we don't understand?" Bel was exceedingly polite but confused.

"Ah, you see....I was thinking of the tragic death of Signora Patty when my wife entered the room. I made the mistake of saying something unfortunate, and my wife interpreted it as directed to her. She was, shall we say, unhappy with me?" He was definitely amused. "To keep the peace in my home, and the pasta on my plate, I had to be sure to not bring my work home, but flowers instead. So she must thank you, and your guests, for the lovely flowers." The women smiled, nodding. Many a time both Nate and Jack had been so absorbed in their work that they had made unintentional insults. Flowers go a long way to help a spouse not resent work spilling into home life-- wine, or chocolate, worked well also, Bee mused. She thought of the many times Jack had had to wait for her to finish editing a chapter or two, and resolved to bring him home something special.

Cautiously, Bel asked "What were you thinking about that put you in the doghouse?"

"Pardon? I was not in a house with dogs." He frowned, searching for the correct interpretation. Bel hastened to clarify. "I'm sorry! It's a phrase that means a husband has done something to make his wife cross enough that he is sent out to sleep with the dog, rather than in his bed."

"Ah. I understand." He thought for a moment. "I was thinking about why *Signora* Patty had an asthma attack, all of a sudden. It seemed very random." He was serious now. The sisters waited, wondering what would come next.

"I have asked *Signor* James to join us as well. We will continue when he joins us." As he spoke, James and Bill entered the room. Monseglio looked from one to the other. James spoke first. "Bill is my partner, Lieutenant. We wanted to hear your news together." Although calm, Bee could see his jaw tighten, expecting a negative reaction from the Lieutenant. "*Si, si,* I know." He spoke calmly. "I am looped on this."

James looked at Bee, who shook her head slightly with a smile. James shrugged, and the conversation continued. Monseglio cleared his throat. "There has been a new development." James sat up straight, shoulders rigid. "It seems that the coroner has discovered the cause of the asthma attack that prompted the respiratory failure." He looked from one to another, their full attention on him. "I shall spare you the details, but it is his job to do a thorough examination. He was able to identify the food in her stomach." Here he paused, searching for the appropriate terms. "There was only tiramisu--and peanuts."

James gasped. "But she's--she was--allergic to peanuts! Why would she eat them?" Monseglio eyed him. "Exactly."

There was silence in the room as the information was digested.

Bee broke the silence. "Where would she have gotten peanuts? Sophia's tiramisu doesn't have peanuts in it. That's what we all ate for dessert that night." She looked troubled.

"Precisely why I am here." Monseglio put his empty coffee cup down. "We removed all the food from the kitchen here yesterday. No peanuts anywhere. We have conducted a thorough search of *Signora* Patty's room. We did not find peanuts, but we did find something." Bel could have sworn he was enjoying his dramatic phrasing, almost as though he were performing the role of detective.

"What?!" James practically shouted, and Bill put a reassuring hand on his arm. James took his hand, and a deep breath. "Sorry." He continued in a normal voice. "What did you find?"

Monseglio waved away the apology. "Upon investigation, we found a container. It had the same chocolate smeared on the sides as on the plate." He spoke triumphantly, proud of the detective work his crew had done. The others were not as impressed as he. "The tiramisu! It was brought in. It was not from *Signora* Sophia." Bee and Bel breathed a sigh of relief, unaware until that moment that they had been holding their breath.

"But…" began Bel. Bee coughed, but Bel continued. "But if it wasn't from here, why were there peanuts on it? No one makes tiramisu with peanuts." It was a logical question, but Bee wasn't thrilled with where the question was leading.

"Again, correct." Monseglio truly seemed to be enjoying the spotlight. "But all of you have told me how much everyone enjoyed the dessert. And how you asked what the secret ingredient was. And you all--" here he searched for the word, "you all were most emphatic in your praise, saying that the nuts made all the difference, it was the best you ever had?"

The four listeners nodded, unsure where he was going with his reasoning. "And you heard *Signora* Patty, leaving to go up the stairs?" He continued, encouraged by their nods. "She must have gone out for tiramisu, purchasing it from a local cafe. Unable to resist trying to replicate the flavor you all applauded, she must have purchased some nuts to sprinkle on top."

With a flourish, he drew from his pocket, a small plastic bag. In it, a crumpled wrapper was balled up. In bright letters, it read "*Arachidi kiddie*" with a picture of a smiling child.

"Peanuts!" Bel whispered.

"Your Italian is much better than *Signora* Patty's." Monseglio looked at her approvingly. "*Arachidi* means peanuts," he explained unnecessarily to James. "Your late aunt was looking for nuts to top her tiramisu. She purchased *arachidi*, not *nocciola*."

He stopped, giving them a moment. "It seems quite clear that she poured the nuts on top of the tiramisu, and ate the whole slice. There was very little else in her stomach, perhaps making her reaction to the peanuts even swifter. I'm sorry to tell you this." He looked at James, whose face was pale.

"The coroner assures me that death was swift. She did not suffer long." His words were intended to be comforting. "Her airwaves shut down immediately. Even if she could have called for help, there was virtually no chance she would have survived." He shook his head. "The case is closed. You may proceed with your plans with the undertaker. The embassy has been notified that the cause of death was anaphylactic reaction to an allergen, causing respiratory arrest. You have my sympathies."

James' hands were shaking, and he buried his head in his hands. Bill put his arm protectively around him, and drew him close. James began to sob. The sisters rose, and Monseglio followed them into the now empty breakfast room.

"But…" Bel began, and Bee stepped on her foot, hard. "Oh dear! Did I hurt you? I'm so sorry!" Bel winced, tears springing to her eyes. "I think you broke my toe!"

"Nonsense!" Bee helped her into a chair, leaning over her solicitously as she settled her. "Be quiet!" she hissed at her sister, before turning back to Monseglio with a smile.

"Thank you, Lieutenant, for all your hard work on the case. Especially that outside of working hours!" She smiled at him, and he bowed. "You must be pleased to have this wrapped up so quickly. I know we are."

He smiled modestly. "Indeed. It was a priority for my department. Those higher up do not like it when a tourist dies. It is a great relief to them to find she died because of her own, dare I say it, greed?" His face showed his disgust.

"And your tour? Will you go on to Assisi?" He wasn't really interested, Bee thought. Just basking in his self-congratulatory glory.

Bel shook her head. "We're very excited to have an extraordinary bit of luck. We've all been invited to be walk-ons in the opera tonight. Tomorrow, we'll get everyone to their respective airports or train stations and they will head home. Bee and I will head out to Verona for a few days' rest before we fly home."

"Verona! A lovely place. My wife is from Verona. You will enjoy it." He was in an expansive mood. "Her cousin runs a little osteria in Verona. It's called *Ghiottone d'Oro*--the Golden Pig. Tell them Monseglio sent you. He will treat you well."

He bowed over their hands again, and left, striding down the hall. He stopped at the family room door, where James and Bill were standing. He shook their hands, and continued out the door.

"Seriously?" Bel was enraged. "You had to break my toe?"

232

"Sorry! I didn't mean it to be so hard. I needed to shut you up before the Pink Panther got your ideas into his head and the whole mess got re-opened."

"But he never even checked the box for fingerprints! Or the bag!" Bel fumed.

"Let's just be grateful for small favors," said Bee. "Maybe it happened just the way the Lieutenant said. At any rate, those clues are disposed of now. There's nothing more for us to do."

Bel sighed. "I don't know, Bee. Something about this makes me very uncomfortable. But if James didn't murder Patty-" "Shhh! " hissed Bee. "Here he comes!" James and Bill walked into the room, and the sisters pasted smiles on their faces. Neither woman was able to lie well; they had been rigorously trained to honesty as children. This had been a major disadvantage for both at certain times. The confusion engendered when required to lie put them both at a disadvantage. Blushing, stammering, babbling took center stage.

James and Bill stopped briefly, thankfully. They didn't ask any questions, which was a great relief. James simply said, "Thanks for being there with us through that. What an awful experience." They murmured their sympathies, and the two men moved on.

Bel was about to start fussing again, but Bee held up a warning finger. "Unless you want to share your skivvies with the group, we need to get upstairs and change now. And I mean now!" Bel's mouth clamped shut, and she jumped to her feet and headed toward their room. "It's a miracle! She's healed! The lame can walk again." Bee called after his sister. The only response was a very rude hand gesture.

They quickly changed into the clothes Bee had laid out for them, and made it back in the lobby in time to greet everyone. There was an electricity in the air--Bel couldn't quite decide if it was excitement or nerves about the opera, or if word had gotten around that Patty's death had been officially declared an accident. She thought about all the secrets that had been shared--what an odd, guilty group. They must be vastly relieved to not have to relive their sins before the police. Her thoughts were interrupted by Bee gently but firmly shoving her into the van.

After a short ride, the excited group pulled up to the Teatro Dell'Opera, a luscious edifice consisting of sweeping stone curves. There was a resemblance to a pyramid in the multiple steps leading to a fantastic view of the city of Florence. Bel had, characteristically, rattled on in the van, describing the architecture, the history of opera, and other cogent facts. Bee realized immediately that the group were only half listening. As Bel nattered on about Florence being the birthplace of opera--the first one ever performed right in Florence in 1597--Bee heard a low buzz from the group. Polite to a fault, they were giving Bel token attention while they whispered about the upcoming ball scene and their backstage experience. Soon, Paolo drew the van up to the front entrance to the opera house. "I will join you soon," he said, "Sophia arranged for me to be in the ball scene also!" Caroline's eyes lit up and she waited for him while he parked the tour van.

Inside, they were hustled to the costumer. They had a quick glance at the interior of the opera house--more gorgeous sweeping curves, and seating for five thousand in the audience. The style and magnificence of the building--inside and out--were incredible. Bee and Bel took a moment to appreciate the interior, never having had time to visit on their previous tours. Too soon, a large, dark-haired woman was calling and clapping her hands, motioning them to follow her. The group hustled backstage, where racks upon racks of glorious costumes hung. For women, there were ball gowns in deep, jewel colors, reds, purples, blues and greens, some with slashed sleeves, most with ruffs and lace. Mary's eyes widened when she saw the variety and the styles. "Velvet and silk--oh my!" she said. "I can't believe I am going to wear something this beautiful in this life!" Caroline, ever practical, was already hunting through the gowns, and found a brilliant green one, with long, slashed sleeves, and brocade trim. The costume mistress explained that size was not an issue--all of the dresses could be pinned and pulled to fit well enough for the one ball scene.

"*Basta!*" she exclaimed. "Quick, quick!" The women immediately pulled out gowns in colors they thought would flatter. Bee chose a lovely maroon, and Bel found a deep blue gown for herself. Bel heard Bee moaning

234

behind her. "Help, Bel! " she hissed. "This damn dress is too small!" Bel tugged and pulled, and got the gown over Bee's hips. "More gelato?" she asked sweetly. "Well, that blue gown isn't exactly swimming on you!" Bee replied. Bel winced, and the two made a pact to watch the caloric intake in future, both well aware that it would not last past the next meal.

Margo's trim figure looked especially lovely, with an embroidered blue gown that showed off her figure to advantage. Lucy looked a bit uncomfortable in cream lace, and stood rather stiffly at Margo's side.

When the women were dressed, they turned to the men, and Caroline led them in quiet applause. The men were gorgeously arrayed in velvets and satins as well. Paolo looked like a knight in a surcoat of green, with a lace ruff that matched Caroline's. His brown eyes gleamed with pleasure when he saw how lovely she looked. Hooking his arm in hers, he waltzed the redhead around the dressing room. James and Bill wore similar tabards, red for Bill, and purple for James. They were incredibly handsome, and strutted around imperiously. "Wow!" Bee exclaimed. "You two were born in the wrong century!" "Too true," murmured Bill. Charles had chosen a surcoat in cream, with ermine trim and puffed sleeves. Mary took his arm and whispered something to him, making him grin. Sophia and Roger swept into the room, dressed in matching deep, rich scarlet court clothes. Sophia was positively radiant, and Roger looked as a regal as the proud nobleman he was portraying. They gave a royal wave in response to the oohs and ahs of the group. Roger spoiled his image by breaking into a grin, remarking "Bloody marvelous!"

The wardrobe mistress called the group together. "Now you wait," she whispered. "The singing start now." She showed them to an area where they could surreptitiously watch and listen from behind the curtains. The group waited for their cue; other extras joined them silently as the moment neared for the ball scene and the drinking song. A few nervous titters were quickly hushed, and when the stage direction was given, they marched onto the stage as a group. Bee could feel her eyes beginning to water. The set was so lovely--an elegant 16th century royal palace--and the costumed singers were so opulent, that she nearly lost her balance in the dazzle.

"Oops!" whispered Bel. "Stay with me!" The extras had been instructed to simply mouth appropriate words during the drinking song scene. The professionals sang with gusto, and Bee determined to buy a copy of the opera for herself. Too soon, it was time for the group to exit, and although they were sorry to finish their scene, getting out of the bright lights was a relief. And, in truth, getting out of the tight and constricting costumes was also.

The mistress whispered to them to remove their costumes, and, turning their backs, they did so. Hands reached for street clothes, and more than one sigh was heard as the gorgeous clothes were returned to the racks. "Oh, I wish we could dress like this now," sighed Bee. "These long gowns cover a multitude of sins!" She saw Bel grin, and decided to leave it at that. She moved aside a few hangers to make room for her dress. She froze. "Bel!" she hissed. "Look under the rack!" Bel followed her gaze and soon saw what Bee had noticed. Sliding her foot beneath the rack, she cautiously slid out a packet of peanuts. The sisters exchanged a worried look.

"Who?!" Bel whispered. The rest of the group was at the door, listening to the remainder of the scene. Bee shook her head, perplexed. There was a burst of applause from the doorway, indicating that the scene had ended. Lucrezia had died, a woman of power, but sad and alone, unloved by her son and husband. Bee shivered. It was creepy to find the peanuts in a room where the tour guests had gathered.

There was no time to discuss it--the stage manager had called everyone to the stage to discuss the final adjustments. Bill and James were delighted to discover they would be crossing the stage, flourishing their opulent wine goblets. Mary was to be positioned at the side of the stage, providing a lovely tableau beside a seated Charles. Margo was in front, too, but seated. She was too short to be seen in the back, so she was provided with a basket of flowers to offer to the ball guests. Paolo and Caroline were to walk along the back, arm in arm--a task that suited them just fine. Bee and Bel were ladies in waiting, standing still along the side lines. While not front and center, they were pleased to be able to stay put and watch all the action. Sophia and Roger had the privilege of promenading with the Duke.

236

Bee was thrilled that Sophia's cousin, as Lucrezia, had enough influence to give the couple such an incredible experience. Lucy alone had not been called by the stage manager. He continued giving directions, assigning spots. Finally, he turned to Lucy, whose cheeks had small pink spots. "You." He said imperiously. "I do not like your dress." She blushed and looked humiliated. Oblivious, he continued. "You are like an exquisite birthday present wrapped in the wrong paper. You should be in something rich, and full of color. Not that pale color for you. You will be in royal purple, and you will sit with the Duke when he is ignoring his wife." He turned away, concentrating on the next scene. Totally shocked, Lucy was rooted to the spot until the costumer scurried to her side, practically dragging her backstage to fit her into an elaborate gown.

Lucy reappeared, a few minutes later, a completely new persona. Instead of a stiff, shy older woman, in her place was a ripe, sensuous lady, graceful and beautiful. The director looked up from his notes, took in the vision, and smiled. "*Bella!*" he practically crooned the word. He took Lucy's hand, kissed it, and went back to his notes with a smile and a wink. This time the pink spots on Lucy's cheeks were from pleasure. The costumer escorted her back to change out of the dress until time for the evening performance, but not before her friends had gathered around her to snap pictures.

After the dress rehearsal, the group gathered to follow Sophia's cousin's advice--it was time for a late lunch/early dinner, and then a quick nap before returning to the opera house for the real performance that evening. There was an electric charge to the conversations--the group was pumped to perform. They headed to the nearest cafe, mindful of the suggestion to eat lightly--stage nerves and heavy meals were not a good combination. The group chattered excitedly, barely tasting their food, reviewing the afternoon. Lucy blushed at the gushing compliments her change of dress had produced.

Paolo drove everyone back to the hotel, promising to have the bus ready and waiting in plenty of time for everyone to get back to the opera house for photo ops--many a Christmas card would feature the opulent costumes.

Bee and Bel gratefully collapsed onto their beds, ready to be off their feet and out of tight garments. "What are we going to do with the extra 20 pounds?" Bee moaned.

Bel looked at her. "Twenty?!"

Ignoring the rude comment, Bee sat up. "The peanuts! Bel, what about the peanuts?!"

Bel sighed. "The peanuts. Murder weapon or snack food?! And who the hell brings peanuts to the opera?"

Bee whispered "A murderer! A murderer brings peanuts to the opera!"

Bel rolled her eyes. "Don't you think you're being just a wee bit melodramatic?"

"Am I?" Bee challenged her. "Look at the facts. We have a small group. One of the members is allergic to peanuts. The group knows it. The group hates her. She dies of an allergic reaction to peanuts. The group goes to the opera, backstage. An empty bag of peanuts is found exactly where the group has gathered. Do you really think it's a stretch to put those facts together?"

Bel considered, sighing. "Well, I concede the logic. This time! But... it also doesn't prove anything. It could still be a coincidence--you have to admit that, too." She looked at Bee, eyebrow raised.

Bee snorted, "There are too many stinking coincidences." And she rolled over and started to snore.

Chapter Thirty-Two

Paolo had the bus parked at the door of the hotel, ready to go. He had a basket of roses, and with a great flourish, handed one to each of the group as they boarded the bus. Caroline was the last to get in, and she was handed a dozen beautiful roses. The redhead buried her nose into the flowers, and her pink cheeks glowed. Paolo beamed, and the group applauded. The romance was officially public.

The short ride to the opera house was full of nervous laughter and teasing remarks about the personas each of them would assume in the opera. Once in the dressing room, the chatter stopped as everyone found their finery and began the challenge of donning the heavy period clothing. Bee and Bel agreed to serve as each other's dressers, making the task easier.

They giggled and posed for pictures together and alone, and kept repositioning themselves, vying to be the one in the back, hiding the voluptuous curves. Nearby, the others were posing and laughing too. Soon the warning chimes rang out, and they obediently hushed, and filed into the wings of the stage.

They stood transfixed, watching the high operatic drama unfold. Sophia's cousin had a beautiful voice, and played a convincing Lucretzia. Scene after scene, her voice soared in the beautiful opera house, and the group was mesmerized. They were startled when the stage director gave them the signal to prepare for their scene--a good thing, as it gave them very little time to have stage fright. They watched in awe as James and Bill strolled confidently across the stage, as if they had done it all their lives. Mary slipped into her position at the edge of the proscenium, looking lovely, but Bee noticed her hands were shaking as they grasped the bouquet she held.

At last it was their turn, and Bee and Bel grinned at each other, clutched each other's arms, and stepped out into the footlights. It was hard to see the audience--a dark mass at the end of the stage. They strolled--after Bel stumbled on her dress--to their position. Then they could relax, and watch the scene unfold in front of them.

Suddenly, Bel's nails dug into Bee's arm. Trying not to visibly react, Bee reached out her foot to kick her sister. Anticipating the movement, Bel deftly moved an inch away, removing her ankle from danger. "Stop!" She hissed, while keeping the smile pasted on her face.

"Look in the front row!" Bel hissed.

Slowly turning her head, Bee focused on the front row--the only one visible to the performers. She gasped. There was Assogot, looking entranced by the spectacle. He was drinking in the experience, his eyes sweeping the stage, devouring the players, costumes, and set. Bee and Bel watched him, unable to look away. They knew the instant he saw them--his eyes widened in shock, and his phone came out of his pocket. He looked around furtively, and they could see him point it in their direction, then quickly return it to his pocket. Bel's hand on Bee's arm tightened, and they began to shake with laughter--so much so that they nearly missed their cue to exit the stage at the end of the scene. Hurriedly, they joined the exodus, swept up into the processional.

After the final opera scene--melodramatic, but exciting--the group gathered to tour the backstage area and meet the principals. Many of the singers did not speak English easily, so Bel translated the group's gratitude for the experience and their praise for the singers. The opera company members were gracious, but hurried, ready to remove their heavy stage makeup and leave. Bee and Bel thought a nightcap would be a fitting end to the lovely evening, but Lucy smiled shyly and said that she had other plans. Bee raised an eyebrow. "Someone more interesting than us?" she inquired sweetly. Lucy ducked her head and acknowledged that she had a late-night date with the director. Margo sighed happily and wished her well, saying,

240

"Don't hurry back on my account, Lucy. I am going directly to bed when we get back to the inn!" Bee and Bel gave a satisfied nod to each other; they had often seen the transformative power of travel make changes in the lives of their participants.

Bee asked Paolo to drive them to a little cafe near the inn, where she knew that the limoncello was excellent. There were a number of recipes for the strong lemon cordial, but this cafe always served the traditional drink, made of lemons, sugar, and grappa, and nothing else. It was sweet and delicious, brought to them ice-cold. Bee cautioned the group not to drink it too quickly, "It's meant to be savored," she said, "and it will give you a walloping headache tomorrow if you drink too much of it or put it down too fast." Bel winced. She tended to be greedy when she found a taste she loved, and had overdone it one night on their first Italian tour. Bee was well aware of this, as they had been together. She prissily reminded Bel of the effects of limoncello whenever she got the chance. "In fact," said Bee, "Bel can tell you..."

"Enough!" snapped Bel. Bee subsided, a chaste smile on her face.

Back at the inn, the sisters climbed wearily to their room, saying a fond goodnight to the group members. Tomorrow they would all say goodbye, and head back to their homes. It was a moving moment, with everyone realizing the trip was nearly at an end.

Sinking onto her bed, Bee remarked, "I think these people are the nicest, most interesting group we have had so far." Bel agreed. "And I can't wait to be rid of them!" Bee and Bel laughed together; although they had grown fond of all the participants, the tragedy of Patty's death and the subsequent drama had exhausted them. The need to present a positive, supportive front in the wake of each member's confessions had taken its toll. Both women were beginning to have a strong desire to head home. Husbands, pets, friends, children--and laundry--were calling them.

"Bel," said Bee tentatively, "who do you think was eating peanuts? Do you suppose it has anything to do with Patty's death?" In response, she heard a gentle snore. Bee knew that Bel would not awaken once she had started purring. The conversation was over.

Chapter Thirty-Three

Bel, as usual, was up with the sun. Bee groaned as she heard her sister banging about the room. She sighed, knowing her rest was over. It would be a long morning, as they helped each guest head out.

Bel plopped herself down on Bee's bed, bouncing. "Are you awake? Are you awake?"

"Are you annoying?" Bee muttered. Bel ignored the remark. "Oh, good--you're awake! I've been thinking."

"Always dangerous. What about?" Bee gave up on sleep, and propped herself up, looking at her sister warily.

"What would you think of bagging Verona? I'm tired, and we never really got to shop in Florence. We're flying out of here anyway." She tried to look innocent, but failed.

"Ok, spill. What is the real reason?" Bee was suspicious.

"Well," said Bel, drawing the word out slowly. "I wonder if we could search for vendors selling peanuts in the area."

"Oh, Bel, no!" pleaded Bee. She thought for a minute. "I guess we wouldn't have to disclose what we found out, if anything. I admit I'm really curious about who did this to Patty. If nothing else, if we could solve this mystery, we would know who was potentially dangerous, and..." at this point, she trailed off.

Bel had her, she knew. Bee could never rest leaving a mystery unsolved. "Okay," agreed Bee, "Let's devote our last couple of days to a little peanut research, and if there's shopping to be had, all the better. But then we let this go, deal?"

"Deal." Bel was tempted to argue, but knew better. Bee had "that" look on her face, and Bel knew not to press her advantage.

With renewed enthusiasm, the two dressed and ran down for breakfast and prepared to send off their tour group. As usual, they had prepared a small photo book for each guest--bless Paolo and his technological abilities--and they had these ready to go. In each were photos of the cities they had visited, a list of the participants, the reading list, and the recipes from their Tuscan dinner. Each individual was pictured, as well as each couple. Previous guests had been very appreciative of the small gesture, and it had become their signature farewell. They had talked over the delicacy of this trip's photos, and decided they would include Patty, out of respect for James and Bill. It had been hard to find a photo where she had not been either scowling or smirking.

In the breakfast room, the usual early risers were already in place, savoring their coffee. Bel's teapot was ready and waiting--Sophia would get plenty of stars on Yelp from them, Bel reflected, smiling to herself as she poured the fragrant tea. Bee was already settled at their favorite table by the window. They ate slowly, enjoying the leisurely meal. The last day of a tour was rather like the last day of class, Bel thought. There were some students you hated to see leave, and others you were grateful to shake hands with and try to forget. She caught Bee looking at her, amused. She knew what Bel was thinking. Later they would relax and talk it over. She shook her head and smiled.

The group gathered for their last official meeting of the tour. Bee and Bel had coordinated everyone's schedule with Paolo, who would be ferrying people either to the train station or the airport. Bee hoped the tour group members would remember to tip Paolo--unlike other trips, he had become a quasi member of the group through his relationship with Caroline, but he still had earned the tips. She made a note to check on that later, with a small sigh. The accounting on this trip wouldn't be pretty. With effort, she focused on what Bel was saying.

244

"We are very grateful to have had the opportunity to get to know all of you. We know this tour had very painful moments." They had worked hard on figuring out how to acknowledge both Patty's death and her obnoxious behavior and not embarrass James, and that was the best they had come up with.

"Still, we hope you will take home wonderful memories, and wonderful friendships."

The group laughed as Caroline raised her hand, Paolo's hand firmly clasped in hers.

"We hope that your trip was much like the books you read to prepare for the trip; an opportunity to learn something new, to look at history--yours and Italy's--in a new way, and create something that you will enjoy referring back to for years to come." There was applause as she finished, and she took a bow. Bee stood, too.

"We have a little memento for each of you." She quickly passed out the books, amid thanks and a few tears. Bel handed out the transportation schedule, saying, "We'll be at the door to say goodbye to each of you personally. If you have any questions before you head out for your return home, please let us know. We would appreciate it if you would give Sophia and Roger a nice review--they certainly have been terrific in accommodating us in so many ways." There was a bust of emphatic applause, made timely by Sophia's appearance with a full coffee pot. She smiled and waved, and blew a kiss at Bel. She was wearing a figure-hugging skirt, and Bel was tickled to see the little bump. The next visit would be very different, and Bel made a mental note to bring along a baby gift.

They lingered for a while, answering the typical departure questions. Of the remaining guests, most were keeping to their original plans. Caroline was staying an additional week to visit Paolo's parents and help him prepare for his move to the U.S.

James and Bill were staying another few days to wait until Patty had been cremated, so they could personally bring her remains home. They had decided to head to Venice to relax while they waited--Bee thought it was a very good plan. It would be nice for them to have memories of Italy that didn't include Patty in some awful way.

Charlie and Mary were headed to the airport as planned. They were the first to head back to the states. Their luggage was packed and ready to go. Paolo and Charlie headed up the stairs to carry it down. Mary stayed behind, and grasped Bee and Bel by the hands.

Taking advantage of Charlie's absence, Bel quickly and quietly asked if Mary had sufficient funds for the trip home. Curious, she looked at them and nodded slowly.

"Why do you ask?" Bee and Bel exchanged glances. "We overheard Charlie at the bead shop. We don't mean to pry--we were just concerned." Bee looked uncomfortable. Mary laughed, and hugged them. "Oh, that!" She exclaimed, amused. "He's just tight-fisted!" Her face grew serious. "Thank you." The little woman's eyes filled with tears. "You have been wonderful. It was a wonderful trip, and you handled all the unpleasantness so gracefully. I'm so grateful."

"But of course!" Bee and Bel spoke in stereo.

Mary shook her head. "No, I mean it. You listened to our sad story, and didn't accuse us of…" Her voice shook and tapered off. Bee enfolded the Iowan in a big hug that concluded the conversation.

As the couple departed, Bee asked that Charlie and Mary consider recommending To Be tours to their friends. "Sure, if we still have any," said Charlie. The sarcasm caused Mary to wince. "Well, we are looking forward to new beginnings, Charlie," she said. "I know we will meet a lot of new people when we move." Charlie's tense face softened as he looked at his wife. "You're right, Mother," he said. "And I would recommend this tour without reservation." The sisters thanked him, and hugged the couple. Paolo herded them gently into the van, and they set off for the airport.

Margo and Lucy had come outside to wave goodbye. Theirs was an evening flight, and they sat down and conferred with Bee and Bel about the day's' plans. Over a leisurely second cup of coffee, it was revealed that Lucy had a lunch engagement--much to the delight

246

of her listeners--the date last night had been well worth extending, and she and the opera director would be enjoying a romantic picnic somewhere in the country. It was surreal to see the New England lawyer blush like a teenager. She whispered that "he" was coming to the states in a few weeks and had invited Lucy to join him in New York for the weekend--and she had accepted! She shyly asked Bee for restaurant recommendations in the city, and Bee promised to email her a list of romantic dinner destinations. Bee sensed new doors were opening for Lucy, and was thrilled to have been a witness to this blossoming. Margo was laughing, shaking her head emphatically at Lucy's polite suggestion that she join them for the picnic. The two set out for some last minute shopping before the picnic, giggling like school girls. Margo looked relaxed and carefree, possibly for the first time on the trip, Bee thought. The idea left a sour taste in her mouth. Why now? Bee wondered. She wanted to talk that over with Bel.

It would have to wait, as Sophia and Roger stopped by the table to confirm last minute details with Bee and Bel. They were, Bee suspected, relieved to have the group gone. Much as they were fond of Bee and Bel, it certainly hadn't been an easy or pleasant visit. Grimly, Bee thought of Patty, making things uncomfortable long after her death. She was sure that cleaning out her room had been up to Sophia and Roger--the maids would want nothing to do with handling the dead woman's things. She gave an involuntary shudder, and Bel threw a sharp glance at her. She quickly rearranged her face, and focused on the conversation at hand. She didn't need any of Bel's pert remarks about her daydreaming. She poured another cup of coffee, and smiled broadly at Bel. That'll make her nervous, she thought mischievously. Bel gave her The Look, which made her smile even more. What the heck, she thought. It's back to yoghurt and granola in three days. She helped herself to another pastry with hazelnuts and chocolate. This time she got the eyebrow. Ah, things were back to normal at last, Bel thought. When Sophia and Roger headed back to their office, Bel turned to Bee. "What was that about??" Bee tried hard to look innocent. "What are you talking about?"

Bel snorted, "The Cheshire Cat look. I was wondering if the Mad Hatter was dropping in on your little tea party, but then I decided you were the crazy one." Bee then tried to assume an injured look.

"Oh, please." Bel rolled her eyes. "And by the way, don't think I didn't notice the pastry." She looked disapprovingly at her plump sister. Sophia hurried up to the table. "Bel! I didn't forget! Here's that almond tart you were asking about." She placed the wrapped sweet in front of Bel and hurried back to the kitchen. Bee started to laugh, more at the expression on Bel's face than the irony of the situation.

Bel had the grace to turn bright red. "Well..." she stopped. "Well." She shrugged, opened up the wrapped tart, and bit into it.

By the time they finished in the breakfast room, Paolo had returned from the airport. Bill and James were waiting in the salon for their trip to the train station. Bee was touched to see that despite all the worry and stress of this trip for the couple,they had a thick envelope in hand for Paolo. James clasped him by the hand and thanked Paolo for his fine service. He spoke in a low voice, but Bel could just catch Patty's name and James' apologetic tone. Paolo gratefully accepted the tip, and helped carry the luggage to the van. Before they climbed aboard, James and Bill approached the sisters. "Ladies," said Bill, "I know I speak for both of us when I tell you how impressed I am with your tour, your compassion, and your sensitivity. This all could have been so much worse without you both guiding us through the nightmare of Patty's behavior and her death. Thank you sincerely." He made a courtly bow, kissing each of their hands in turn. James did the same, then opened his arms and offered a huge bear hug. "And thank you so very much for not judging me," he whispered. "You two are treasures and we will never forget you." Bee sniffled a bit as the men climbed aboard the van. Waving, she watched them drive away, and turned to her sister. "Bel," she mused, "I think..." Turning, she saw that Bel was already mounting the stairs to their room. Bee hustled after her. What was she up to now?

Bee opened the door to their room, falling over Bel's suitcase, which had moved to an inconvenient spot just inside the door. "Bel, ouch!" Bee said, rubbing at her shins. "Did you need to put the bag right there?" Bel was not listening, she realized. Her sister was madly rummaging through her tote.

"Bee, have you seen my notebook? I can't find it, and I wanted to check something about Margo's background." "No," moaned Bee, still clutching at her shins. "Where did you have it last?" "Right here, in my bag," said Bel. The sisters looked at each other, their faces beginning to register alarm.

"Are you sure you put it there? Remember that time in Scotland when you were sure you had put our plane tickets in your bag? We had the entire place searched but the tickets were in your coat pocket. THINK. Stop pacing, and talk me through it."

Bel stopped, closed her eyes, and opened them, a grim set to her jaw. "First of all, I didn't leave my suitcase here. Unless you moved it, someone else has."

Bee shook her head, watching her sister as she placed the tote on the bed.

"You know me. I don't put my suitcase out until the last possible second. I might need something." Normally, Bee would make a witty remark about what her sister might need, but she was well aware of how distressed Bel was and kept her mouth shut, waiting. "I had almost everything packed, in both my suitcase and my carry-on, including my notebook. I didn't want to leave it out in case Sophia or one of the maids came in. I put it underneath my wallet so I would be able to put my hands on it immediately." She reached into the open tote, pulled out her wallet, and pointedly put it on the bed, nodding to the empty space beneath it. Bee took a breath, and said cautiously, "Let's just take everything out to be sure. I believe you, but it may have slipped and shifted when the tote was moved."

"Moved by whom?" Even distressed, Bel's grammar was flawless. "Who would move my tote and my suitcase? And why?" She stared at Bee.

Bee felt her stomach lurch. They had navigated such troubled waters on this tour, but it had never seemed to touch them personally. She felt so violated, thinking someone had been in their room, pawing through Bel's things. She could only imagine how Bel felt, knowing that her belongings had been subject to deliberate ransacking. For the first time on the tour, she felt threatened. Bel emptied her tote, unceremoniously dumping the contents on her bed.

"It's not here." Her voice was flat and calm--always a sign that Bel was really, really angry. "I think this proves that Patty didn't die naturally. Someone was afraid we figured it out."

Bee sat down on the bed heavily. She was suddenly weary. She wanted to go home. Home to her routine job, home to her nice, boring house, and most of all, her husband--how she missed Jack and his reassuring calm. "Who the hell could...why the hell would....oh, hell." She stopped, frustrated.

Bel answered the unfinished sentence. "Precisely. Who and why are the only questions." She thought for a moment. "Actually, the only question is who. We know why--they don't want to be identified as a murderer. Pretty simple, really." Her eyes narrowed, and she tapped her fingers against the table, drumming them while she thought.

Bee shook herself, thinking fleetingly of Jack. It was no time to wring one's hands and pretend to be a damsel in distress. She realized she was more angry than afraid. Now all she wanted was to catch the bastard. She looked over at Bel--the drumming had stopped. Bel was looking at her, amused. How did she know?!

"We'll fight the good fight, Bee. The real question is, what do we do if we do figure it out? Do we turn them over to the authorities? We had already decided to let it go. Does this change anything? Remember, these are all people we know, and we know how Patty abused them, some of them more than others. What do we do with our knowledge?" She looked at Bee, and held out her hands mimicking the imaginary scales of Justice.

Bee sighed. "I don't know. It seems like this just changes things, doesn't it? And yet...there's no one on this tour that I would be happy about seeing charged with murder."

They sat in silence for a while. The knock at the door startled them both and they jumped to their feet. Sophia called to them through the door. "Bel? Bee? Are you in there?"

Laughing shakily, Bee answered the door. Smiling, Sophia held up a small, black spiral bound notebook. "Did you leave this at breakfast? One of the maids found it at your usual table when she was clearing up after breakfast."

Bee hugged Sophia, who was startled by the warm embrace. "Oh, Sophia, we have been turning the room upside down looking for it! Thank you!" Her quizzical look indicated that she was pleased, if a little surprised, by the enthusiasm the little notebook's return prompted. As the door closed, Bee turned to a red-faced Bel. Without a word, she tossed the prodigal notebook back to her. The wild rollercoaster of emotions had left her momentarily speechless--but only momentarily.

"I swear, Bel! You make me crazy. The last fifteen minutes have been more stress than my nerves need. This is like Scotland all over again, but worse, since you had me thinking a murderer was in our room!"

Bel paid no attention, but flipped through the book. Silently, she held it up for Bee to see. It was clear from across the room that pages had been ripped out. "I told you it was in my bag. I didn't bring it to breakfast."

"Oh, damn. Here we go again." They stared at each other.

Chapter Thirty-Four

Bill, James, Charlie, and Mary had left the city. Caroline was preparing to leave with Paolo. Margo and Lucy were on an evening flight back to the States. Who would have had the time--and the nerve-- to go into Bel's tote and steal the book? Bee and Bel went over the notebook, reviewing what pages remained and trying to piece together which pages were missing.

They slumped in their chairs, realizing nearly everything to do with the tour participants' histories had been torn from the notebook. Only a few of Bel's cryptic scribbles remained, and they turned out to be unrelated--notes on museums and galleries for future visits.

"Now what?" Bee knew better than to suggest that it would be easy and appropriate to simply close the book and go shopping.

Bel shrugged. "We could close the book and go shopping. But I'll be damned if I'll stop trying to figure this out." She closed her eyes, and Bee knew she was recreating the pages in her mind. She waited a few minutes, giving Bel a chance to sort her thoughts. When she opened her eyes, Bee asked her questions quickly, before Bel could start on something new.

"Bel? The questions are still the same. Who did it, and what do we do about it? Do we want to send any of these folks to prison for ridding the world of Patty? We have absolutely no proof, and what are we going to do with the information if--just if--we do actually discover who did it?" Bel looked away.

"You do realize it's an ethical question we'll be haunted by for the rest of our lives?" Bee persisted. "If we continue, we are forced to make a decision on someone's fate. Either we send a person to prison for revenge that was probably well deserved, or we let a murderer go free. Do you really want to be the one making that decision?" Bee's voice was low but urgent.

"Right now the case is closed. The Italians have made their official decision. What happens when we tell them they're wrong? Do we get accused of withholding evidence? They're not going to appreciate being made to look foolish, and I rather think the kindly Lt. Monseglio will make sure he doesn't make any more mistakes. Each and every one of us on this tour would instantly be very thoroughly investigated. Is that what we want? And if you do discover something and choose not to say anything, what then? Can you live with that information?"

Bel turned back to her sister's troubled face. She put out her arms, and grasped her sister's shoulders. "I think…" She hesitated, then sighed. "I think it's time to go shopping." Bel picked up her bag, and held out her hand. Bee jumped up, and they went out the door, leaving the notebook on the bed.

Out in the Tuscan countryside, Lucy and her director enjoyed a romantic picnic. He had brought a loaf of fresh semolina bread, a flask of olive oil, and a bottle of wine. Lucy laid a wedge of cheese, a plate of figs, and a jar of peanuts on the blanket. They toasted their new friendship.

Bill and James sat back in their seats, watching the hills slide by as the train carried them away. "Hungry?" Bill asked. James nodded, and from his backpack Bill pulled a jar of peanuts, and spilled some into James' outstretched hand.

Charlie and Mary settled into their seats as they headed back to the States. The flight attendant offered them soft drinks and peanuts. "No, thank you, dear. I have my own." Mary smiled sweetly.

Caroline and Paolo pulled up to his parents' home. Paulo turned to Caroline and asked "Are you nervous, *Bella*?" She laughed, and put her arm in his. "No, not with you beside me. I just hope they like me." The door flew open, and Paolo's mother embraced them both, kissing Caroline heartily on both cheeks. Laughing, the redhead presented them with a basket filled with wine, bread, olives, and peanuts.

254

Margo had her suitcases open on the bed. She carefully folded her clothes and methodically placed them in her bags, casually popping peanuts into her mouth as she sorted through the gifts she had purchased for her beloved nieces and nephews.

In the kitchen, Sophia and Roger finished cleaning up after the extended breakfast service. They retired to the salon, once again their private domain. Roger poured them each a glass of sparkling water, toasting the departure of their last guests before renovations began. Sophia put her feet in his lap to be rubbed, and sighed contentedly as he massaged her tired feet and she munched on a small bag of peanuts.

Back in Tokyo, Katsu Takahashi invited his extended family over to see his photos of his trip to Italy. He offered his guests a very fine Italian wine he had brought home, and small bowls of figs, olives, and wasabi peanuts were passed. "*Futago?*" asked his sister, pointing to the picture of two plump American women. "Are they twins?"

"No, no-- *kureiji!*", he answered, and leaned in to tell her the odd story of the crazy women who haunted his every stop in Italy.

Bel and Bee, passing a bag of roasted peanuts back and forth, shopped until they dropped.

To Be Tours Killer Italian Dinner (hold the peanuts)

Aperitivo: Pear, Gorgonzola and Walnut Bites with Prosecco

Prima Piatti: Pasta With Sausage and Fennel with Chianti Classico

Secundo: Veal Piccata, served with Roasted Sesame Potatoes and

Sisters' Stuffed Artichokes, with a Super Tuscan

Dolce: Sophia's 'Family' Tiramisu with Moscoto d'Asti

Bee's Pistachio and Cranberry Biscotti with Limoncello

Pear, Gorgonzola and Walnut Bites

After a long day of museum tours, this will make you forget your aching feet!

2 ripe pears, sliced about $1/_5$" thick
½ loaf good Italian bread
Gorgonzola, sliced about $1/_5$" inch thick
½ c. walnut halves

Place thinly sliced pieces of bread on a baking tray. Place one slice of pear on each; cover each pear slice with a piece or pieces of gorgonzola. Top with a walnut half. Bake at 350 degrees about 10 minutes, until the gorgonzola melts. Serves 4 hungry people, or 8 polite adults.

Sisters' Stuffed Artichokes

Bee and Bel love this dish--great for parties, and it uses the whole artichoke, unlike the Italians' zest for discarding all the leaves.

    4 artichokes
    3 cloves garlic, minced
    ¼ cup minced parsley
    1 cup dry bread crumbs- seasoned or plain
    Salt and pepper
    ¼ cup toasted and chopped pine nuts (or walnuts)
    A few tablespoons of olive oil

Cut stems off artichokes and remove just the thick, tough outer leaves. Cut the thorny leaf tops off with a serrated knife; artichoke should be flat on top. Pull the leaves apart to expose the hearts, and scoop out the choke with a spoon. Heat your oven to 350 degrees. Stir together the remaining ingredients, adding enough olive oil to make the stuffing moist. Put the stuffing in the center of each artichoke, and pull the leaves over the filling. Put artichokes, stem end down, in a lidded dish, and sprinkle with salt and pepper. Add water to reach ⅔ of the way up the sides of the dish. Cover tightly and bake about 45-60 minutes, or until tender. To serve, drizzle each artichoke with a little olive oil.

Bee's note: this recipe is a bit more virtuous than her favorite one for artichokes, which consists of boiling them in water and then dipping each leaf-- and the luscious heart-- in melted butter.

Sausage and Fennel Pasta Perfection

This is Bee's favorite pasta dish, perfect when you need a soul-satisfying meal to take your mind off murder...

> 1 lb. uncased mild Italian Sausage (or Hot, if you like it spicy...)
> 1 large bulb fennel
> 1 large onion
> 2 T Olive oil
> 2 T tomato paste
> Peperoncino flakes to taste
> 1 box (approx. 12 oz) of your favorite pasta
> Parmesan cheese

Heat olive oil in a LARGE pan--all ingredients will end up in this pan, so you'll need a big one. Cook pasta as directed on box, except cut the cooking time by a minute. Drain, reserve one cup of water from cooking the pasta before draining it. Set pasta aside.

Slice onion in half, then into "crescent moons", and add to oil. Cut fennel into matchsticks, discarding the tough outer leaf. Save some of the feathery green fronds to garnish. Add fennel to the pan, and saute until tender. When tender, push to one side of the pan, and add the sausage, breaking it up into small bits as it cooks. When the sausage is no longer pink, incorporate the onions and fennel and continue to cook until the sausage is lightly browned. Push all ingredients to the side, and add the tomato paste (if you haven't discovered it yet, find the tomato paste in a tube--it's so much easier to use, and you don't waste any!), and stir just until the tomato paste begins to cook. Add the peperoncino flakes. Stir all the ingredients together, until evenly coated. Add the cooked pasta, and half of the reserved water. Stir and cook for one minute. Add remaining water if needed for the sauce. Serve, garnished with the fennel fronds, and top with parmesan cheese.

Lucia's Veal Piccata

A wonderful dish to serve if you have the time to relax and enjoy your meal, preferably with a delicious red wine, sparkling conversation, and a sister who happily cleans the kitchen if you cook. This serves 8 if you have a first course, four if you don't.

2 large lemons, juiced
2 T capers
1 T chopped fresh thyme
1 c chicken broth
¼ c dry white wine
¼ c plus 1 T heavy cream
1 bay leaf
¼ t salt
½ t freshly ground pepper
8 thin pieces of veal cutlet
1 c flour (Wondra is best)
1 T butter
Chopped parsley for garnish

Preheat the oven to 200 degrees. Line a baking sheet with aluminum foil, then cover with multiple layers of paper towels.

Combine the lemon juice and the capers and thyme in a small bowl and set aside.

Combine the broth, wine, cream, bay leaf, salt and pepper in a small saucepan and bring to a boil over medium heat while stirring. Reduce heat to medium, and let sauce reduce to about ⅔ cup (about 10 minutes). Discard the bay leaf, and remove from heat.

Place one or two pieces of veal in a zippered kitchen bag, and pound with a meat mallet until slices are ⅛ inch thick. Season both sides of veal slices with salt and pepper.

Place flour on a plate, and lightly dredge the veal slices.

Heat the oil in a large skillet until the oil shimmers. Place slices in the pan, in batches so it isn't crowded in the pan. Cook for about a minute on each side until golden brown. Transfer to the baking sheet, and place in the warm oven until remaining slices are cooked.

When all the slices are cooked, add the lemon juice, capers and thyme to the pan. Cook for 3 minutes, then add the reduced broth mixture. Remove from the heat, and stir in the butter. Season with additional salt, pepper, and thyme as needed. Plate up veal, pour sauce over each portion, and garnish with parsley.

Roasted Sesame Potatoes

Incredibly simple, so delicious!

One and a half Idaho potatoes per person serving

2/3 c sesame seeds per 4 persons servings

Olive oil (in a spray mister is helpful)

¾ t kosher salt

Preheat oven to 400 degrees. Wash and peel potatoes (you may leave them unpeeled if you feel strongly about it, or are running short on time)

Slice potatoes approximately ¼ in thickness--a mandolin is a great help here!

Place slices on a baking sheet in a single layer, and lightly brush or spray with olive oil. Dust lightly with salt. Sprinkle on enough sesame seeds on each slice so the potato surface is barely visible.

Roast in oven 20 minutes, or until potatoes are tender. Serve immediately.

Sophia's 'Family' Tiramisu

This dish, classically Italian, was actually invented in the late 1970's. It's to die for.

Coffee dip:
1 ½ cups espresso coffee
2 teaspoons sugar
Dissolve the sugar in hot coffee, then cool.
Zabaglione filling:
4 egg yolks
½ cup sugar
½ cup marsala wine
1 lb. mascarpone cheese, room temp
1 ½ cups heavy cream

Beat yolks in the top of a double boiler until fluffy. Beat in the sugar and then the wine. Put over simmering water and whisk until the mixture thickens. Mash the cheese until creamy. Add zabaglione to the cheese and beat well. Whip the cream to stiff peaks and fold into the zabaglione/cheese mixture.

Assembling:
40 ladyfingers
2 Tablespoons unsweetened cocoa powder
1 cup toasted and ground hazelnuts

Quickly dip each ladyfinger in the cooled coffee. Line the bottom of a 12X8 inch baking dish with the cookies. Spread ½ of the cream mixture over the layer of cookies. Sprinkle half of the ground hazelnuts over the cream mix. Repeat the cookie and cream layers. Top with the rest of the hazelnuts and dust the whole concoction with the cocoa powder. Refrigerate at least three hours before serving.

Bel's Lazy Tiramisu

As she always has better things to do than cook, Bel hunts for quick and delicious recipes. Just a tiny slice of this cake will transport you.

> 3 Cups mascarpone cheese
> 1 ½ cups confectioner⬚s sugar
> ¼ cup Marsala wine
> ¾ cup cold heavy cream
> ⅔ cup water
> 4 teaspoons instant coffee powder
> 1 large pound cake (purchased), sliced crosswise into ⅓ inch slices
> Unsweetened cocoa powder
> 1 cup hazelnuts, toasted if you wish, ground (optional)
> ¼ cup toasted hazelnuts, chopped coarsely (optional)

Using a mixer, beat cheese, 1 cup of the sugar, and the wine on medium speed until well blended. Add the cream and beat until fluffy; set aside.

Combine ⅔ cup water, ½ cup confectioner's sugar, and instant coffee in a small saucepan and bring to a boil, stirring occasionally. Remove from heat and set aside.

In a glass baking dish about 11 inches long and 2 inches deep, arrange cake slices to cover the bottom completely. Brush half of the cooled sugar mixture over the slices, then top with half of the cheese mixture. Sprinkle with half of the ground hazelnuts, and all of the chopped nuts (this step is optional, but yummy). Top with remainder of the cake slices and repeat the first layer. Cover with plastic wrap and refrigerate at least 2 hours. Dust the top with the remainder of the ground hazelnuts and sift unsweetened cocoa over the top of the desert to serve. Will feed 10-12. Calories: who cares!!

Bee says the classic Tiramisu recipe uses ladyfingers dipped in espresso instead of purchased cake brushed with instant coffee. Try it that way, if you have too much time on your hands. Bel does not.

Bee's Best Cranberry- Pistachio Biscotti

Bee and Bel love these crisp cookies- not as hard to make as you might think, given the prices they command. Best yet--you will never want boxed biscotti again after trying these. Perfect with coffee or tea. Outstanding with Limoncello. But then, what isn't?

    1 cup shelled pistachios
    1 cup dried cranberries
    2 1/2 cups flour
    1 cup sugar
    1 teaspoon baking powder
    ¼ teaspoon salt
    2 large eggs, room temp
    2 large egg whites, room temp
    1 Tablespoon grated orange zest
    2 teaspoons vanilla
    1 large egg white, slightly beaten

Preheat oven to 350. Place nuts on a cookie sheet and bake about 7 minutes-check often to avoid burning. Cool. Combine cranberries with hot water to cover and soak for a few minutes. Drain, pat dry. Line a cookie sheet with parchment paper. Put flour, sugar, baking soda and salt in a bowl and beat on low speed just until mixed. Stir in cranberries and nuts. On a floured board, knead the dough a few times, until dough comes together. Divide dough into 3 pieces and shape into 3 logs, about 12 inches long. Put logs on the cookie sheet and flatten logs to a size of 2 ½ inches high and about 14 inches long. Brush with egg white; bake until golden brown, about 25 minutes. Cool on a rack about 8 minutes; lower heat to 325. Cut logs on the diagonal with a serrated knife, making each slice about ½ inch. Bake about 8 minutes on each side, Cool. Store up to 3 weeks in a lined tin. Bee's note: this makes a lot of cookies, but they won't last long. Go ahead, put them in a tin, but then you'd better hide it!

Limoncello

Bel says: this takes time to make, but it is so worth it! Very little effort involved, just patience, which is not really one of my virtues. Be sure to use a huge jar, as you will have about 13 cups of liquid.

> 6 ⅓ cups (1 ½ liters) 75% alcohol (2 bottles Everclear grain alcohol)
> 6 ⅓ cups water
> 2 ⅓ pounds sugar (1 lb.= 2 cups)
> 14 lemons

Wash, then peel lemons, removing the yellow peel only (white is bitter). Place peels in a glass jar and cover with alcohol. Seal tightly and rest out of direct sun for two weeks.

Then heat the water in a pan, mix in the sugar, stirring, and boil for 5 minutes. Cool for one hour, stirring occasionally. Add syrup to the jar and mix well. Cover and rest one month, out of the sun. Strain out the peels, bottle and freeze.

Will keep as long as you need. Do not inform husband that it's available. Makes a great gift item if you are crafty. Bee is. Bel is not.

Reading List

Dante Alighieri--<u>The Inferno</u>: 14th Century epic poem of Dante's journey through Hell. Dante remains the "favorite son" of Florence, and there are many sights and events dedicated to him throughout the city.

Dan Brown--<u>Angels and Demons; Inferno</u>: fascinating plots and subplots, wealth of factual detail on Rome and Florence, including historical symbols and sites, blended with fictional characters and scenarios.

G. K. Chesterton--<u>St. Francis of Assisi</u>: a must for the visitor to Assisi, detailing the life of St. Francis.

Machiavelli--<u>The Prince:</u> classic story of Renaissance politics and power, published in 1532. The political treatise is thought to be the first work of modern philosophy.

Irving Stone--<u>The Agony and The Ecstasy</u>: the story of Michelangelo. Stone moved to Italy and apprenticed to a marble cutter to learn the trade to better appreciate the genius and mastery of his subject.

William Shakespeare--<u>Two Gentlemen of Verona</u>: comedy set in Italy, considered to be Shakespeare's first play. The play is centered around the themes of friendship and infidelity.